"THE DRONES ARE INVISIBLE TO RADAR."

The Able Team leader's jaw set firmly as he scanned the shadowy terrain ahead. "If they had stealth robot tanks, then they could build a stealth helicopter."

A red light buzzed on the control console. "We're hot! Target radar lock!" the pilot announced as he wrenched the chopper hard right.

Strapped in, Lyons felt the jerk like a dog on the end of a leash. Out of the darkness, he saw a flaming halo growing in intensity and following the helicopter's thrashing movements.

He knew exactly what the flaming halo was—the rocket exhaust of an antiaircraft missile, the lethal shaft of its warhead forming the black void in the center of a hellfire ring.

Death shrieked at the men of Able Team on a jet of flame.

Other titles in this series:

DON PENDLETON'S

STONY

AMERICA'S ULTRA-COVERT INTELLIGENCE AGENCY

MAN ®

EXTREME ARSENAL

A GOLD EAGLE BOOK FROM
W★RLDWIDE ®

TORONTO • NEW YORK • LONDON
AMSTERDAM • PARIS • SYDNEY • HAMBURG
STOCKHOLM • ATHENS • TOKYO • MILAN
MADRID • WARSAW • BUDAPEST • AUCKLAND

First edition February 2007

ISBN-13: 978-0-373-61971-9
ISBN-10:   0-373-61971-5

EXTREME ARSENAL

Special thanks and acknowledgment to
Douglas P. Wojtowicz for his contribution to this work.

Printed in U.S.A.

EXTREME ARSENAL

To Sam, for teaching our troops in Iraq and saving lives in Thailand after the tsunami. Some people might believe that God sends disasters to destroy the world, but He doesn't. He sends good men and heroes like you. Come home safely, my friend.

PROLOGUE

Yuma Proving Grounds, Arizona

Dane Whitman watched the MidKnight Mark II armored combat drone roll across the Yuma proving grounds. He glanced over at General Stephen Rogers and smiled.

"How's she holding up?" Whitman asked.

"Still quiet on the seismic detectors," Rogers said as he looked at the monitor. He swiveled the flat screen so that Whitman could look at it. The general hovered the cursor over the infrared sensors. "Even its heat signature is nearly invisible. Good work."

"Stealth and armored combat never worked that well, hand in hand, but this is a revolutionary new design," Whitman replied. "With the MidKnight, we can hit the enemy with impunity. Don't want to risk a Marine platoon on foot? Send in a small squadron of MidKnights."

Rogers pursed his lips. "What about regular tanks?"

"That's the joy of this. The MidKnights are slave

drones. One operator can handle and coordinate two of them. The range on the remotes are fairly limited, so our operators will need to be close. What better place than wrapped in the Chobam armor of an M-1A tank?" Whitman asked.

Rogers nodded. "But what about the tanks themselves?"

"The hypersonic vibrational dampeners are modular designs," Whitman explained. "They can be installed in M-1As with ease."

Rogers frowned. "So why use the drones?"

"To increase our armored ability. Instead of sending out large squadrons of tanks, we have two armored vehicles and four drones able to do the work of a squadron, with more firepower and superior coordination," Whitman said. "And with less risk of someone with a cheap, shoulder-mounted rocket launcher taking out a tank crew."

Rogers looked dubiously at the monitor.

Suddenly one of the MidKnights exploded. Chunks of armor plating and flames erupted as if from a metallic volcano.

"What in the hell?" Rogers demanded. He stood in the control booth, eyes locked on the field below. Another of the MidKnights detonated in an orange blossom of flame and debris.

"Sir!" Lieutenant Aaron Blake spoke up. "There's something else out on the field!"

"Impossible!" Rogers bellowed. "This testing ground is protected on all sides. There are no access roads…"

The control tower shook.

Whitman held on to his chair, but Rogers and Blake

were tossed to the floor. He glanced down to see a spiked disk pass near the bonfire of one of his drones. A long, thick tail rose from the thing's back. Its bulbous tip spit out another flash of fire. He watched the low, armored intruder's head spit twin lines of flame that smashed the tent with the MidKnight operators to shreds.

The millionaire inventor held his breath as more of those attackers became visible, their tails alive with jets of fire. Rockets speared out of the sides of the blunt tail tip and destroyed a hangar building.

"How in the blazes did they get here?" Rogers asked.

"Ankylosaurs," Whitman whispered. "They look like Ankylosaurs."

"What?" the general shouted.

"Ancient armored dinosaurs…" Whitman said. His eyes widened as one of the disk-shaped drones pivoted and opened fire on the base of the control tower with their heavy machine guns.

"Pull off of the field!" Rogers shouted into the mike. "Get out of the line of fire!"

Whitman looked at the monitor. In its infrared lens, the bodies of Yuma defenders flared hotly as they were pierced by lances of automatic weapons fire. Several had already fallen, turning from yellowish white to cool blue. Except for the flaming muzzles and rocket shell launchers, the Ankylosaurs were all but invisible to infrared and radar. He clicked through various detectors. The intruders were stealthier than his own designs. While the MidKnights and the Ankylosaurs were both invisible to radar, the black, spiked monstrosities had a null heat profile except when their weapons fired.

Glass shattered in the control room and Blake's torso exploded as 25 mm shells ripped through him. Whitman recoiled, soaked with hot, fresh gore. Slimy gobs of pulped flesh dropped to the floor as he shifted position. Rogers stared in pained shock, for a moment at the head of the lifeless officer, and it took a moment for Whitman to focus on the fact that all the general held was a head attached to the grimy taillike spinal cord, ribs sticking up like insect legs where they'd been shattered.

"Get out of here now," Rogers said resolutely. "This tower's no protection against those things."

Whitman hit the eject button on the DVD recorder drive.

"Come on, man!" Rogers shouted.

"The sensors have information on the attackers. We can use it!" Whitman replied.

"Think about your designs another—"

"No! To learn who is attac—" Whitman began. Something hot burned below his back and he suddenly felt very tired. The glimmering disk in his hand seemed too heavy to hold up and he flopped facedown on the floor.

"Whitman!" Rogers shouted. "Oh, God…"

Whitman didn't know what the man in the green suit was talking about. His mind drifted. "Ankylosaurs…"

"Don't talk," Rogers said. He gripped Whitman's lapels and pulled him along toward the steps.

Whitman was glassy-eyed in shock, his brain not registering properly. His breathing was difficult. He looked back over his shoulder and saw a pair of legs, half a pair of them actually, blown off just above the knees. One was flopped on its side, but the other leaned against a counter, as if it were still standing.

"Hey…" the weapons designer muttered as he was dragged over the top step.

"Save your strength, Dane. It'll be okay," Rogers whispered. "It'll be okay…"

Whitman looked drunkenly up at the man. He thought he should know this nice person's name, but it escaped him. All he could think of was the dinosaurs, the Ankylosaurs. He smiled.

He loved dinosaurs. He always liked to read books and watch movies about them…and when he went to the museum…

His eyes blinked lazily.

"Dane, hold on dammit," Rogers gritted.

"I like the museum…" Whitman whispered, his head resting on the cold stone step. He closed his eyes, imagining an era when leviathans roamed the Earth.

Death took the genius as he smiled dreamily.

GENERAL ROGERS FELT for a pulse and found none. His lips pulled back tightly, and he looked down at the mirrored disk the man died to retrieve.

"To learn who attacked," was what he'd said before the 25 mm cannon shell had blasted his upper thighs into a messy spray of vaporized flesh and bone.

Rogers took the disk and slipped it under his jacket. "Okay, Dane. I'll make sure the right people get this." The general took off down the stairs, reaching under his jacket and drawing out the SIG-Sauer M-11 pistol from its concealed holster. The little handgun wouldn't do much against an armored juggernaut, but it was something that gave him some confidence. He wasn't completely helpless.

As he reached the base of the tower, he glanced at a gaping hole in the wall. Two soldiers were strewed in the rubble on the steps, and Rogers knelt to check on them. Both were dead.

Numbing anger washed over him. These soldiers were under his command, and they had given their life in a rush to his side. His jaw set, he shook off his shock. He needed to contact the rest of his men and insure their safety. He looked down and spotted a field radio.

He plucked it from the corpse's belt and heard the sounds of the Yuma Security Task Force as its members tried to coordinate a defense against the attacking robots.

"This is General Rogers. All security forces fall back! Those things are too powerful to stop!" he ordered. "Fall back to shelter and do not engage!"

Rogers sensed danger and threw himself to the base of the steps. The impact jarred the old soldier's bones, but the drop saved his life as machine guns and cannon fire tore at the steps he'd just occupied. He looked at the radio and stunned realization hit.

The attackers drones had homed in on his transmission. He lurched to his feet and raced for the door. He pressed down the lock transmit button and called into the unit, "Cease radio communication! They're targeting anything that transmits!"

Gunfire chopped at Rogers's heels and he tossed the communicator away from him as he continued his mad dash across the field. The deadly line of autofire that hounded him swung away and ripped apart the ground where the radio bounced. The shock wave of a grenade detonation buffeted the general's back, but Rogers continued to rush toward a stone bunker. The Ankylosaurs, as Whitman called them, paused, seemingly confused.

Rogers smiled. His last message had gotten through. The drones had nothing to target. One of the machines suddenly whirled toward him.

Radio targeting wasn't their only means of detection, Rogers realized and he threw himself into a ditch instants before heavy-caliber machine gun fire slashed the ground he'd just vacated. The general flopped facedown in the mud and curled tightly to the bottom of the runoff ditch.

The rumble of the Ankylosaur's approach thundered in his ears and he looked up at the looming robot. A blunt, bearlike head adorned with two 25 mm cannon barrels and belts for the weapons swiveled along the ditch. Multifaceted lenses swept across Rogers and he held his breath. Those lenses had to have been infrared sensors. The thing would spot him...

The Ankylosaur pivoted, as if continuing to search for him. Chilled and drenched, Rogers felt his teeth begin to chatter and he clenched his jaw shut. The cold mud caked him and obscured him from IR detection. Only the momentary snap of chattering teeth had drawn the murderous robot's attention.

Sonar or vibrational sensors, Rogers realized. His ears throbbed with the hum and chatter of low-frequency sonics buzzing through the air. Just like Whitman's design for the MidKnights. The ULF sonics provided an obscuring cloud of null-sound that counteracted both a vehicle's audible signature and the vibrations it released as it moved. That's how it had sneaked up on the testing grounds unseen. But from where had it come?

There was no time to answer that question.

Rogers stayed deathly still, counting his heartbeats, wondering whether the next pump would be his last. The two barrels leveled at him, like the murderous black-eyed sockets of the Grim Reaper himself. The general had served his country his entire life, and fought to make sure his men would be safe. At least he knew he'd give up that life having given his soldiers the chance to be safe.

A thunderbolt struck the head of the machine and hot, flaming wreckage sprayed all over Rogers. He recoiled from the sudden wave of burning splinters, but when he looked up, he saw that he was unharmed. He patted his jacket and felt the DVD, still intact, nothing had burned or marred his jacket where he'd secreted it.

"General!" a voice shouted. The Ankylosaur opened fire, and Rogers rushed along the ditch away from the autofire. He looked back to see the tail boom of the wounded battle robot swivel toward his troops.

Throwing all caution to the wind, Rogers leveled the muddy M-11 pistol at the raised launcher. He opened fire, burning off the entire 13-round magazine and the hot 9 mm ball round in the pipe. The tail boom sparked as the high-impulse bullets struck home, then flashed brilliantly.

The general's stomach dropped as he realized that the robot tank had launched one of its rockets, but the fireball was too bright to be the flare of the miniature missile's engine. The Earth shook and the tail boom separated from the attacker robot. The explosion flattened the general and knocked the empty pistol from his hand.

He had to have hit the machine rocket as it entered the launch tube; a one in a million shot that had saved the lives of his men.

More antitank missiles and the deep-throated thumps of heavy-caliber antimatériel rifles filled the air.

A young man raced into the ditch, a smoking missile tube in his hands.

"Sir…" Corporal Vance Astrovik called as he swung a rifle off his back. "Sir, are you okay?"

Rogers nodded. "I ordered you men to clear the field."

"We wouldn't leave you behind," Astrovik stated. He saw that the general was soaked with cold muddy water, and bent down to scoop up a helmet full of cold goop. The soldier poured it over his own head and face, then crawled to the edge of the ditch.

"Don't speak. They have some sort of audio detectors, as well," Rogers whispered as he crawled to the corporal's side.

"Fall back, sir. I'll cover your retreat," Astrovik told him.

Rogers knelt to pick up his muddy SIG, then shook out the excess gunk. He slammed home a spare magazine and watched the machines. "Sorry, son. I lead from the front."

Astrovik managed a weak smile.

"Look out!" he suddenly blurted. The young corporal knocked Rogers down to the bottom of the ditch as a crescendo of fire and thunder filled the air.

Rogers glanced up to see the damaged Ankylosaur being hammered by the other units into a mangled pulp of unidentifiable metal. Rockets and explosive cannon rounds left a scorched hulk behind. The robots weren't going to leave much for the Yuma experts to look over after their raid.

Rogers and Astrovik slid from the bottom of the ditch and watched the squat little drones whirl and roll frantically into the distance, disappearing through the scrub. One of the armored machines trailed smoke from a fire, but the general's men wouldn't be able to track it.

Looking around, General Stephen Rogers saw that the test base had been all but flattened. Every vehicle was now a twisted mass of crushed metal and rubber. Some blazed from explosive shells that lit the fuel in their ruptured tanks, but there was nothing on wheels that would allow them to chase down the retreating armored assault drones. Rogers cursed under his breath.

A bugle clarion split the air and Astrovik turned on his radio.

"Our spotters lost the drone toward the old mine pass," Astrovik quickly told Rogers. "They're retreating."

Rogers nodded and took the radio. "Can we get air support?"

"General Rogers?" It was Gunnery Sergeant Pym. "I have Lieutenant Van Dyne calling in. U.S.A.F. states they'll have medevac helicopters here in twenty minutes, but defensive air cover is only thirty seconds away."

"Good man," Rogers said.

A heartbeat later, fighter jets roared through the sky overhead. He couldn't see what they were against the night sky, but as soon as they passed, he could tell by their single cones of exhaust that they were F-16s of some form. He hoped that they had air-to-ground weaponry.

One F-16 cut loose with its 20 mm cannons; the air ripped with the shredding rattle of high-velocity explosive shells. Both jets suddenly swerved as spears of flame lanced into the sky toward them. The drones' rockets sailed into the night, missing their intended targets, but giving the attackers time to escape even further.

"General, we've lost the intruders," Van Dyne broke in. "They're invisible to FLIR and radar... The Air Force can't pick them up on sensors or visually."

Rogers breathed out a harsh sigh.

"I want a team to follow those things' heading, Lieutenant," Rogers ordered. "Call in a mountain operations Ranger team and have them set up with antitank weaponry."

"It'll be a few hours, sir," Van Dyne answered. Despite the carnage, her voice was calm and focused.

Rogers looked in the direction where the Ankylosaurs escaped. The old mine pass was a dead end. Those drones were as good as caught.

But something nibbled at the back of the general's mind.

He doubted that their assailants were going to be found. Not for a long time.

Rogers thumbed the DVD from his jacket.

Those nightmare robots would be seen again. And from what he'd seen so far this night, they had proved to be an irresistible force for destruction.

"God help us," Rogers prayed softly as the F-16s orbited the burning base.

CHAPTER ONE

England

The London fog rolled in on cue as David McCarter took to the streets with his friend Pat. They walked arm in arm, McCarter his usual brisk, ground-eating stride slowed to accommodate the blond woman's pace. She walked with her temple rested against his shoulder.

They'd just left the cinema after watching a controversial film and were engaged in light banter concerning the plot.

Something moved in his peripheral vision as he turned to press his point and he stopped. His combat instincts cried out that trouble was brewing.

Pat felt McCarter's muscles tighten, as rigid as those on a marble statue. "What's wrong?"

A black-clad figure, wielding a submachine gun, darted across the street to climb a small privacy wall around a home. McCarter pushed Pat into the shadows of a house's entranceway and shielded her with his back.

"There's some drama happening," the Phoenix Force leader whispered softly. Drama, in the slang of the SAS, involved guns and imminent violence. "Stay out of sight, no matter what."

Pat's lips pulled tightly into a thin, bloodless line. "You don't have your mates with you."

McCarter reached under his jacket and slid out a tiny Charter Arms .38-caliber revolver and pressed it into her hand. "Don't do anything stupid. If anyone with a gun pops into view, let him have the full load."

Pat nodded nervously. He gave her hand a quick squeeze and turned toward the house. He was in mid-draw of his favored Browning Hi-Power when he spotted two more mysterious figures dart into view. One pivoted and dropped to a knee to aim at McCarter, who lunged out of the path of a line of silenced autofire. The SAS veteran's handgun was out by the time he struck the cobblestone road, its luminous front sight a fuzzy green ball. The glowing dot interrupted the torso of the gunman. He fired two quick shots and rolled frantically so as not to provide a stationary target for the other gunner.

The black-clad wraith that he'd hit twisted to punch another burst of silenced bullets into the road. McCarter leaped behind the fender of a Mini Cooper, its chassis rattling as slugs struck home.

"Dammit." The enemy gunman grunted. "He's behind cover!"

"Who the..." the other assassin whispered as he stepped onto the sidewalk. McCarter swiveled and took aim at the second attacker's knee. He tapped off another shot and was rewarded by his target toppling off balance. The victory was brief, though. A salvo of suppressed gunfire rattled against the bumper of the Mini Cooper in response to the Phoenix Force leader's attack. "That hurt, you miserable..."

McCarter popped up and fired over the roof of the vehicle. This time he pumped out three shots. Sparks flew as bullets exploded against his enemy's helmet. The gunman staggered backward, then shook the cobwebs out of his head. The Briton ducked back behind the body of the car as the Mini Cooper's windows detonated under a hail of automatic weapons fire.

As chunks of broken glass rained down on the Phoenix Force leader, he bit back a growl of frustration. The three head shots would have brought down anyone. Even one bullet would have slipped into the gap between the helmet and the goggles of an armored opponent. But the sparks that exploded showed McCarter that even his custom of loading one hollowpoint and one NATO ball round wasn't enough to penetrate whatever they were wearing. The mix of expanding and deep penetrating ammunition was the Briton's insurance against opponents who wore body armor. At this range, the NATO ball round should have cracked through even a Kevlar helmet.

The two hardmen were betrayed by their shadows as they approached. They assumed that they had the Phoenix Force commander boxed in, and that was their mistake. As long as he had breath in his lungs and his heart still beat, he wouldn't give up. He glanced back and saw Pat huddled in the doorway. If the gunmen got any closer, they'd be able to see her, and the tiny Charter Arms .38 would be even more impotent against their protective armor.

McCarter exploded into action. He charged the gunman in the street and fired directly at the assassin's face. The armored attacker froze at the sight of the Englishman's sudden attack, and was blinded by the point-blank muzzle-flashes and 9 mm rounds smashing into his armored faceplate. The gunman let out an inarticulate yell that gave McCarter all the opportunity he needed. He threw his empty handgun aside and grabbed his enemy's submachine gun. With a savage twist, he pried the weapon to one side and slipped behind his black-clad opponent's body. The other gunman tracked him and opened fire on instinct.

McCarter's human shield jerked as slugs punched into him. He hauled the armored assassin's arm around to grab the killer's weapon. The black-clad body slumped and turned into deadweight as the Briton clawed the subgun out of its grasp. With a kick, the Phoenix Force commander threw himself to the ground and out of the path of another burst of fire.

For a moment McCarter thought that the weapon in his grasp was a mini-Uzi. It had the same feel, but when he triggered it, the bullets that erupted tore through the Mini-Cooper's door as if it were made of tissue paper. The surviving gunman jerked as the slowed slugs hit him. He charged around the back of the vehicle.

The sound of a revolver split the air and sparks erupted on the gunman's body. Pat had seen the killer and she followed McCarter's advice. It was enough to distract the murderer and he twisted to pump a burst into the doorway, but McCarter cut him off and emptied the machine pistol's magazine into the armored attacker.

This time, the gunman folded over and dropped to the ground, dead. McCarter discarded his empty magazine and frisked the corpse for spare ammo. He looked up to see Pat's pale face, eyes wide with fear. He winked at her. "Chin up, love."

She nodded.

He checked the top round in the machine pistol and saw that it was a bottle-nosed bullet. It took a moment for him to figure out what the cartridge was, when he remembered the Saab Bofors Dynamics CBJ MS personal defense weapon. Based on the mini-Uzi, it could be modified to fire 6.5 mm armor-piercing bullets from a bottle-necked 9 mm case. The extra powder charge behind the narrow slug allowed it to pierce Kevlar and ceramic trauma plating with all the authority of a rifle round. He charged up the Bofors and headed for the low wall when he noticed another of the armored gunners crawl into view.

"What the…" the assassin demanded, then saw the lean-faced Briton, armed with the deadly machine pistol. He dropped out of sight before McCarter could trigger the weapon, so the Phoenix Force warrior leaped to the top of the low wall and went prone. He aimed his machine pistol into the darkness, then lined up on the glint of a streetlight on the curved dome of the dark assassin's helmet.

McCarter didn't give his enemy a chance. He cut loose with a salvo of high-powered slugs that chopped into the armored helmet. Chunks of bullet-resistant material flew, smashed to splinters by the Bofors slugs.

He dropped to the lawn and raced toward the house. Through the window, he spotted an armored gunman line up his shot on a cowering woman.

"Not on my watch, mate." McCarter growled as he triggered the Bofors CBJ. Glass shattered and the assassin jerked violently. He still stood, which told the Briton that it would take a close-range salvo, without the interference of even a pane of glass, to neutralize the enemy. He charged the window and dived through even as the would-be assassin recovered.

McCarter felt the heat of the gunner's burst cut closely over him. He triggered the Bofors one last time and stitched his adversary from crotch to throat. The woman screamed as the armored man's corpse smashed violently against the china cabinet. The ex-SAS commando crossed to her and saw that she was uninjured.

"Is there anyone else in the house?" he asked. She looked at him, her dark brown eyes pools of fright.

"*Yo no…*"

"*Esta otros en la casa?*" McCarter quickly corrected. He knew his accent and grammar were horrible, despite his practice with his teammate Rafael Encizo and Rosario Blancanales of Able Team, but he still got the point across.

"*Mi tio,*" she stammered. Her uncle. She pointed, knowing that gestures were easier to understand.

McCarter held his hand out, palm down. "*Abajo.*"

She nodded. She would stay down, and wisely

crawled behind a sofa. The Phoenix Force leader turned and moved deeper into the house. Chances were, there were at least one or two more killers in the building. He dumped his depleted magazine and fed in a fresh one.

McCarter reached the bottom of the stairs, then ducked back as the floor erupted. A hail of gunfire chopped the floorboards to splinters and would have sliced him off below the knees. Crippled and mutilated, he would have been easy pickings for the assassins.

"Hurry up!" a voice shouted. McCarter spotted an apple resting in a bowl by the stairs. He reached for it, pulled the stem out and spit it. Then he hurled the phony grenade up the stairs. "Shit!"

The gunman lurched into view, flushed from the top of the stairs and into the Phoenix Force commando's line of fire. McCarter ripped off a short burst that smashed the gunman's arm to a useless pulp. He swiveled the muzzle and ripped the assassin across the knees. He was going to need answers, and since these guys spoke better English, he picked the one on the steps. The gunman and his weapon slid down the stairs. McCarter rushed to the fallen killer and punched a short burst at the man's outstretched wrist. The black-clad hardman had nearly reached his weapon when the 6.5 mm Bofors rounds completely severed the limb.

"Stay put, mate," McCarter said as he kicked the submachine gun farther down the hall as a precaution. "I want to chat with you in a bit."

He charged up the stairs and saw the last of the armored assassins surge into the hallway. McCarter dropped to the floor instantly, a scythe of burning lead tearing the air where he'd stood moments before. He blasted the black-clad killer across the shins. The high-powered CBJ rounds splintered bone and pulped flesh in their passage, and dumped the murderer to the floor. McCarter rose to go after him, but dropped back down as the hit man wouldn't give up. A Bofors bullet grazed the Phoenix Force leader's shoulder after it punched through the top step.

"Bloody bastards don't know when to quit." He popped up and swept the floor with the submachine gun, turning the landing that the gunman laid upon into a mass of splinters, shredded armor and gore. The Bofors locked open, empty, and instinctively he reloaded the last magazine into the weapon. He wasn't going to be caught off guard.

McCarter approached the last corpse. Bare skull poked through the shattered helmet.

He entered the room that the assassin had just left, then froze. A bloodied sheet covered an immobile lump in the middle of the bed. McCarter shook his head. He'd been too late for the victim. He stepped over to the body and turned on the lamp to look at the man. His features were familiar, but the Briton couldn't quite place them. He frowned and heard the sirens of police cars outside.

The Phoenix Force leader stepped back outside and looked down the stairs. The gunman who'd been deprived of his limbs convulsed, shrieking in pain. McCarter went to the base of the stairs, stripped his machine pistol of its magazine and popped the round out of the chamber. He dropped the empty weapon and laced his fingers behind his head, elbows up.

Two armed policemen burst through the door, the muzzles of their Glock 17 pistols leveled at him.

"There's a dead one in the sitting room, one at the top of the stairs, and they murdered the owner of this home," he offered. "My name is David King. I'm former SAS…"

He turned to let them see that he was unarmed. One officer rushed over to frisk him.

"You've got empty holsters on your hip and ankle," the policeman said.

"I lost my Browning in the street, and my companion has an empty revolver," McCarter replied. "I gave it to her to protect herself."

The policeman fished out his wallet. "You have permits for the handguns, and to carry them concealed. You must be pretty important."

"I'm supposed to be armed. There's an unarmed woman in the sitting room. She speaks Spanish, and she's very frightened. She's the niece of the home owner," McCarter explained.

"Does she speak English?" the other officer asked.

"No. I tried," McCarter replied.

"Do you speak Spanish?" the officer who frisked him asked.

McCarter nodded. "Not fluently, but I can get by when I'm not under pressure."

"Could you help, then, sir?" the policeman asked. "You can lower your hands now."

McCarter relaxed. "Sure. No problem. Bring my friend in?"

The policeman nodded and spoke into his radio. It

was going to be a long night, and McCarter didn't want Pat stuck out in the cold dampness alone.

McCARTER SCREWED HIS KNUCKLE against his eye socket, fighting off the need for sleep. The sun burned in the window, shining on him like God's flashlight. He glanced toward the sofa where Pat slept fitfully, curled tight with her shoulders drawn against a chill that was deeper than her bones.

"Thank you for your patience, Mr. King," Inspector Byers said. "You'll be in the London area for a while?"

McCarter nodded.

Stony Man Farm had enough pull with the British government to arrange for the Phoenix Force leader to leave the city should he be called away on an emergency mission.

"All right," Byers said, reluctance coloring his words. "You're free to go. Just keep in touch."

McCarter shook the detective's hand. "Much obliged, mate."

He walked over to Pat and touched her shoulder. Her pale eyes flickered open immediately.

"What now?" she asked.

"I'm taking you home, love," McCarter answered. He helped her to her feet and laced his arm with hers. Together they walked slowly to the front door and left the crime scene. A police car was out front, waiting to take them wherever they wished.

They remained quiet on the drive back to her flat. It wasn't difficult to fake exhaustion. McCarter could feel the passage of blood cells through his cheeks like the rumble of underground trains. Pat leaned against his shoulder, a warm reassurance that she was all right. His empty holsters felt all wrong, though. The police had, understandably, confiscated the side arms for evidence in the shooting. Byers was thorough, and McCarter bit back his discomfort at being disarmed. Even his spare magazines and strip of .38-caliber cartridges to reload the Charter Arms had been taken away.

Hal Brognola would move heaven and earth to make sure those weapons were retrieved from the evidence locker and replaced with sanitized replicas. The originals bore too many of the Briton's fingerprints and their serial numbers would be traced to David King, his cover persona. All records of the investigation would eventually be purged of any mention of the Phoenix Force commander, the levels of secrecy that Stony Man Farm operated under restored to protect their phantom war against those who thought themselves above the law.

McCarter's mouth was pressed into a tight, brooding frown. Six trained commandos with high-powered weapons and bulletproof armor and helmets hadn't been sent to eliminate *any* old man living in obscurity in London. The bastards he'd fought were too good.

It would have been easier if he hadn't gotten involved, but McCarter hadn't become one of the most experienced warriors in the world because he didn't care. When people needed help, he acted, the consequences of doing the right thing be damned.

They left the squad car when it stopped at her apartment building, and McCarter saw Pat safely to her door. Minutes later he was in a taxicab and back in his room at a nearby hotel.

He went to his luggage, opened a bag and pulled out a spare pistol rug. McCarter unzipped it and revealed a Glock G-34 in 9 mm Parabellum and a smaller Glock 26 in the same caliber. He held up the blocky pistol. The members of Phoenix Force were evaluating the handguns, and as the leader of the team, he had reluctantly accepted the pistol to wring out at a couple of ranges with his fellow SAS men. Calvin James and Rafael Encizo had been the first to fall in love with the Austrian-built handgun and managed to recruit Gary Manning and T.J. Hawkins to their side. The fact that the two men had been able to shoot the gun under water, and had done so in combat, only endeared it further to the experienced divers. The grip, though a little more square, was similar in feel to his Browning. In 9 mm, the G-34 had a 4-shot greater capacity to his beloved Browning, with only a shade more height and thickness to compromise its concealment. Since he usually dressed in oversize, often rumpled clothing, that was no problem.

"The times, they are a changin'," McCarter murmured as he checked to make sure the chamber was loaded. Assured that the Glock was hot, he holstered the gun. The New York 1 trigger, in Glock nonclementure, meant that it was a trigger-cocking only action, only needing a smooth, 7-pound pull of the trigger to fire off a shot. At first he was iffy about the lack of a thumb safety, but the New York trigger's pull was enough to stave off a discharge and the pull of the Safe-Action trigger was as slick and complementary to precision shooting as the single-action trigger of his favored Browning. Plus, the members of the SAS that McCarter had been catching up with had been sold on the Glock family of handguns. The British elite troopers were very excited by the light, safe pull of the new series of pistols. As a bonus, the G-34, while being concealable, had a rail on the dust cover that allowed the men of Phoenix Force to attach laser-aiming modules or various flashlights for low-light combat.

He stuffed the Glock into his waistband. He loaded the little Glock, as well, and deposited it back in the pistol rug.

He zipped it up and carried it to the nightstand. The cell phone looked like a metallic dead rat, a reminder that, for all intents and purposes, his vacation was now over.

Though on a busman's holiday, McCarter was also in London to reinforce some old contacts in the SAS and MI-6, and he'd decided to spend some time with Pat. He plucked the cell from its resting spot in his suitcase and pressed the speed dial, reaching the Farm's secure number.

Barbara Price, as usual burning the midnight oil, took his call after Stony Man's computers pronounced his signal clear of prying ears. "David?"

"Hi, Barb. I came across a situation in England," McCarter explained.

"I know. David King showed up on Scotland Yard's background check," Price stated.

"That's why you're awake—to chew me out, eh?" the Phoenix Force commander asked.

"You know, it's usually Striker or Carl who can't take a decent vacation without getting into a war," Price responded.

"I felt left out," McCarter quipped. He then broke into an account of the men he'd encountered and the murder of the old Hispanic man.

"We've been running a check on the victim. Interpol's firewall is giving Aaron's team a headache," Price said. "The name we entered activated their cybersecurity and clamped things down tightly."

"Bloody inconvenient of them," McCarter snapped.

Price sighed. "It's for the best. The firewall is under their witness protection protocols. It should be too tough to crack."

McCarter frowned. "That's why he seemed so familiar."

"You might know who it is?" Price asked.

"Try Roberto DaCosta," McCarter suggested.

Price muffled the receiver and passed on the information. McCarter waited, knowing it wouldn't take long.

"David?" Price asked.

"What'd you find out?"

"Roberto DaCosta was a Catholic bishop from El Salvador. He testified against the old Organización Democráticia Nacionalista—ORDEN—regime and the ESA. Able Team once pulled security for him against one of their teams," Price responded. "It was a brutal, dirty mission."

McCarter frowned. "Well, I was too late to help him out. ORDEN... Did they hire American mercenaries?"

"Why do you ask?" Price inquired.

"They spoke English and they sounded American," McCarter responded.

"They have recruited experts from all around the world, but right now, ESA is pretty much a dead issue," Price responded. "Most of them are either dead, deported or serving jail time. Again, a lot of ORDEN and their death squads went down hard under Able."

"Maybe someone had a plan to undeport," McCarter replied.

"Someone's trying to make a comeback?"

"Start the guys rattling cages," McCarter answered. "I'm going to check out a few more things on this side of the pond."

"Do you want Phoenix over there?" Price asked.

McCarter shook his head. "No. They could be put to better use working in tandem with Carl and his boys until we pick something up."

"All right. I'll make sure one of Hal's irregulars is on the case to get your pistols back," Price responded. "Do you need to acquire some weapons?"

"I've got the evaluation Glocks."

"Really? I never thought you'd be happy with the new Glock," Price responded.

McCarter patted the gun stuffed into his waistband. "It's not that I have to be happy. If I'm going to trust this gun to protect my boys, then I have to trust it to protect my arse."

"I'll mark this day in history," Price joked.

McCarter chuckled. "I'll never hear the end of this, will I?"

"Nope."

"I'll be in touch," he told her.

"You'll leave your phone on?" Price asked.

"Yeah, I'll keep my phone on. If you don't reach me, leave a voice message," McCarter replied. He hung up.

CHAPTER TWO

"Black seven on red eight." McCarter's voice cut through the darkness.

Christopher Reasoner looked up from his table, solitaire cards splayed out. "It doesn't count as a win if you get help, David."

McCarter, in a knee-length black peacoat, stepped from the shadows. He looked like a floating head in the darkness beyond the pale cone of light thrown down by the desk lamp. "Like you'd have noticed?"

Reasoner moved the stack over under the red eight, then placed a blotter sheet on top of them. "What's up, David?"

"I'm looking for a ship that came in a while back, say within the past week," McCarter replied. "They paid to be left alone."

"You know as a dock authority, I'm supposed to subject all craft to a search," Reasoner answered. He laced his fingers together and gave the SAS veteran his most honest look.

McCarter clucked his tongue and shook his head.

"Chris, don't give me that crap. Someone came in. They didn't do any offloading. I'm thinking, they came from South America."

"David, you're hurting my feelings. When have I ever been duplicitous with you?" Reasoner asked.

McCarter rolled his eyes then leaned forward. He motioned with his finger for Reasoner to come closer. The man glanced toward the door. McCarter tilted his head, a warm friendly smile setting the dock man to ease. Reasoner bent nearer to McCarter, then felt a hand clamp over the back of his head. Before he could resist, his face hammered down into the blotter and he felt his nose crunch sickeningly.

"Bloody hell!" Reasoner howled, streams of blood pouring from his nose like a waterfall.

McCarter yanked the man's head down into the table once more and Reasoner's eyes crossed from the pain. The official's fingers clawed at the rough green construction paper, crumpling it as his tormentor hauled him up, glaring at him angrily.

"Listen, you little tosser," McCarter snarled. "The people on that ship shot at me and nearly shot a close friend."

Reasoner coughed. Red droplets spattered and disappeared on the heavy wool of McCarter's coat. "Oh, fuck me…"

McCarter pushed Reasoner's face into the puddle of blood forming on the crumpled blotter. He applied his full weight to Reasoner's neck, and the official kicked at the smooth concrete floor.

"My neck!" Reasoner sputtered. "You're breaking my bloody neck!"

McCarter sighed and leaned back, letting Reasoner sit up again. "You were a whiny bitch back at the regiment. How long does it take to grow a pair?"

Reasoner reached for a drawer, then heard the snick of a safety. He froze and looked down the nearly half-inch diameter black hole of a muzzle. "I'm getting a box of tissues for my face, you right bastard!"

McCarter nodded, his aim unwavering. "Go ahead and get the box. If you touch anything else, though…"

"You'll kill me?" Reasoner asked.

McCarter smiled. "I'm a better shot than that. I'll just make you wish you were dead, and still leave you able to write the answers I want."

Reasoner saw McCarter shake his head behind the big square slide of the pistol leveled at him. He set his box of tissues on the desktop, pointing out to the SAS man the .357 Magnum revolver resting in the top drawer. The dockman's eyes narrowed. "Were you born a bastard, or did you take lessons?"

"I'm a natural, but that doesn't mean I don't keep training. The amateur trains until he gets it right. The true professional trains until he never gets it wrong," McCarter answered. "Nice Maggie. Hand it over by the barrel."

Reasoner set the revolver on the desktop and sighed. "Okay. A ship called the *Kobiyashi* came in the other day."

"Japanese registry?" McCarter asked.

"Mix of Asians and Hispanics on the crew. Liberian registry, as usual," Reasoner replied. He pressed a wad of tissues to his upper lip and it soaked immediately through and through.

"Where was its last stop?" McCarter inquired.

"Since when did you start taking to plastic pistols?" Reasoner interrupted. He was trying to stall and regain his composure. "Isn't that the new Glock?"

McCarter glared at Reasoner. The 9 mm hole in the business end of the pistol glared at the official with only slightly less intensity and intimidation. After a long, uncomfortable moment, McCarter spoke up. "You like eating through a straw?"

"A straw?"

"Liquid nourishment. Actually, you wouldn't taste it without a tongue, since they'd stick the tube through your nose and straight into your stomach."

"So like I was saying. The *Kobiyashi* was just out of Panama," Reasoner replied. "Came across the canal. Before that they were in the Pacific."

McCarter frowned. "Any idea where?"

"Up in the armpit between Baja, Mexico, and the mainland," Reasoner said. He wiped more of his blood off his chin. "Why?"

"I'm writing a book," McCarter answered.

Reasoner nodded. "Then I'll keep the words short and easy for you to spell."

A thunderbolt went off in Reasoner's right ear, hot flames licking at his eyes. The official screamed and covered his head. Hot stickiness filled the inside of his head and when he opened his left eye, he saw a wisp of smoke rise from the barrel of McCarter's pistol.

"Sorry. Underestimated the muzzle-flash," McCarter replied. It sounded as if he was trying to speak through a pillow. Reasoner reached up and found that his right ear was still there, burned and tender from the nearby muzzle-flash that clamped his right eye shut, but he came away with fresh blood.

"What…"

"I think I blew the eardrum. Sorry, mate," McCarter answered.

Reasoner shuddered. "You're insane."

"I just don't have any patience for smugglers," McCarter responded. "Or the bastards who make it easy for them."

"Listen…" Reasoner began.

"You were kicked out of the regiment for selling off our equipment," McCarter said. "Your lawyer kept you from becoming some bloke's boyfriend in prison, but if it were up to me, you'd be lucky to take a long drop off a short rope."

"I didn't sell to the Provos," Reasoner answered. "And it was old gear…back stock."

McCarter was unmoved. "What berth?"

"They're setting sail in five minutes. You'll never catch them," Reasoner replied.

"Leave it to me," McCarter said. "What berth?"

"Thirteen," Reasoner answered.

"Close your eyes, Chris," McCarter ordered.

The official closed his good eye. "You're not going to shoot me, are you?"

Silence.

It took Reasoner nearly five minutes for him to get up the courage to see if McCarter was still there.

MCCARTER KNEW that he was going to be cutting it close. Not only was he armed with only a pair of pistols that weren't ones he was familiar with, and Reasoner's .357 Magnum revolver, but he was all alone. A takedown of a ship would need at least two more people, as Able Team had proved several times. He'd have preferred to have all four of his Phoenix Force teammates on hand to throw in against the smugglers on the *Kobiyashi*.

It would have to do. The Phoenix Force leader didn't want to lose track of the boat. Already the sailors were undoing the moorings. The bow's rope, big and fat, was being hauled up over the railing while two sailors unwound the stern cable. Crewmen jogged up the gangplank.

"All aboard!" came the call from the deck.

It was now or never.

One more thing slowed the Phoenix Force leader. There was a possibility that the entire crew on the ship wasn't implicated in the transport of a team of assassins. McCarter was audacious and ruthless, but he wasn't a cold-blooded murderer and when he fought, he fought against those he knew were killers and had deadly intent. He'd fall back to the handguns as a means of last resort, which meant that he was even further behind the curve.

"Hey! We're casting off," a Filipino sailor called to him. The round-faced seaman was stocky, his shoulders betraying a burly strength. "You can't come aboard."

"Official business, no time for a chin-wag," McCarter said as he barely slowed, sidestepping the Filipino.

The stocky sailor grabbed McCarter's arm and pulled open his jacket to reveal a revolver. The former SAS commando pivoted and broke the Filipino's nose with the point of his elbow, then plucked the revolver from the man's waistband. "I told you, no time to talk, mate."

A second sailor rushed up, but instead of helping out his stunned shipmate, he reached for his own weapon. McCarter sighed and pistol-whipped the man across the jaw with the barrel of the Filipino's revolver, twisting the newcomer's handgun out of his grasp. A sweep of his feet across the man's ankles, and the Briton dumped the man to the ground. With a quick flip, he had a revolver in each fist.

"Anyone else want to slow me down?" McCarter growled.

The other sailors who were handling the moorings looked at the armed man, dressed in black and packing a brace of handguns after three quick strikes. They didn't want to see what he could do with bullets and took off running. McCarter let them flee and continued up the gangplank.

A figure rushed to the railing and McCarter spotted a submachine gun in his grasp. Uzis weren't standard issue for security forces on a ship, so he threw himself flat on the slanted walkway. Both revolvers spoke with thunderous reports. Twin .38-caliber slugs chopped into the gunner and threw him onto his back before he could aim. Autofire ripped from the dead man's assault weapon into the night sky.

"Good news and bad news," McCarter muttered to himself as he leaped to his feet and raced to the deck. "Good news, now I know who the bad guys are. Bad news, they got bigger guns than I do."

On deck, he looked both ways and watched as an-

other pair of gunmen burst from the wheelhouse. Their
weapons were an odd mix, one carrying a battered
AK-47, the other packing another of the compact Bofors CBJs. McCarter took the CBJ gunner in the face
with two slugs from his right-hand weapon, and put a
bullet from the other revolver through the wrist of the
AK man's trigger hand. The rifleman screamed as he
clutched his ruined limb to his chest, his weapon forgotten as it tumbled over the rail.

McCarter rushed toward the wheelhouse and discarded the partially spent revolvers. He skidded to a halt,
scooped up the fallen assault rifle, shouldered it and
looked for more targets. The wounded gunman above
pulled his sidearm and leaned over the railing. The
Phoenix Force commander sidestepped before a bullet
exploded on the metal at his feet. Then he pulled the
AK's trigger.

Nothing. He racked the bolt and chambered a new
round, the old case spinning from the breech. He tried
to shoot again, but there was still nothing. The injured
guard fired again, twice, but upside down and using the
wrong hand, his accuracy was off, not that McCarter left
himself as a stationary target. He popped the magazine
and saw that the casings were green and rusted from too
many years at sea.

As another shot chased him, the Phoenix Force veteran dived behind the bulkhead, leaving the AK-47 behind. Poor weapons maintenance would have gotten
him killed. He reached for the alloy-framed Glock
G-34 and drew it, the safety snicked off reflexively. Mc-
Carter suddenly felt very comfortable with the new

handgun. It was blockier than his sleek Browning, but
the muzzle thickness helped add to the heft that made
the balance feel almost like his confiscated pistol.

The door crashed open and a fat thug with a shotgun
burst onto the deck. McCarter didn't wait for the newcomer to aim, triggering the G-34 twice. High-velocity
127-grain hollowpoint rounds slammed into the big
guard, and it was as if the man had hit an invisible force
field. The shotgunner collapsed to the walkway with a
sigh and a thud. McCarter leaped over the dead man and
cut into the door he'd exited.

A black-armored phantom with the same gleaming
helmet as he'd encountered the night before loomed at the
top of the stairs. McCarter dived into a hallway as armor-
piercing slugs smashed the floor where he'd stood instants
before. Tucked into a shoulder roll, he somersaulted another few feet and came up facing the stairwell. He let the
Glock hang in his left hand, yanked out Chris Reasoner's
.357 Magnum revolver and thumbed back the hammer.

The armored assassin stepped into view and received
a hot blast of 125-grain lead, screaming along at nearly
1500 feet per second. The 9 mm might not have penetrated the goon's armor, and the hollowpoint round
didn't do much better, but the high-powered bullet did
flatten the machine gunner. McCarter snapped up the
Glock and punched a single 127-grain bullet into the
gun of the attacker, wrenching the Bofors autoweapon
from the killer's grasp.

McCarter followed up with a solid kick to the helmeted man's chin. A sickening crunch sounded and the
gunman was stilled. The Stony Man commando's gam-

ble had paid off. There was no way the automatic weapons and body armor would have gotten through aircraft or train customs, but the bribery at the docks and the nature of boat smuggling would have made it all but impossible for someone to truly check out the ship. Security was tight in the post 9/11 era, but short of dismantling the freighter, there would have been no way to find everything.

The stunned, armored assassin struggled to get up, but McCarter stooped and pulled the helmet off the killer. "Who're you working for?"

The hit man looked down the muzzle of the 9 mm Glock. "I'm not going to talk."

McCarter growled and pistol-whipped the armored killer into nerveless unconsciousness. Boots pounded on the metal grating that made up the steps, and he shifted his aim back to the stairwell.

The first gunman into the open caught a .357 Magnum slug in the groin. Pelvis shattered, his legs stopped working and he plopped into a heap in the hallway. Two more guards tripped over the fallen seaman, their weapons clattering as they struggled to stay up. McCarter caught one of the pair as he bent to grab his assault rifle and punched a 9 mm round through the joint of his shoulder and neck. Bone and muscle were destroyed instantly as the hollowpoint tunneled deep and stopped in the sentry's left lung. The body smashed face-first into the floor and flopped to one side.

"Don't do it!" McCarter ordered the other gunman as he reached for a revolver under his sweater.

The guard paused for a moment, but a slamming

door behind the Briton spun his attention away. He dropped to the ground as another of the thugs cut loose with a charge of buckshot. Pellets zipped over McCarter's head and crashed into the paralyzed gunner, a salvo of shot blowing him off his feet.

The Phoenix Force leader took out the shotgunner with two shots from the thundering Magnum revolver, then turned to look at the carnage.

"I'm dying, man," the wounded gunman whispered, blood rasping in his lungs.

McCarter looked helplessly at the bloody chest of the seaman. He was skilled enough in battlefield medicine to stop lethal blood loss from a single bullet wound, but the chopped hamburger that remained in the path of the 12-gauge's violence was larger than the Briton's fully spread hand. He tore a wad of cloth from a corpse's shirt, but by the time he made a compress out of it, the wounded sailor had expired.

McCarter frowned in frustration. He'd come onto this ship to get answers, not to leave behind total carnage. He shook his head in disgust and checked the load on Reasoner's revolver. Three shots remained in the cylinder, so he stuffed it away as a backup weapon. He checked the load in the Glock and the 17-shot reservoir was still more than half full. He pocketed the partially depleted magazine and fed it a fresh stick.

McCarter holstered the Glock and picked up the Bofors, but cast it aside when he found that the receiver had been smashed by the 9 mm slug he'd punched into it. Instead, he picked up an old battered Sterling. Remembering his encounter with the rotten ammo in the AK-47, he pointed at a wooden crate marked "shoes" and pulled the trigger for a short burst, using the cargo to absorb any ricocheting rounds. The submachine gun burped to the SAS veteran's satisfaction and he frisked the dead man for spare magazines. He found two more curved 32-round sticks for the Sterling and pocketed them.

He moved to where the latest gunmen had entered the superstructure on the freighter, and saw an assembly of figures heave something long over the side. McCarter shouldered the Sterling.

"Don't move!" he warned.

A pair of black-clad assassins dived over the railing as another man spun. McCarter triggered a burst into the gunman. Bullets sparked against ceramic trauma plating and the gunman's helmet, and the Phoenix Force pro rolled back through the door to escape a salvo of 6.5 mm armor-piercing rounds. As it was, only falling to the deck had saved him as the Bofors bullets punched through the steel bulkhead above him.

The torrent of withering fire kept McCarter pinned long enough for whomever was on the deck to escape. When there was a lull in the shooting, he swung out and saw that the railing was clear. Only the churning white water produced by the Zodiac boat's engines gave any indication where the enemy had gone, and by the time he rushed to the bow of the ship, they were out of range for the machine pistol he carried. Even though he'd fired on the run, there was no sign that the Sterling had done anything. He let the submachine gun hang on its sling and let out a sigh of frustration.

He had prisoners, though.

It was a beginning.

Not a satisfying beginning, but it would have to do.

MCCARTER LIT a cigarette, then took a pull from his can of Coca-Cola Classic. He replayed the interrogation of the armored assassin, mind reeling from the implications of the man's answers. He tried to push aside what he'd had to do to get those answers.

Phoenix Force had a long career of capturing and interrogating prisoners. While they used mostly psychological trickery to get their answers, bad cop/good cop scenarios and such before they had acquired Calvin James's medical expertise and the use of drugs, there had been a few times when McCarter had had to bloody his hands.

Combat against armed and capable opponents was one thing. Torture, though, was something that disgusted him. But without a trained medic to monitor heart rate and examine the prisoner for heart defects, the Phoenix Force commander had to do things the old-fashioned way.

"Torture is inefficient," his predecessor and mentor, Yakov Katzenelenbogen, used to say. "People will say anything to stop the pain, and it's too time-consuming a process."

McCarter winced inwardly. He felt like he'd let the old man down, but he'd needed what answers he could get.

Not only was the mission at stake, but now that he understood what was going on, all of Central America was threatened. He closed his eyes and fought down guilt for doing horrible things to vulnerable, defenseless flesh.

It was one thing to pop Reasoner's eardrum and to smash his face into a tabletop a couple of times. A little rough-housing was needed to convince the traitorous scumbag that it was in his best interests to spill information.

The assassin, however, required work. McCarter did what had to be done. Unease bubbled and roiled inside of him as he sifted through the memories of pleading cries for mercy to get to the information about the designated mission of the assassins.

Roberto DaCosta had been assassinated by a hired crew of killers. While the assassin hadn't known much about who had hired them, he had known that after they left the port, they were to rendezvous with a sea plane several miles offshore to return to Central America for further sweeps.

Whatever happened, someone was going to have to back up the mastermind's play. Denied his cadre of nearly invulnerable murderers, or most of them, there would be a mad scramble to refill the ranks to continue the operation. McCarter thought about those who had escaped on the Zodiac boat. The motorized raft would have the speed and range to make the rendezvous with time to spare. There would be no way to intercept them, and they would report back to their boss that they were no longer working in secrecy.

McCarter realized that instead of flushing his targets, he might have driven them back underground, deeper into hiding.

The flight would keep him in the chase, but Phoenix Force and Able Team would be busy elsewhere, hunting down leads. He'd contacted the Farm via cell phone, and that would give them a head start. Maybe they would be able to intercept the escaping assassins, though it was doubtful.

It had been pure luck that allowed McCarter to stumble on this operation, and Barbara Price made noises that there was another emergency in the works that would occupy Able Team's concentration. She didn't give details over the cell phone. Even though their communications were over secure lines, operational procedure was that she didn't share information that the Phoenix Force leader didn't need to know. If Able Team pulled off their mission in time, maybe they could assist afterward.

Until then, Phoenix Force was on its own.

McCarter knew one thing, though.

It was better than being all by himself. While he didn't feel helpless without his teammates, it would be good working with his friends, the four men he considered his family, once again.

Standing together, the five warriors of Phoenix were truly an irresistible force.

CHAPTER THREE

Yuma, Arizona

Hermann "Gadgets" Schwarz looked at the assembled scorched garbage strewed across the tabletop at Yuma.

"We've had some of our best tech experts look over this," General Rogers told the Able Team genius as he poked at a charred circuit board. "Nothing that survived could be identified or traced to a manufacturer. At least not with the technology we have on hand."

Schwarz shook his head slowly as he picked up the burned circuit board piece. "You've cataloged and photographed all the pieces, where they were placed in the remote drone?"

Rogers nodded. "Yes. Our techs are attempting to reverse engineer the design, but the missiles and explosive 20 mm shells smashed the machinery and electronics apart brutally."

Schwarz looked at his notebook. "You have a very

concise description of their sensory and stealth capabilities, however."

"Mostly through close personal experience," Rogers stated.

"How close?" Schwarz asked.

Rogers looked at the floor between them, then took two paces back. "About this range."

Schwarz released a low whistle. "You like to lead from the front, sir."

The general shrugged. "I'm responsible for my men. It didn't hurt that I was on the run for my life, but... Son, I don't know who you're supposed to be, but these things attacked and killed my people, my friends. This place, for all its secrecy and military regimen, is a home for us. We're as close to a family as we can get here. Do you know what I mean?"

Schwarz glanced toward the entrance where Rosario Blancanales and Carl Lyons stood. They conducted interviews about the Ankylosaur raid with other members of the proving ground staff. "Heart and soul, General."

"I want to find whoever's responsible for this and bring them to justice," Rogers said. "If you need anything, I'll make sure you get it."

"Thank you, sir," Schwarz replied. "Is it okay if I take some of the wreckage to your lab? I want to work with it."

"No problem," Rogers answered.

Schwarz gave the general a reassuring smile. "We'll get these guys. They might be able to run, but they won't hide for long. Not from us, sir."

He picked up several pieces and set them in clear plastic bags.

Rogers and the Able Team genius crossed to the entrance of the hangar, where Lyons and Blancanales both stopped and greeted their friend with a nod. Blancanales reflexively gave the general a smart salute, which was returned.

"Another ex-military man?" Rogers asked.

Blancanales nodded. "For security, that's about all I can say."

"I understand," Rogers answered.

"I'm hitting the lab to look at some of these components. I think I can pick something out of the bits and pieces," Schwarz said. "Think the two of you can handle the recon without me?"

Lyons rolled his eyes. "No problem. I think we can track a few killer robots without you. Go nerd out and we'll tell you about the exciting hike we took later."

Schwarz sighed. "You're too good to me, Ironman."

"That's something I thought I'd never hear." Lyons grunted. "C'mon, Pol. Saddle up and head 'em out."

"'Rawhide,'" Blancanales quipped. He pointed toward the 4-wheeled ATVs and slipped on his helmet. "Able style."

"Don't let Cowboy hear you say that," Lyons said, referring to John "Cowboy" Kissinger, the Stony Man Farm armorer.

"I don't think Cowboy ever rode a horse in his life," Blancanales answered.

Lyons threw one leg over the seat and sat down. He revved the engine and slipped on his helmet. "Sure you wouldn't rather come with us?"

"I don't think there's going to be anything in the

mine," Schwarz replied. "But if there is, bring me a few chunks back."

Lyons nodded. "Have a good time."

Lyons, Blancanales and the team of MPs rode off on their four-wheelers.

Logic told Schwarz that there wouldn't be any trouble, but something nagged at him. "General? Could you have someone set the lab up for me?"

Rogers looked after Lyons and Blancanales as they left. "You've got that feeling, too."

Schwarz pulled a spare helmet off the ATV they'd set aside for him. He checked the rifle stuck in the saddle, then made sure his personal weapons were secure. "I've learned never to distrust my instincts. As soon as they pulled away…"

"I understand. Don't waste time gabbing with me," Rogers told him.

Schwarz fired up the ATV and rushed off to join the rest of Able Team.

THE PLATOON OF RANGERS that Able Team hooked up with had the mine entrance hemmed in. The powerful Fabrique Nationale M-240 machine guns rested on bipods. The 7.62 mm muzzles stared into the darkened cave, ready to unleash a torrent of armor-piercing thunder against anything that made a move out the front. A trio of Dragon antitank missile pods rested on their legs, the big fat tubes similarly aimed. The Dragon warheads had the power to tear apart any modern tank, and if they couldn't stop the Ankylosaurs, they would at least bring down a huge section of mountainside.

Tons of rubble would stop even the killer robot tanks.

Carl Lyons waited for the Rangers to set up the mighty M-2 .50-caliber machine guns. That would finish the ring of steel that would hem in any escaping drones. He pulled his rifle from the ATV's saddle sheath and snapped back the bolt, chambering a .50 Beowulf rifle round into his weapon's breech. The magazine held twelve of the massive rounds in the same space that a normal M-16 would have held a full thirty shots. He traded firepower for purely awesome stopping power. While the .50 Beowulf round was only half as long as the rounds fired by the M-2 machine gun, it was still a significant powerhouse. Kissinger had given Able Team several magazines of tungsten-cored slugs, designed for use against armored vehicles.

Just in case.

Lyons checked the light on the muzzle of his rifle, then looked to the others.

"M-16, Viking style," Blancanales said. He couldn't quite hide the tension in his voice.

Schwarz slipped on a pair of Wolf Ears hearing protectors and clicked them on. "Give me a sound check."

Blancanales and Lyons wore the same hearing protectors. Advanced electronics and padding would prevent ruptured eardrums caused by the thunder of automatic weapons in a cave, but sensitive microphones would pick up softer sounds that could betray an enemy. The three men of Able Team had trained with the Wolf Ears long enough to know that they worked under stressful, nasty and dirty conditions. When they were forced to use full-power, unsuppressed weapons in a tunnel, they often made the effort to wear the hearing protector-amplifiers.

"Testing," Lyons whispered.

"Yabba dabba doo," Blancanales spoke softly.

"You guys are confusing me as to which one's the caveman," Schwarz quipped.

Lyons slipped his goggles down over his eyes again. He made sure they didn't displace his Wolf Ears. "Funny. Remind me to laugh later."

"Whenever I do, you hit me with a newspaper," Schwarz answered. The Able Team leader only narrowed his gaze. He wasn't known for his sense of humor, especially this close to a possible engagement.

"Lock and load your rifles," Lyons ordered as he picked up a large lantern. "I'm on point."

Blancanales and Schwarz put aside their banter and fell into step behind Lyons. They spread out and stalked into the mine entrance.

Blancanales paused and shone his light on the ground. "This floor has been graded."

Lyons knelt and ran his fingertips over the hard-packed earth. "No signs of treads. Gadgets?"

"They weren't hovercraft," Schwarz replied. "But what dust there is has been smoothed out. Look… There are rails."

Lyons walked over and tapped his flash hider against the bent metal. "Something heavy rolled over this. There's gouge marks on it, too."

Blancanales looked at the scarred and mutilated metal, then stared deeper into the tunnel. "Some other machine?"

"A digger?" Schwarz asked. He moved farther down the tunnel, then squinted through his goggles. "Someone knocked a back door through to Yuma's testing facility."

Schwarz pulled out a map from his case and flicked his light on it. "The Bear gave me some maps to help me figure out how the attack drones could have escaped."

"This mountain range is heavy-duty granite, though," Lyons said. "Right?"

"Mountains usually occur when tectonic plates collide. The higher the mountains, the newer they are and the more force behind their collision. The Blue Ridge Mountains, where the Farm is located, are very old and worn down, but there are fissures and caves throughout them. Geological surveys try to map them out, but you can't find them all," Schwarz answered. "Whoever made this attack had this place geographically staked out."

"And they had just the right size digger to punch a hole big enough from a naturally formed cave, or even an underground river to pop up in this mine," Lyons finished. His brow furrowed. "It's been nearly fifteen hours since the initial attack. We might have lost the trail."

Something rumbled in the darkness.

"Or not…" Blancanales spoke up. He shouldered his rifle and looked through its scope. "Something big's moving in."

Lyons snicked the safety off on his Beowulf. "Pull back."

An engine revved and roared, and floodlights snapped on. The Able Team leader pivoted and opened fire, .50-caliber, tungsten-cored slugs erupting from the muzzle of his rifle. The heavy slugs sparked violently on machinery. Through the lights, the three Stony Man commandos saw the whirling shapes of multiple drill heads spin wildly.

"Aw, hell," Schwarz muttered as he cut loose with his own weapon. "We found the digger!"

"Fall back!" Lyons bellowed as the machine continued to close.

Blancanales triggered the M-203 attachment under his Beowulf. "Fire in the hole!"

A tunnel-shaking explosion, deadened by the sonic filters on the Wolf Ears, flared. The drilling machine was cast in stark relief. The moment that the high-explosive flashed, three rotating cones of multiple drills were visible, gnashing stone-chewing teeth flickering wickedly like the mouth of some hideous dragon.

The digger paused for a brief moment, shaken by the high-explosive grenade fired by Blancanales, then lurched forward again. Lyons shoved the Able Team veteran behind him and held down the trigger for an extended burst of heavy-caliber, armor-piercing slugs.

The spinning drill heads bounced slugs all over. The machine was all but indestructible as it bore down relentlessly on them.

Lyons dumped the empty magazine from his rifle, then looked back at Blancanales, who forced a fresh grenade into the breech of his launcher.

"I told you to move it!" Lyons growled.

A canister sailed over the two men, interrupting the Able Team commander.

"Heads down!" Schwarz called.

Lyons grunted as Blancanales kicked him out of the way and aimed at the ceiling above the digger.

The double-shock wave shook the whole mine and rolled over Lyons as if it were the treads of the deadly machine itself. Rock tried to flex, but shattered and crumbled. The pressure wave blew the Wolf Ears right off Lyons's head, and he shook off the thunderbolt that cracked between his ears.

A clap on his shoulder brought him out of a temporary daze and he saw Blancanales shouting at him. The man's lips moved, but nothing was coming through the ringing in his skull. He glanced over and saw the digger, its drill bits still whirring wildly. It had stopped, though, one light torn from its housing by the shearing force of the double explosion.

"—said are you okay, Ironman?" Blancanales asked.

"Yeah. What did you do?" Lyons asked.

"I dropped some of the roof on that thing, and Gadgets flipped some high explosive under the belly of the beast. Looks like he took care of at least one set of treads, and the collapsed rock pinned the rest down."

Lyons blinked and saw Schwarz, highlighted by the remaining floodlight on the drill, his rifle aimed at the ground, looking around the sides of the machine when the thing lurched. Schwarz stepped back and fired a short burst into the drill head, but only succeeded in raising more sparks as heavy tungsten bit into solid steel.

"I don't think it's dead!" Lyons mocked as Blancanales helped haul him to his feet. They kept out of the range of the churning teeth. He looked around the front, then saw Schwarz shoulder his rifle and fire a single shot.

Smoke billowed and the trio of drill heads slowed.

"Spotted the motor and tried to take it out with a burst," Schwarz explained. "Pull back some. I'm going to roll a grenade under the other motor."

Lyons nodded, and he and Blancanales pulled back. The Able Team leader donned his Wolf Ears again and clamped them tight over his head. Schwarz raced back to them, and a new detonation rumbled in the confines of the tunnel. Blancanales and Schwarz spoke again, but it was muffled by the hearing protectors. Lyons tried the microphone switch and shook his head, removing the headset.

"That did it," Schwarz replied. He looked at the Wolf Ears. "Problems?"

"Yeah," Lyons answered.

"Let me look at it," Schwarz told him. "Go check on the digger."

Lyons nodded and followed Blancanales. The drill bits no longer moved, and Pol slid his frame between the digger's chewing drill points and the ground. It was a little too close for the brawny ex-cop's tastes, in case the machine managed one last surge of power. It could easily chew his friend to a pulp and Lyons wouldn't have a chance to rescue him.

"Looks like we have room to get behind it," Blancanales called. "The tunnel is pretty clear. A little rubble from the cave-in, but other than that…"

"Can you check to see if this thing's fully down for the count?" Lyons asked. "I don't want to have you stuck under this bastard with your shins chopped into ground beef."

"Sure, hang on. Gadgets's first grenade peeled open the bottom, and I can see a few engine parts," Blancanales explained. He clicked on a pocket-size flashlight, then drew an Emerson folding knife. The sturdy blade sliced through cables, though the Able Team commando hissed as a slight jolt burned his fingers.

"You okay?" Lyons asked.

"Yeah. I cut through the main battery cables, and a little bit of the charge came up the blade. I wasn't in good contact with the metal, though, so nothing more than a small burn," Blancanales replied. "Taking care of the generator cables now, too."

The floodlight cut out, and Lyons snapped on his pocket light. Schwarz tapped him on the shoulder and he accepted his Wolf Ears back. "What was wrong?"

"The shock wave knocked the battery wires loose. I stripped the insulation, hand wound it back together again, and taped it up. It won't be perfect," Schwarz said, "but you can hear, and the protectors will keep your eardrums safe. I'll solder it into prime shape when we get back to base."

"Good," Lyons answered. "All right. Tie some rope around your rifle and pack. Pol's going to haul our stuff through so we can get past this hunk of junk."

"You think we might find something at the other end," Schwarz replied.

"Yeah," Lyons answered.

Schwarz looked at the machine, then frowned. "Hang on."

He reached into his pack and pulled out a meter. "Pol! Shut off your comm for a minute! You too, Carl."

Lyons nodded and did as his partner said.

"I'm picking up some readings," Schwarz said. "A carrier wave."

"But Pol killed the power," Lyons replied.

Schwarz backed up and continued to look at his field meter. "It's got its ears live for something. Wait… starting to pick up a signal the closer to the entrance I get. Pol?"

"I'm checking," Blancanales called back. "Yeah! I feel this thing packed with plastic explosive."

"Let me get in there," Schwarz ordered. He pulled out another device and handed it to Lyons. "This is a jammer. Stand right where I was, and keep this thing on until I tell you to turn it off. Someone's transmitting a detonation code to some explosives in the machine."

"Enough to bring down the tunnel and take out a search party," Lyons mused.

"You catch on fast," Schwarz replied. Blancanales slid out from under the digger and Schwarz slipped underneath after clamping wire cutter handles in his teeth.

Blancanales crouched and added his light to Schwarz's efforts under the machine. Lyons, no expert at demolitions disposal, stood with the jammer, sullen and silent. He didn't like standing by helplessly, but he knew that his lack of experience with disarming explosives would only be a hindrance. Gadgets and the Politician were weaned on C-4 from their A-Team experience. If anyone could handle the booby-trapped juggernaut, it was his partners.

Lyons took a deep breath and waited for the deadly digger to be tamed.

Rosario Blancanales accepted the central processor from Hermann Schwarz.

"Save that. Bear and the others are going to have a field day working on its programming," Schwarz told his old friend.

Blancanales nodded. "How did this thing move without radio controls?"

"The processor. It must be an artificial intelligence unit. Fairly basic. We set off the digger's motion detectors as soon as we got too close," Schwarz answered. Something snapped in the hollowed gut of the machine. "Damn. We woke it up. It's got infrared sensors."

Blancanales shook his head. "As soon as it got the detonation signal, it would have dropped the whole mountain onto us."

"Or whoever went in. I'm thinking that they expected a platoon of soldiers, sweeping the darkness with IR to keep from being 'seen,'" Schwarz replied. "It would have been like waking up Ironman with a floodlight in the face."

Schwarz shimmied out from under the machine with a handful of radio components. "The detonators."

"Look like standard radio units," Blancanales replied.

"They are, but we can trace them. I'll pull out the C-4, and then we'll get the Rangers to pull out the digger," Schwarz told him. "We're going overland."

Blancanales smiled. "The transmitter for the detonation signal would likely be manned."

Schwarz nodded. "Beats a tunnel fight, especially if the drones rolled through an underground river. We don't have scuba gear with us."

"Good thinking," Blancanales congratulated. "I'm sure Carl would like the breathing room too."

Schwarz took out the squashed blocks of explosives and set them apart from the detonators. "Scorched earth, and a bunch more dead soldiers. The bastard behind these robots is starting to piss me off."

Blancanales knew that the electronics genius was a mellow, slow-to-anger man. It stemmed from his Southern California upbringing, and the endless patience it took to work with ever-shrinking electronic components. The fact that he mentioned being upset meant that Schwarz's blood had to have been boiling. Though he was part of the Stony Man Farm operation, he was still a veteran of the United States Army, and the death of brother soldiers always struck him hard. And unlike Carl Lyons, who mastered his berserker's temper long ago, Schwarz got very cold when he got angry.

"We'll take care of this," Blancanales told him. "That's our job. Revenge for the good guys…semiofficial style."

"Prosecution to the max," Lyons added. He picked up the C-4 to take it to the Rangers at the entrance. "I heard you two talking. We're going overland?"

Schwarz nodded. His lips were drawn tight, trying to control his emotions.

"I'll see if we can get a pilot," Lyons replied. "Gadgets…"

Schwarz glanced up.

"They're dead. They just don't know it," Lyons reassured.

Schwarz nodded tightly, as if the muscles in his neck were coiled to the breaking point. "I gotcha, big guy. Prosecution to the max."

THE CANYON WAS too tight to land a UH-60, but a Hughs 500D "Little Bird" could set down nicely. The pilot was a clean-cut kid named Lieutenant Tim Sarlets.

"You boys call for a ride?" he asked.

"Yeah," Schwarz replied. He climbed into the shotgun seat. He had one of his radio monitors in his lap, and looked at the Army pilot. "We're going to be doing a little circling, triangulating a radio signal. Think you can do that?"

"Sure thing," Sarlets answered. "Any other requests?"

"Keep us low," Lyons told him. "We don't want whoever we're triangulating to spot us coming."

Sarlets gave the big, blond ex-cop a short salute. "Roger that. I kind of figured you didn't want to be seen."

"I like this guy. Can we keep him around?" Blancanales asked.

"We'll have to ask the boss," Lyons responded.

Loaded up, the men of Able Team strapped in and the Little Bird rocketed skyward.

CARL LYONS PERCHED in the open side-door of the helicopter. In the darkness below, somewhere, a radio transmitter broadcast a signal that was intended to kill dozens of American soldiers on their home soil. On top of a massacre by armored juggernauts, the tragedy would have been compounded as more brave men died and the trail to the murderous masterminds would have been closed off by a collapsed mountain.

His knuckles flexed white around the grip of his Beowulf M-4. He'd replaced the magazine of tungsten-cored antimatériel rounds with a load of 350-grain jacketed hollowpoint bullets. Even against a living opponent who wore body armor, they'd shatter bones and mangle muscle behind Kevlar. Through the night-vision goggles attached to the helicopter helmet, the terrain beneath him was a weird, alien world of green hazy stone and deep shadows. He spotted movement and shouldered the Beowulf, but held his fire as a goat trotted out of a dark recess. Lyons lowered the rifle and shook his head.

"Anything yet?" he asked, impatience gnawing at his core.

Schwarz looked up from his map. He marked off another zone where the radio signal started to fade. "One more sweep, Ironman."

"Good." Lyons grunted. He double-checked the 40 mm high explosive round in the M-203 launcher stored under the barrel. Just because it was unlikely that they would run into the deadly drones that swept down on Yuma didn't mean he didn't want to have something that could devastate the slaughtering robots.

Schwarz's murmurings, readings of the field monitor as he registered signal strength, were a low drone, a constant reminder that this was slow, tedious work. Lyons strained his ears, listening for the readings. He picked up Gadgets's mutters of a lower signal strength and tensed even before the electronics genius made his announcement.

"That's the box," Lyons stated. He pointed toward a ripple of shadows and outcroppings. "Sarlets, put us down. We're on foot from here."

"I've got no clean spots to land. This is rough terrain," the pilot answered.

"That's good news," Blancanales replied. "They couldn't bring heavy antiaircraft along."

"How about a crane helicopter?" Schwarz asked.

Lyons shook his head. "This place is too close to Yuma to pull that kind of—"

"The drones were invisible to radar," Gadgets reminded him.

The Able Team leader's jaw set firmly as he scanned the shadowy terrain ahead. "If they had stealth robot tanks, then they could build a stealth helicopter."

A red light buzzed on the control console. "We're hot! Target radar lock!" the pilot announced as he wrenched the helicopter hard.

Strapped in, Lyons felt jerked like a puppy on a leash. Out of the darkness, he saw a flaming halo growing in intensity and following the aircraft's movements as the chopper thrashed.

He knew exactly what the flaming halo was—the rocket exhaust of an antiaircraft missile, the lethal shaft of its warhead forming the black void in the center of a hellfire ring.

Death shrieked at the men of Able Team on a jet of flame.

CHAPTER FOUR

Virginia

T.J. Hawkins sighed and slipped his Glock 26 into its hip holster. A second, identical tiny Glock was holstered at his ankle, and two 12-round magazines were clipped to his belt. He looked over to Calvin James as the man checked the loads on his .45-caliber Colt Commander and his backup short-barreled Colt Python.

"Jet Aer G-96 in an ankle sheath," James told Hawkins.

"We're going to CIA Headquarters. They're just going to try to take our weapons away anyhow," Hawkins replied. "Why do we have to run this drill every time we go out armed?"

Gary Manning and Rafael Encizo both shook their heads as they made sure of their weapon loads.

James, a tall, black man, held up his hand to the others. "T.J. hasn't done as much legwork as we have, guys. Just because we've had some pretty soft travels for the past few years with him on military flights and not a lot of street-level investigation…"

Manning, a brawny Canadian, nodded. "I know. You were dropped in without being told how cold the water was with us. Since the majority of our activities lately have been paramilitary operations, T.J. hasn't been given much exposure to the classic Stony Man Tourist Luck."

"Stony Man Tourist Luck?" Hawkins asked.

Encizo, a handsome Cuban, grinned widely. "Whatever can come out of the woodwork will come out of the woodwork."

"Terrorists at the airport," James began.

"Thuggee assassins with strangling scarves," Manning added.

"Don't forget wolves," Encizo admonished Manning. "Of all the times to have been without my PPK…"

"And ninjas," James stated.

"Like *cucarachas*." Encizo spit.

"This is CIA Headquarters, guys. Not downtown Beirut," Hawkins explained. "Sometimes I think Mc-Carter's feeding you paranoid pills."

"We tried," James said with a sigh.

Manning slipped a magazine full of .357 Magnum slugs into the grip of his Desert Eagle and stuffed it in his shoulder holster. "No knives. But I have an Impact Kerambit wrench in my right front pocket."

The others nodded.

"Come on," Manning ordered. "T.J., you drive."

Hawkins saluted the Canadian with an index finger touch to his brow. "Yes, sir."

AGENT SAM GUTHRIE looked at his desk clock and saw that his noon appointment with the four Justice Department agents was only minutes away. He closed the top button of his shirt, readjusted his tie and made sure his shirt was tucked into his suit pants. Being a tall, slim man, it was hard to find clothes that fit him so that he matched the image of a neat, suave spy. At least the short bristle of his graying blond hair was hard to mess. He turned off his computer and stepped out of his office.

"Want anything from the commissary on my way back, Xian?" Guthrie asked his secretary.

Xian, a pretty Vietnamese-American woman, gave him a warm smile. "No thanks. My roommate Dawn packed some quesadillas for me and I picked up some pop on the way in."

"All right. I'll catch you later," Guthrie said, and left for the meeting, which was being held outside in a court-yard. The small park was ringed with white-noise generators concealed under bushes to prevent eaves-dropping. It was also in sight of several low-profile guard emplacements, with Marine sharpshooters on duty. It may have seemed paranoid, but Guthrie knew from recent history that even Langley wasn't immune to attack.

The four "Justice Department" agents looked like a motley crew to Guthrie—a tall, slender black man, a barrel-chested Caucasian, a stocky, swarthy Hispanic, and a lean, but average-looking Caucasian.

"I'm Roy. That's Rey, Farrow and Presley," Manning stated. "Hal Brognola arranged this interview."

"Right. Something about an old acquaintance of

mine," Guthrie replied. "It wouldn't be Roberto DaCosta, would it?"

Manning nodded. "What have you heard?"

"That he was murdered last night," Guthrie replied. "I used to work with him down in El Salvador."

"Doing what?" Encizo asked as Guthrie directed them to a granite table with matching semi-circular benches.

"We were investigating ORDEN and the ESA, the governing body of El Salvador and their pet killers, back in the eighties," Guthrie replied. "Roberto was an asset within the organization, and he kept us up to date on ORDEN's less than legal operations."

"Death squads," James challenged.

"Among other things," Guthrie responded. "Even back then, we weren't too excited to be associated with professional murderers. Once the Sandinistas murdered an American missionary in Nicaragua, and it appeared as a full-page spread in *Newsweek*, we became a lot more gun shy about who we worked with."

Guthrie shook his head at the thought. "Roberto wanted out desperately, and I arranged for his relocation to London after ORDEN collapsed. Even though someone went to town exterminating the death squads that made up the ESA, it really wasn't safe for him in-country anymore."

Encizo nodded at the answer. He remembered Able Team's wars with Fascist International, the primary supplier of right-wing death squads to Central and South America. Though he'd only been involved in one operation against the Reich of the Americas, he kept up with after-action reports and knew that when Able put Fascist International in its collective grave, the world became a better place to live. He ruminated for a moment on how much of a link there might be between a revived FI and the assassination of DaCosta.

"Did DaCosta keep close tabs on things back home?" Hawkins inquired.

Guthrie shrugged. "I tried to limit my contact with him. I didn't want to compromise his new location."

"You still refer to him as Roberto, though," James stated. "He was more than just an asset."

Guthrie frowned. "You picked up on that."

"We've been around a few times," Manning said. "What did you hear?"

"His nephew is on the run from something," Guthrie replied.

"What happened?" Hawkins asked.

Guthrie shook his head. "I don't know. That much didn't get back to me, but I started trying to find him through my own resources…"

The throb of a helicopter cut through the air and caught the attention of the assembled men.

"Classic Stony Man Tourist Luck," Hawkins muttered loud enough for James to hear over the approaching aircraft before the hiss of rockets split the air. Rooftop targets spit up geysers of flame, and Hawkins realized that the helicopter had just destroyed the heavy antiaircraft emplacements nestled atop the office buildings.

The ex-Ranger would have laughed if he hadn't seen the weapons pods bristling like stubby wings on the sides of the helicopter. Instead, he dived across the marble table and threw Guthrie to the ground.

From the towers, Marine marksmen opened fire, but their rifle bullets only sparked ineffectually off the hull of the sleek gunship overhead.

A line of machine-gun fire chopped across the courtyard and a .50-caliber slug smashed a crater in the center of the marble table that Phoenix Force had been sitting at.

Manning dumped the magazine out of the butt of his Desert Eagle and stuffed in a clip of 180-grain, keg-shaped hunting loads. It wouldn't be much more effective than the rifles the Marines had in the towers, but the combat rounds he had loaded previously would flatten like spit balls against an armored aircraft. Encizo unleathered his Heckler & Koch USP and pumped out a half dozen 9 mm Parabellum rounds before he ducked behind his heavy stone bench.

A rocket lanced from the wing pod and blew a Marine sentry in his perch to oblivion. Another two helicopters popped out over the main computer center, but unlike the slender-tailed, bulb-headed dragonfly that swept death and destruction over the Langley compound, these were ugly, reptilian sharks, disgorging rappelling lines and black, armor-clad killers.

"Look familiar?" James asked Guthrie.

"Nope," the CIA agent replied as they got to their feet. James pushed Guthrie toward the shelter of another marble table as the deadly bug-shaped gunship pivoted and spotted them.

Manning fired two shots from his Desert Eagle, aiming the accurate weapon at the barrel-like rocket pod hanging off the side of the helicopter. The 180-grain keg-shaped slugs hit the drum-size target, but one round sparked wildly off the rocket launcher and ricocheted into the main body of the gunship. The second bullet punched through the thin, precut sheet-metal cover of the artillery rocket pod and glanced off the top of the tube. A fearsome jet of flame erupted from the front of the pod as the explosive dart was detonated by a .357 Magnum penetrator. The gunship rocked, but the pod was well-designed, containing and funneling the explosion into a thrust of superheated gas and shrapnel that peppered the windows of a building.

Explosive bolts fired and the heavy, drumlike canister tumbled off the stub-wing and sailed toward the ground. Hawkins had taken cover behind a tree, and was drilling 9 mm slugs at the bottom of the helicopter. His rounds had little effect, and he leaped wildly as the rocket pod smashed through the branches of the tree and cracked the concrete where he'd been crouched instants before.

Hawkins whirled and looked at the pod. A red light began flashing rapidly on its top, and the Phoenix Force warrior knew that the electronic box wasn't going to be healthy for anyone in the courtyard if it reached its peak. He aimed his stubby little Glock 26 and hammered out the remnants of its magazine into the black transmitter. The metallic box crumpled and shattered, sparks flying as battery capacitors discharged. Hawkins took a deep breath as he realized that being close enough to recognize the remote detonator for what it was, was also near enough to ground zero to be vaporized by the self-destructing rocket pod.

He shook off the thought of being that close to death and fumbled a 12-round magazine into the butt of the tiny Glock, his hands trembling with the aftershocks of an adrenaline rush that slipped him into overdrive. Hawkins took cover behind a tree beside the inert rocket pod and took three quick breaths to get his thundering heartbeat back under control. A burst of .50-caliber slugs tore through the dirt and punched into the tree trunk, spraying Hawkins's hair with splinters.

Rafael Encizo rushed toward the entrance of the building where the black-armored commandos disgorged onto the roof. A quick glance told the stocky Cuban that this was the computer center at Langley. He hit the doors with his shoulder and bounced off the glass. Electronic locks had shut down the building, and he knew that he couldn't shoot through the clear doors. CIA Headquarters was protected by armored glass that was resistant to even rifle rounds.

The Cuban turned and saw the gunship swivel. He decided to play chicken with the aircraft. It would be a one in a million chance, but the Computer Center was under assault by mysterious invaders, and the CIA would need all the help it could get from the members of one of America's finest fighting forces. The Cuban pro fired off three quick shots at the silhouette of the pilot behind his armored cockpit dome. Even the high-potency 9 mm NATO ball ammo bounced off the heavy curved Plexiglas, but it drew the ire of the gunship's jockey.

The heavy M-2 machine-gun pods suddenly erupted with fire and Encizo threw himself behind the heavy granite cylinder that provided both decoration for the courtyard and antiramming and car-bombing protection for the Computer Center building. Four feet in diameter, the heavy stone block stopped the first salvo of 750-grain, half-inch slugs from the deadly gunship, even though each impact created a four-inch deep crater in the face of the pedestal. Encizo rolled to one side as the helicopter swiveled and tried to get a new line of fire on him. Behind him, the armored glass doors detonated into a rain of cracked shards as armor-piercing .50-caliber bullets smashed through them. The power of the big fifties had served Encizo in opening up the Computer Center, though he was pinned down now.

It wasn't hopeless, however. Three other members of Phoenix Force were in action in the courtyard.

Calvin James and Gary Manning exchanged a quick glance, and the black ex-SEAL and the burly Canadian leveled their .357 Magnum sidearms at the tail boom of the gunship. James's short-barreled Colt Python wasn't designed for long-range shooting, but across the forty yards to the NOTAR tail boom of the gunship, it was plenty accurate and powerful. Manning's massive Desert Eagle had proved itself capable of hitting targets five times that distant. Heavy-duty penetrating slugs from both mighty Magnum weapons hammered into the tail boom. James's 158-grain lead slugs and Manning's 180-grain hunting rounds struck the air vanes that directed forced thrust to stabilize the helicopter in flight. The NOTAR was protected from ground fire, its vulnerable tail rotor replaced by a powerful fan housed in a cylinder of armored metal. However, the directing vanes needed to be exposed to allow the helicopter to turn in one direction or the other.

The .357 Magnum maelstrom directed at the tail boom vents smashed the louvers out of place, wrecking them on their pivoting mechanisms. The gunship jerked as the pilot fought to keep the aircraft straight.

"T.J.! Go with Rafe!" Manning bellowed.

The Southerner nodded and broke for the Computer Center as the Cuban raced into the now-excavated entrance.

James rushed across the courtyard as the helicopter and gunner fought to keep the gunship in the air. He skidded to Manning's side behind another marble table. "Any plans to deal with the chopper?"

"It's moving too erratically for us to target any more vulnerable points," Manning answered. The big Canadian's eyes narrowed as he watched the aircraft dip, then swerve. The machine guns ripped wildly, blowing out windows in another building. "Still, if it keeps shooting, it'll kill people in the buildings, even without aiming."

James popped the cylinder on his Colt Python and thumbed two fresh rounds into the revolver. "I wish I'd brought a rifle or a grenade launcher..."

Manning looked over to the jettisoned pod, then back to James. "How about a rocket launcher?"

James grinned. "How're we going to set it off?"

"I'll improvise," Manning replied.

The two Stony Man commanders rushed toward the rocket pod.

THE SECURITY GUARDS spotted Encizo and Hawkins as they rushed into the lobby, guns drawn, but the Phoenix Force warriors had out their badges. Recognition of their authority had saved them from a mistaken-identity shooting.

"It's a war outside!" one guard snapped. "What the hell is going down?"

"Two helicopters dropped a squad of commandos on your roof," Hawkins replied. "Are you getting any reports from upstairs?"

The sentry keyed his radio and heard static and screams over the speaker. "This is all we've got."

The other guard nodded anxiously. "We were going to evacuate the building, but with that gunship out there…"

"Keep an eye on people down here," Encizo ordered. "We'll take care of things. Do you have any shotguns or submachine guns?"

"I'll take you to the security office," the second guard said. "All we have are—"

A wraith in black burst into view, heading toward the security office. The newcomer's head was wrapped in a shiny black helmet, making him look almost insect-like, an alien invader out of a science-fiction movie. Hawkins, Encizo and the two security guards all acted as one and unleashed a swarm of 9 mm slugs at the black-clad invader. The swarm of bullets knocked the intruder down, and Encizo rushed up to the fallen invader, keeping the muzzle of his HK leveled at the helmeted face.

The black-clad killer suddenly jerked to life and

swept the muzzle of his machine pistol at the Cuban, but he kicked the frame of the weapon. His armored adversary's grip was too strong to dislodge the gun, but Encizo had saved himself from a chestful of bullets. He fired point-blank at the assassin's head, but jerked away as his 9 mm slugs rebounded off the shiny helmet. The invader twisted and hooked the Cuban's ankle with one arm. Off center, Encizo struggled to maintain his balance as his opponent rolled and toppled him. The machine pistol's muzzle swung up toward Encizo's face, the unblinking eye of the barrel threatening to be the last thing he ever saw when a hurtling form crashed into the downed pair.

Hawkins wrapped his forearm around the intruder's throat. "Stick him, Rafe!"

Encizo didn't need prompting as he drew his Cold Steel Tanto fighting knife. The reinforced chisel point flashed for a moment, then plunged through the tough black fabric across the invader's chest. It took every ounce of the Cuban's weight and strength to penetrate the body armor, and even then, the razor-sharp blade lodged in the killer's rib cage.

"Cristo." Encizo cursed as he redoubled his efforts to eviscerate the bulletproof attacker. A second surge of the muscular Phoenix Force warrior's frame against the invader's armored chest, and the full six and a half inches of reinforced, chisel-bladed steel snapped through bone and bullet-resistant material. Pulling with all his might, Encizo dragged the deadly knife through the marauder's stomach, slitting him open like a fish.

The black-clad intruder thrashed in Hawkins's grasp for a moment, then died.

"Holy shit," Hawkins gasped. "What the hell is this bastard wearing?"

"Good stuff," Encizo answered as he plucked the machine pistol from the killer's lifeless fingers. He dumped the magazine and checked the top round, a bottle-necked, greenish-black tipped slug. "Teflon-coated tungsten penetrators, 6.5 mm."

"Same caliber as the creeps David ran into in London," Hawkins said as he handed Encizo spare magazines. He plucked a handgun from the dead man's holster and checked its load. "Same ammo for this one, too...but it's a high-capacity 1911."

"You take that one until we can find one of these things for you," Encizo replied, holding up the Bofors PDW.

Hawkins holstered his mini-Glock and took two spare magazines for the high-cap 1911. "Twenty rounds per stick. Not that bad a piece."

"Come on. If they penetrated this far, then they're probably all over the building," Encizo responded.

The two Phoenix Force commandos left the security guards to retrieve their heavier weapons to protect the CIA employees in the lobby.

GARY MANNING EXAMINED the pod as Calvin James watched the lurching gunship. The big Canadian ducked as a scythe of .50-caliber slugs ripped the air over his head, ignoring James's exclamation as the salvo came too close.

"Hurry up, Gary," the black ex-SEAL admonished.

"That thing's taken out a lot of windows and sections of wall."

Manning pulled his Impact Kerambit wrench from its sheath and chopped its reinforced fiberglass point between the seams that formed the end of the drum. He twisted hard and broke off the tip, but pried apart the metal enough for him to fit his powerful hands in. The Canadian's massive shoulders swelled as he wrenched the metal pod open, his face beet-red from the effort.

James tried to ignore his friend's display of nearly superhuman strength, but even with a deadly gunship spraying lethal streams of fire overhead, it was a sight to behold. The drum popped open and armored tubes were visible inside. Manning swallowed hard, breathing deeply, then planted one foot against a tube and wrapped both of his paws around another. "I need your Taser, Cal."

The tall ex-SEAL nodded. "Think it's got enough of a charge to set that off?"

"It should. These things don't need that much voltage to fire." Manning grunted as he flexed against the tube. Metal crumpled and wrenched as the brawny Canadian hauled on the rocket tube. He'd freed one end, levering it out of the pod when James tackled him to the ground. A heartbeat later a thunderstorm of bullets hammered into the ground, destroying what was left of the tree stump. Dirt and wood chunks rained on the prone Stony Man commandos.

"Thanks," Manning replied, breathing hard.

"Anytime," James answered. "You're going to end up with a hernia."

"The needs of the many outweigh the needs of the few," the Canadian replied as he returned to the rocket pod. It had been left untouched by the stream of lead that nearly chopped the Stony Man warriors to pieces. Manning braced himself again before the pilot could swing the helicopter around.

"He's not shooting the other rocket pod," James noted. "He must not want to hit his own people inside the Computer Center."

Twisting steel shrieked as Manning ripped the rocket tube free.

"It's loaded," he said softly, exhaustion having crept into his voice. James knew Manning possessed prodigious endurance, regularly running in marathons and engaging in weight-lifting contests with Carl Lyons, Able Team's muscular commander. For him to show weariness meant that he'd tapped reserves of strength that the Phoenix Force demolitions expert had rarely touched. "Fire off your Taser, Cal."

James nodded and fired the X-26 point-blank into the dirt. The launching probes shot out, but he released the trigger, preventing the battery's capacitor charge from draining. Manning grabbed the probes and hooked them up to the wire leads at the base of the rocket pod.

James slid his slender but strong frame under the tube and shouldered it. "You aim."

Manning nodded as he wrapped the wire leads around the electrical probes at the tip. He stepped clear of the back of the rocket tube, sighting along the top of the bore as the black ex-SEAL grunted under the weight of the armored cylinder and its explosive payload. The wobbly helicopter saw what the two Phoenix Force warriors were doing and struggled to come level with them, its machine gun muzzles swiveling onto the pair.

"Gary..."

"If we miss, that's it," Manning admonished. The enemy gunship stabilized for one moment and pointed straight at them. The initial machine-gun bursts slammed into the earth on either side of the Stony Man commandos.

"And we're in their blind spot," Manning added. He pulled the trigger on the X-26 Taser. The little pocket-size unit cut loose with its charge, and the rocket motor fired to life. The 77 mm warhead leaped out of its tube and speared through the bulbous head of the gunship, lancing it like a soap bubble filled with napalm. The shock wave bowled over James and Manning, flaming wreckage fluttering down in a burning snow that ignited patches of the Phoenix Force warriors' suits.

The hot licks of flame jolted the two stunned Stony Man fighters and forced them to roll to put out the burning tongues that flared on their clothes.

Their immediate emergency over, James and Manning surveyed the area. Others in the courtyard had been hiding behind stone walls and marble tables, and those who had been injured were being tended to by fellow employees.

"Come on," James said, helping Manning to his feet. "You got enough left to deal with a marauding force of ninja killers?"

"I guess I'll have to."

The Canadian pulled his sleek Desert Eagle and followed the black commando into the Computer Center.

CHAPTER FIVE

Yuma, Arizona

Carl Lyons perched like a gargoyle cast in bronze and black, his knees deeply bowed, hard blue eyes scanning the rolling hills that had proven so treacherous the night before. He glanced back over one bulging shoulder. "Anything on the radio?"

Hermann Schwarz shook his head. "This place is a blanket of space noise."

Lyons looked at the approaches to their cave. "Pol?"

"Sarlets is sleeping now," Rosario Blancanales answered. "It was the least I could let him do after we hauled him through this range."

Lyons grimaced. "I hated moving him, too, Pol. But if we stayed at the helicopter…"

"I know, Carl," Blancanales replied. "I made sure he'd recovered from shock before he went to sleep. I don't think he has a concussion, so he'll be able to rest."

Lyons looked at his watch. It had been nearly dawn

when the enemy missile had torn off the stabilizing rudder on their chopper. Sarlets, despite receiving a six-inch jagged shard of shrapnel in his abdomen and burns across his right arm and leg, managed to get them onto the ground in one piece. Their priority was to get the Army pilot to safety before a hunting party showed up to finish off the helicopter.

The bottles of Ringer's solution that Schwarz and Blancanales insisted Able Team carry on every mission, from their experience in the Green Berets, had proved invaluable in keeping Sarlets from dangerous blood loss while Blancanales sewed and taped his stomach injury shut.

"He's lucky. If the shard had sliced his bowel or intestine, we'd have to deal with a serious infection," Blancanales, the Able Team medic, stated.

Lyons slid his rough hand over the receiver of his Beowulf M-4, watching the approaches. "A small enough favor. There's still a few man-size germs running around."

"You think that there'd be an assault squad attached to the missile launcher?" Blancanales asked.

"Otherwise we wouldn't be under radio jamming in the area," Schwarz answered. "We've been out of contact with the base for four hours, though. General Rogers might have someone looking for us by now."

"And risk another helicopter crew and search team being shot out of the sky?" Blancanales asked. "This was a trap, and we fell for it hook, line and sinker."

"Rogers will send a search party," Lyons said. "But he'll make sure that they're covered, and it takes time to set up that kind of security."

Suddenly the Able Team commander lifted his closed fist and the trio fell silent. Schwarz and Blancanales drew their silenced pistols while Lyons moved forward and nestled in the shadows of a rock. The big ex-cop pulled his silenced Para-Ordnance 1911, pointed at his eyes, then to the right-hand gully. The Stony Man warriors set up in their hides, and Blancanales hefted a small rock.

Lyons gestured with his fist and Blancanales whipped the stone at the wall. The loud clatter resounded and two shadowy shapes blurred just behind the corner of an outcropping.

Silence reigned uneasily in the rocky canyon for several long, heart-stopping moments.

Then a dull, snorting rumble filled the air. Lyons braced himself against a verbal reaction, but he knew that the exhausted, injured and unconscious Sarlets couldn't help it. He was snoring.

His lips drew tight into a mirthless smile a moment later, and he silently egged on the sleeping pilot to continue his unconscious racket, wishing that Sarlets could snore even more loudly.

Come on, you scumbags. We're all asleep here, he thought. He snicked off the safety on his silenced 1911. Fifteen rounds of .45 ACP were ready to go, right out of the spout. The luminous tritium front sight's glow wasn't needed in daylight but the lime green dot was a round, perfectly cut indicator of where his shots would go. Blancanales and Schwarz were also primed with their suppressed .45s, ready to take their attackers in silence.

One form stepped out of the shadow of a rock, lean and clad in black from the top of his insectlike helmeted skull to the bottom of his boots. Lyons and the others held their fire, waiting to pull the rest of the hunting force into their ambush.

The black-clad assassin stepped forward. Lyons didn't like the black shiny faceplate, which kept him from seeing his target's eyes. The stalker could have been looking directly at any one of them, fully aware of their presence, but choosing not to react until it was too late. The gunman paused looking into the cave, then aimed a small, Uzi-type machine pistol into the depths.

Directly at Sarlets.

Lyons acted instantly, bouncing three .45-caliber hollowpoint rounds off the helmet of the murderer before he could trigger his weapon. Unfortunately, the Able Team leader's intent was to smash the bullets through the faceplate, killing him, not simply staggering him. A stream of high-velocity slugs chewed the boulder that Lyons crouched behind, one slug punching into the canyon wall just over his head.

Blancanales saw the results of his partner's initial salvo and let his Para-Ordnance pistol drop to the ground, unslinging his .50 Beowulf in one smooth motion. The heavy-caliber rifle erupted with a deep-throated bellow, slugs intended to disable and destroy robot tanks punching through the torso of the armored killer, spraying gouts of gore from the corpse's back.

"Christ!" a gunman off to the side shouted as their point man's chest erupted in volcanos of blood and stringy tissue.

Lyons transitioned from his 1911 to his own carbine and chopped out a storm of 300-grain tungsten-cored devastators toward the enemy who'd given himself away. Even as he fired, he knew he'd missed, and ducked back as the enemy returned fire.

"Ironman," Schwarz whispered over their com link. "Line's are open."

"They're calling in help," Lyons answered.

"I'm on it," the electronics expert replied. "Keep 'em busy."

Lyons grunted in response and shifted his position to the other side of the T-intersection that branched off into their cave. His shoulder to the wall, with the enemy just around the corner, he was poised to greet any new intruders with a face full of half-inch destruction.

Blancanales fed a 40 mm grenade into his launcher, then gestured with his hand in a splashing motion.

Buckshot round, Lyons interpreted. He pulled back from the corner of the T, to get out of the awesome cone of damnation that Pol intended to rip downrange. Even if the hundreds of .25-caliber pellets didn't penetrate their armor, the shredding shock wave would certainly flatten an enemy. Lyons glanced back and saw Schwarz haul Sarlets out of the mouth of their cave.

"They're calling in a missile strike. We need to move," Schwarz warned.

Lyons nodded to Blancanales, who rushed forward and triggered his buckshot grenade. Blancanales's mounted M-203 thundered and filled the air with a hundred flesh-destroying pellets. The projectiles hit stone and bounced wildly, turning that section of canyon into a no-man's land of hypervelocity steel.

Lyons hooked Sarlets's arm around his muscular shoulders and retreated while Blancanales followed up his thunderbolt with a rainstorm of half-inch-wide slugs to keep the enemy at bay.

He raced after his partners just as a flaming lance sliced into the cave. A boiling wave of fire and smoke rolled from the entrance, intense heat curling Blancanales's hair as he raced along.

"Cutting it close," Lyons commented as he watched for the enemy's efforts to catch up.

"Close only counts in horseshoes and high explosives," Blancanales replied. He ran his fingers across his baked hair, feeling curls snap off. "Then again…"

"You don't get much more high explosive than that," Lyons growled. "Gadgets?"

"Calling in adjusted coordinates," Schwarz called back.

"Jam those fuckers," Lyons snapped.

"On it, but they got off their firing solution," Schwarz replied.

Lyons moved and scooped up the pale, wan Sarlets. "Hang in there, soldier."

"Like I got a choice?" Sarlets croaked. His Beretta M-9 was locked in his fist, ready to fight despite his weakness.

The powerful Able Team commander hauled the wounded pilot like a duffel bag, thick legs pumping as the Stony Man strike team raced toward the safety of a sandstone outcropping. Another fiery bolt of devastation hammered down from heaven, shaking the earth beneath their feet. Lyons stumbled from the shock wave, but fell beneath Sarlets, cushioning the injured man's crash.

"Nice landing," Sarlets told him.

"I owed you," Lyons answered with a smile. Sarlets's lips pulled into a tight, pained grin. He held his protest as the Able Team leader tucked him into a rocky corner for protection. He opened the pilot's jumpsuit and saw that the stitched wound was still taped firmly shut, no seepage dribbling from the edges of Blancanales's improvised bandage. Lyons closed up the jumpsuit and snapped shut Sarlets's armored vest. "Stay put. We'll welcome the bad guys."

"They're deaf and dumb," Schwarz announced.

"Good. I'm getting sick of running," Lyons rasped.

"Give Gadgets and me a moment to swing around their flank," Blancanales told Lyons.

The Able Team leader nodded. "Count off to twenty-five. That's when I'll flush them toward you."

His two Able Team partners took off and the brawny ex-cop fed a fresh stick of 300-grain penetrators into his Beowulf. Lyons glanced back to Sarlets who managed a thumbs-up salute. The blond warrior winked reassuringly, then stalked off to greet their hunters.

"HE'LL START THE FUN at twenty, you know," Schwarz said as they raced along.

"Ironman's greedy that way," Blancanales answered. "Fifteen…"

The two ex-Green Berets had broken speed records to get into position, knowing the impatience of their partner. Schwarz skidded to a halt at an intersection and crouched behind a swell of stone in the canyon. Blancanales took the opposite side of the rocky corridor.

The arrival of the two Able Team warriors drew a startled reaction from a quartet of armor-clad killers twenty yards away. A spray of 6.5 mm armor-piercing bullets raked the canyon walls around them and Schwarz triggered his Beowulf in response.

The drumbeat thunder of Carl Lyons's heavy-duty rifle rattled down the way, and Blancanales smirked. "We beat him to the punch."

"Knowing Carl, he probably rushed us along to distract those creeps," Schwarz answered as he held down the trigger on his flesh-shredding weapon.

Caught in between the three rifles of Able Team, the brutal hunting party was torn to pieces, vehicle-smashing rounds bulldozing thick furrows in flesh and bone after punching through flexible, armored fabric. Had the Stony Man warriors been armed with their usual 9 mm or 5.56 mm autoweapons, the black-clad marauders could have weathered the storm of withering fire.

It was just the enemy's bad luck to have come across Able Team when it was loaded for murderous robot tanks instead of the usual type of terrorists.

Schwarz and Blancanales reloaded, then advanced on the group, rifles aimed at the downed killers, just in case any were playing possum. Lyons fired a .50-caliber slug, point-blank, through the helmet of one of the enemy gunmen.

"That's it," Lyons replied. "Kill the jammer."

Schwarz flicked off his unit and knelt by one of the dead men whose helmet was still intact. It took some effort, but he unsnapped the chin strap and pulled off the protective shell.

"Souvenir?" Blancanales asked.

"These guys weren't wearing any external radio packs that I could tell," Schwarz replied. He tugged on the helmet, then found a pair of wires leading down under the black, flexible armor's collar. He rolled the dead body over, and pulled his knife. He slit the collar open and saw two layers of heavy polymer fiber, with a pair of ceramic plates sandwiching a green copper circuit board. "Built-in body-wide flat panel communicator. Incredible technology. The ceramic and the polymer weave wouldn't interfere with electronic transmissions, but the trauma plates would protect the circuit board."

"Look at that," Lyons pointed out. "When you cut it open, water seeped from tiny tubes."

"Right, the water can be heated or chilled by a small belt unit to keep the wearer from suffering from exposure or heat prostration," Blancanales said.

"Discussing the cutting edge of fashion is fascinating," Lyons began, "but their buddies with the missile launcher will be wondering where these punks went to."

Schwarz slid on the helmet. "Whoa…"

"What?" Blancanales asked.

"All kinds of optics. Night vision, targeting reticles, comm mike… Also built-in audio amplification and filtering, just like the Wolf Ears we wear," Schwarz replied. "All wrapped up in a hard candy shell that bounces .45 slugs like grains of rice."

"Bad guys as well-equipped as we are," Lyons stated. He picked up a machine pistol.

"Uzi?" Blancanales asked.

"No, too small a caliber," Lyons answered as he dumped the clip. "It's a 6.5 mm. Look at the tip."

"Teflon coating for a tungsten core," Blancanales noted. "Armor-piercing, high-end ammunition. Kissinger's still doing ballistics tests on these at the Farm."

"The guy who equipped these dudes has some good connections or is a design genius in his own right," Schwarz replied, doffing the helmet. "The machine pistol is a Bofors design, but there's no manufacturing stamps on any of this stuff."

"You mean, our bad guy is building his own equipment?" Lyons asked. "That'd take some impressive manufacturing facilities."

"Which gives Aaron and the guys at the Farm something to home in on," Blancanales commented.

"Great," Lyons said. "We'll leave these guys here for later. We need to get back to Sarlets."

"Shit!" Schwarz snapped.

Lyons looked up and saw several smoking arcs in the sky, missiles looping lazily upward, then dipping down as they reached their zenith. "They're going to blow this whole stretch to kingdom come."

The Stony Man trio didn't need further prompting to explode into a frantic run back to the wounded pilot.

Langley, Virginia

WHEN RAFAEL ENCIZO burst into the stairwell, he was greeted by the ripping burst of an enemy machine pistol, and only his quick reflexes saved him from being cut in two by the deadly black wraith several landings above. T.J. Hawkins kicked open the door, crouched and fired three shots from his 6.5 mm converted 1911, the armor-piercing rounds punching through the concrete floor beneath the muzzle-flash of the enemy gunner.

There was a grunt of pain as the intruder jerked back from the railing. Hawkins raced to the shelter of a flight of stairs, next to Encizo.

"Think you hit him?" the Cuban veteran asked.

"He didn't sound too happy," Hawkins replied. He dumped his magazine and checked how many rounds he had left. "But I don't think it went through the concrete."

"Close enough to make him reach cover," Encizo answered. "Looked like he was on the fourth floor."

"And there's six stories to this building," Hawkins noted. "Do you remember what was listed in the directory for the top two floors?"

"Information Archiving and Intelligence Analysis," Encizo stated.

"What would they want up there?" Hawkins asked.

"Let's go find out," Encizo answered.

"I was hoping you'd say that," Hawkins replied. He took the lead, his more youthful energy setting the pace.

At the third-floor landing, the enemy gunman popped up again. A hornet swarm of bullets chased at Hawkins's heels, but this time, it was Encizo who brought up the rear as the hardman was flushed. With a pull of the trigger, the swarthy Phoenix Force pro ripped a line of destruction up the center of the armored wraith, puncturing him from groin to throat with half a dozen armor-piercing slugs. Hawkins raced up the steps the last of the distance to the dying intruder and relieved their foe of his machine pistol and a second high-capacity 6.5 mm 1911.

"Look what I got you," Hawkins announced, turning over the handgun and two spare magazines. "The pistol holds twenty shots."

"And it isn't even Christmas," Encizo replied, a smile on his face.

Hawkins stuffed his own pistol into his waistband, picking the automatic weapon for more forceful response to the armored marauders. "I'll take the sixth floor, Archiving."

"I'll take care of Analysis, then," Encizo stated. "Be careful. Their vests are way better than ours, and these guns punch through them like they were paper."

"I'll do what I can," the Southerner drawled. "But we've got a building full of potential hostages."

Encizo nodded. "I know what you mean."

The bottom of the stairwell burst open again and the two Phoenix Force commandos reacted to the newcomers.

"Rafe?" Calvin James's voice called up.

Encizo grinned. "Come on up! We were going to split and check out two different floors."

"Hang on!" Manning called.

It took a few moments for the two Stony Man warriors to join their partners. Encizo noted with concern that Manning looked winded from the sudden rush up the stairs. "What's wrong?"

"Wore himself out bending steel in his bare hands," James replied. "Shit, these guys look like what David described in London."

"Need something that can take care of their armor?" Hawkins asked, offering his pistol.

Manning shook his head. His face was red and flushed, but he wasn't bowed by exhaustion, only breathing slightly deeper than normal. "Cal and I have our .357s."

"Yeah, but one of these guys took a 9 mm NATO hardball we had Dutch-loaded," Hawkins commented. He pressed the high-capacity pistol into the burly Canadian's hand.

Manning nodded and holstered his Desert Eagle, pocketing the spares Hawkins provided. James received a similar weapon from Encizo. "Happy regift, Cal."

James raised an eyebrow. "I'll take the top floor with T.J. You old guys can take the lower floor."

Manning grimaced. "You whippersnappers watch it."

"Yeah, Rafe gave me the speech already," Hawkins said. "C'mon, let's get on top of things."

Encizo and Manning exchanged a look as the others left. "Are you…"

"My back hurts like hell," the Canadian answered. "But I can still fight. People need us now."

Encizo nodded and led the way, concern hanging darkly in his thoughts.

Hawkins eased the door open slowly while James scanned the hallway on the other side in the polished reflection of his Jet Aer knife blade. The ex-SEAL shifted the improvised mirror to his other hand and spotted a gesturing invader, waving his arm as if he were directing traffic. James glanced back to Hawkins and pointed toward the activity. He replaced the knife with the high-capacity 1911 pistol, then started a three-finger countdown.

When the last finger closed into a fist, Hawkins threw the door open with a spearing jolt of his shoulder. Whipping into the hallway, he spotted the armored killer and ripped a burst of 6.5 mm tungsten slugs into his torso. The intruder had only half turned to greet the two members of Phoenix Force before he was cut down, but James spotted another of the wraiths explode out of an office. The tall black man knocked the Southerner out of the way with his own shoulder block and punched a trio of armor-piercing bullets into the newcomer. James's first shot ripped the submachine gun out of the hardman's grasp while the second two bullets parted polymer weave and shattered ceramic plate on the way through to the gunner's black heart.

James quickly upgraded to the Uzi-like autoweapon, and handed Hawkins the corpse's handgun and spare ammunition. The ex-SEAL recharged the partially spent subgun.

"They still have better armor than we do," Hawkins noted.

"Then we'll just have to be faster than these bastards," James answered. "On me."

The Southerner fell into step behind his senior partner, scanning the entrances of cubicles for more black-clad invaders. Only when they turned the corner were they forced to dive for cover.

Hawkins came out of his shoulder roll, tempted to let the highly penetrative 6.5 mm bullets slice through the plastic and corkboard cubicle walls to hammer the enemy. He held his fire, not certain if there were any bystanders between him and his target.

"Looks like they were camped out around a machine," James said. He didn't risk exposure to double-check his initial assumption. "A printer?"

"A server hub," Hawkins corrected. "Just like the guys have back at the Farm."

James grimaced. "Of course. The main computer banks are too well protected from an assault. They're going to introduce a virus into the system."

Hawkins frowned. "Hell of a risky way to do it."

"Not with the armor and firepower they brought," James answered. "They probably didn't expect anyone to disarm one of them."

"Even so, the air cover from Langley AFB…" Hawkins protested.

"Let's discuss this later," James snapped. He dived into the open and cut loose with the machine pistol before somersaulting back behind cover. Enemy 6.5 mm slugs punched through the cubicle wall in front of Hawkins, forcing him to swing out and around.

The Southerner wondered if his partner had taken leave of his senses when smoke billowed at the other end of the office suite. Hawkins grinned. James had wrecked the server hub with his blast of autofire, preventing the introduction of the virus into the computer system. The Phoenix Force warrior raced down another row of cubicles, keeping his head low.

A shiny black-domed helmet was visible over one wall, and Hawkins dropped to one knee. There was only one cubicle wall between him and the target, and he cut loose with a burst. The armored marauder jerked and stumbled into the open, his machine pistol flaring hotly and chewing up the carpet where the ex-Ranger leaped from. A slashing arc of armor-piercing slugs chewed through plastic and corkboard. A round had punched through the prefab wall and the laminated surface of a desk to smash Hawkins in the chest. Only the thickness of the material that the armor-piercing bullet had chopped through had slowed the deadly projectile enough to be stopped by his own concealed, bulletproof vest, even though Hawkins felt as though he'd been smacked in the ribs by a ballpeen hammer.

The wind knocked out of him, the Stony Man fighter slid on the carpet. His legs poked out around the wall, and Hawkins struggled to curl himself behind the bulk of a desk drawer. That had to have been how the armor-clad assassin had survived Hawkins's burst. Even the subtle thickness of plastic and cork had slowed the deadly rounds enough for flexible polymer weave and ceramic trauma plating to save the hardman.

Hawkins was lucky that an additional inch of desktop had been enough to do the same for his lighter vest.

A desktop radio just over his head gave forth a mournful wail of electronic noise, and the Phoenix Force commando realized why there was no instantaneous response from nearby military bases. Langley Headquarters was under a blanket of electronic jamming, cutting off the nerve center of America's intelligence community from any defense mechanisms. The phone lines were also probably knocked out by similar means, leaving Phoenix Force and the security guards as the sole response to three armed helicopters and a platoon of nearly invulnerable invaders.

Hawkins triggered his machine pistol again, firing through the cubicle wall. There were too many civilians on hand for him not to fight. Even one noncombatant would have been too many at risk for him to fall back and retreat. Another wave of enemy missiles ripped into the surface of the desk, smashing chips of veneer and chunks of plywood free. With a surge, the Phoenix Force commando lanced out into the open before a peppering storm of 6.5 mm tungsten rounds crashed into the floor where he'd sat. He triggered his weapon on the fly and caught the armored hardman at groin level, smashing his pelvis under a hammering salvo of destruction.

With his pelvic girdle crushed, the gunman collapsed like a mannequin, howls of pain cutting even through the murderer's armored helmet. Hawkins pulled the trigger again on the crippled opponent, but his machine pistol was empty. He let the autoweapon drop into his left hand and plucked the 6.5 mm pistol out to end the invader's suffering when he heard a shout.

"T.J.!" James's voice cut through the ruckus.

Hawkins fired the hi-cap 1911 on instinct, only moments later realizing that he'd swung the muzzle toward a figure that rushed at him from his blind spot. A spray of automatic fire that chopped up a cubicle to one side relieved Hawkins's momentary doubt that he hadn't put a bullet through one of the very people he was fighting to rescue. However, the black-clad gunman collapsed to the ground, his weapon tumbling from insensate fingers. Hawkins saw the wounded man claw for the handgun in his thigh holster.

"We need a prisoner!" James shouted.

Hawkins hesitated in putting another bullet through the wounded man's helmet, then leaped on him, chopping the barrel of his handgun across the invader's wrist. Hard steel met wrist bone, and despite a protective layer of flexible, bulletproof polymer, the bone proved insufficient to the task. The Southerner slammed the butt of the weapon against the domed helmet for good measure, but with a broken leg and arm, the fight was out of the enemy commando.

"Got one!" Hawkins announced.

Calvin James suddenly appeared, tackling another of the armored intruders through a section of cubicle wall, the aluminum frame collapsing under the weight of the two struggling fighters. James snapped a hard wrist-heel punch into his opponent's breastbone with a thump like a drumbeat. The black ex-SEAL followed up with an elbow that connected just under the chin of the full-head helmet, and the armored killer thrashed wildly, clutching his throat.

"Got one, too," James answered, breathing hard.

"Did you see any of the employees on this floor?" Hawkins asked.

"Not in this section," James said. "Not alive."

Hawkins winced. The man he'd shot in the groin

twisted and wailed for mercy as his blood gushed from his wound. James glanced at the dying killer and started to draw his handgun when the Southerner shook his head.

"He has some questions to answer about the surviving employees," the youngest member of Phoenix Force announced solemnly. Hawkins got up and walked over to the crippled murderer.

James started to tie up their two prisoners with lengths of electrical cord and computer wire.

Then a powerful explosion shook the floor. James and Hawkins looked on in horror as the cubicle farm collapsed into a sucking crater.

CHAPTER SIX

Yuma, Arizona

If Hermann Schwarz and Rosario Blancanales impressed Carl Lyons with their speed in setting up the flanking ambush for the hunting party in the canyon, they surpassed his expectations as they rushed to Tim Sarlets's side before the rain of high explosive could slam down over their heads.

Blancanales and Schwarz scooped up the wounded pilot and dragged him along, with Lyons bringing up the rear in a mad rush to get back to their cave. The first explosion rumbled overhead as warheads detonated atop the table of sandstone and rock facing the cave. The previous missile hit had been only moments before, but to Lyons it felt like it had been days, and thick clouds of dust and the heat of the recent blast still hung in the air in the cave. Though a rockslide had considerably narrowed the entrance, it had also built a barrier against raining stones.

When Schwarz slipped on a rock as he scrambled

over the pile of crushed stone, Lyons picked up the slack and pulled the wounded pilot into the cave. The Able Team leader whirled and clamped one brawny hand around Schwarz's vest and yanked him in moments before another detonating missile sprayed a swarm of slicing, jagged shrapnel as it hit. The two Stony Man warriors hit the ground in the same instant as the shock wave and shrapnel sizzled over the accumulation of the landslide, five feet of piled stone shielding their fragile bodies from bullet-fast fragments.

"We've got to quit meeting like this," Schwarz quipped. "People will talk."

Lyons shook his head in mock irritation and shoved his partner away. "You're not my type anyway."

The electronics genius snickered and crawled on his belly toward Blancanales and Sarlets.

"You holding up okay, flyboy?" Schwarz asked.

Sarlets winced painfully. "About as well as you'd expect. You know I was stabbed with a six-inch chunk of metal only a few hours ago. You're supposed to be going easy on mc."

"You'd rather still be out there?" Blancanales asked, motioning toward the mouth of the cave.

Sarlets shrugged, tired. "Nope."

Artillery shook the ground, but there wasn't any more loose stone in the cave's ceiling to shake free. As it was, the four men covered their noses and mouths with scarves to keep from sucking dust into their lungs as it billowed over the barrier.

Lyons looked to Schwarz. "Do you have a rabbit to pull out of your hat?"

The electronics genius's eyes flashed as a sudden memory struck him. He reached down and turned off his jammer, then pulled out his field scanner.

"Give it a few moments," Schwarz explained as he tuned the passive receiver in his palm. His brow furrowed as he looked for frequencies. "C'mon, give me a lock."

Lyons wanted to ask his partner what he was doing, but he knew the fierce intensity on the man's face. He was in the zone, brain calculating thousands of possibilities, absorbing input.

"Four…" Schwarz whispered softly, continuing his countdown as he fiddled frantically with the scanner. "Zero."

He turned off the scanner and put it away, then pulled out a small notepad, scribbling furiously. Schwarz glanced up from the paper and nodded to Lyons. "One rabbit."

Lyons nodded. "Give it to me."

Schwarz pointed toward the ceiling of the cave. The thunder of the artillery died away, though the choking smoke still billowed out in the canyon. "They kept firing as long as I had this area locked down into a null zone of radio communication. I killed the jammer and swept to see if they were still listening. Their line was open, and I was able to gauge their position."

"How far?"

"Two miles," Schwarz answered.

The Able Team commander grinned. "We can cut across that easily."

"Not with Sarlets in tow," Blancanales replied.

"This place is secure. It survived a hammering from those rockets," Lyons stated.

"And if they send out a scout party?" Blancanales inquired.

"We'll cut across their path and take them out," the big blond ex-cop answered. "Sarlets, can you handle a Magnum just in case?"

Sarlets nodded. "If it's heavy enough."

Lyons handed over his six-inch barreled Colt Python. "I don't do lightweight. A .357 slug should put a serious dent in their armor, especially if you use these."

The Able Team handed him two speed loaders filled with green-tipped slugs. "Teflon-coated, tungsten-cored."

"Technically, your Python is about 9 mm," Schwarz stated.

"Yeah, but it's not a teeny euro pellet. It's built for Americans to knock down Americans," Lyons answered. "Enough jawing. We have some bastards to kill."

Langley, Virginia

RAFAEL ENCIZO ROSE, his back aching where chunks of ceiling had bounced off. A frightened secretary that he'd instinctively shielded whispered her hurried gratitude and took off for the door to the stairwell. He checked on Gary Manning who was throwing his shoulder against a huge bar of concrete. Underneath, a couple of CIA employees struggled, pinned by the concrete wedge.

"Rafe…" Manning called.

The muscular Cuban moved to assist Manning, his own broad shoulders and powerful arms straining to help relieve the massive weight pinning the two civilians. The chunk of ceiling shifted slightly, then rose far enough for the pair of trapped victims to squirm to freedom.

"Move it," Manning said with a grunt of effort. Though one limped, it didn't slow either of the two as they raced to escape the shattered office suite.

Encizo looked to the burly Canadian. "Ready?"

"Drop it on three," Manning gritted.

"Two…"

"One," Manning concluded, and the two muscular Phoenix Force warriors stepped back. The concrete rebar dropped to the floor, denting it but not penetrating to the level below.

Encizo looked for his armor-piercing subgun, but it had been lost in the hectic explosion. Instead, he retrieved the confiscated hi-cap 1911. "Think that was the last of them on this floor?"

Manning nodded. He looked at the crater in the floor, a bowl of reinforced concrete with a hole in the bottom, a window to the next level. "The bastard who triggered the bomb must have realized that there was no way past us."

"So he killed himself," Encizo whispered, fighting off the shock of such desperate action. "These guys don't seem like fanatics, though. Not with their tactics or weaponry."

"No," Manning replied. "It wasn't the method of a fanatic. You know damn well, if he was captured, there was no way that the CIA's interrogation experts would leave him untouched."

Encizo shuddered. He'd been through more than

enough torture in his lifetime, when he had been imprisoned in Cuba, and once when he was part of the dramatic rescue of a hostaged Vatican. While the Cuban military police and the terrorists only had primitive means of ripping the flesh and mind of a victim, Encizo knew full well that with the chemicals and medical technology at the CIA's command, anyone handed over to them would live for a long time in a hell that made a lake of fire seem like blissful mercy.

"Check that side," Encizo said. "See if there are any more survivors."

"Be careful, the floor isn't sturdy anymore," Manning warned.

"Hey!" a voice called down from a hole in the ceiling. The two Phoenix Force commandos looked up to see the dark, handsome features of Calvin James. "You two okay down there?"

"We'll live," Encizo answered. "How's everything upstairs?"

"Shitty," James said. "They killed almost everyone on this floor."

"But we have a prisoner," Hawkins interjected.

"We would have had two, but the floor collapsed and sucked him down," James added.

Encizo glanced around and saw a mangled body, or at least parts of it, sticking out of the rubble near the top of the pile. "At least we have someone to talk to. Cal, check him for a suicide pill."

The Phoenix Force medic nodded and turned back from the hole in the ceiling.

"Y'all need help down there?" Hawkins asked.

"We're mopping up and checking for civilian survivors," Manning returned. "Check the floor below. The bomb blast put a hole through to that level, too."

"I'm on it," Hawkins replied. "Cal, do you need help with the prisoner?"

"Give me a minute. Then you can haul this piece of crap down with us. If anyone's hurt, they'll need lots of medical attention," James said.

The Cuban nodded. Though Hawkins's Ranger first-aid training was among the best in the armed forces, the skills of a Navy hospital corpsman like James were invaluable. If Manning or Encizo found anyone alive on this floor, their first-aid skills would be enough to stabilize the victim long enough for James or a medevac to take over, provided the skies were clear enough for helicopters to airlift people out to a hospital.

Encizo looked through the rubble on the side of the building he was searching, knowing that if he rushed, he might miss an injured civilian, but if he took too long, then the helicopters on the roof would get away, or perhaps even send down more reinforcements to finish their job.

The Cuban Phoenix Force veteran looked out a window and caught a glimpse of a shadow across the side of the building. It was one of the troop helicopters, and it raced off, disappearing behind the buildings on the other side of the courtyard. Encizo tensed, wondering if he'd missed the other craft's departure, or if it was still hanging back, waiting for the remainder of the assault force.

James and Hawkins had captured one of the intruders, though. Letting the assault force's remnants escape for now was only a temporary reprieve. Encizo knew that inside, armed with only a popgun, he wouldn't be able to do anything to slow the other aircraft, no matter how easily the tiny 6.5 mm bullets sliced through body armor. A tiny .25-caliber hole in a human being was disproportionately more fatal than a quarter-inch hole in a heavy combat helicopter.

"Help…" a voice croaked, almost too soft to hear. Encizo holstsered the handgun and moved to the side of the wounded man. While the victim's head and right arm were free, he was trapped beneath the wedge of a filing cabinet. The stocky Cuban examined the filing cabinet, not wanting to unsettle a precariously balanced weight, crushing an innocent person.

"I've got you," Encizo consoled. "Hang on."

There was a look of relief in the man's eyes, but that flashed away in a moment of terrified shock. "Oh my…"

The Phoenix Force veteran spun to the window as the trapped victim's expression changed. The polymer frame of the hi-cap 1911 was locked in his hand even as he wheeled around, staring at the sharklike outline of the transport helicopter as it hovered outside the window. It hung outside, visible in full profile, and instinctively Encizo realized why.

In the open side door of the hovering transport, a gunner with a multibarreled weapon adjusted his aim.

Heartbeats later, at 6000 rounds per minute, the six-barreled XM-134 minigun erupted to life, its high-powered 7.62 mm payload chewing through glass and concrete as if it were soft cheese.

Yuma, Arizona

THE MURDEROUS COMMANDOS in black armor weren't in the mood to hang around the canyon. The remaining killers toiled at booby-trapping their rocket launchers and transmitter.

Lyons's eyes narrowed in cold fury. "Those booby traps look dangerous, Gadgets."

The electronics genius, nestled beside him behind a shelf of stone, nodded. "If they're not deactivated, they could hurt or kill the people trying to disarm them."

"Got something to fix that?" Rosario Blancanales asked.

Hermann Schwarz took out his jammer and adjusted its frequencies. "That's the trouble with high explosives. You store too much of it in a single area, and a powerful radio signal could set it off. Hence those signs around construction sites—no radio playing allowed."

Lyons grinned grimly. "Rock them like a hurricane."

Schwarz returned the grin, focused his transmitter's beam, then aimed it like a gun at one rocket launcher that an armored marauder tinkered with. The broad-spectrum pulse struck the sensitive explosives. There was no guarantee that the ploy would work, but he was draining his jammer's batteries in one shot, sending out a shriek across dozens of bands. The scattershot radio wave connected with something.

A wad of plastic explosive that the raider placed at

the base of the automated launcher's firing system erupted in a ground-quaking blast that hurled the saboteur thirty feet. The way the hardman landed, Carl Lyons knew no amount of armored polymer fiber could protect him. The saboteur's limbs were twisted like a rag doll's. The bulletproof black outfit that he'd worn served only to keep the pulped flesh and crushed bone inside in one man-shaped lump.

Another of the armored cretins screamed in pain as a chunk of shrapnel from the launcher imbedded in his shoulder.

Lyons exploded from behind his shelf and ignored the wounded killer, his Beowulf focused on the helicopter the survivors scrambled toward. On full-auto, the .50-caliber rifle ripped several holes in the windshield. The rotors still spun, its landing gear now inches off the ground.

Blancanales's M-203 grenade launcher gave a throaty roar and plopped a 40 mm HE shell in the open side door of the transport craft. The grenade detonated on impact and pulverized the door gunner and another raider who had crawled halfway into the passenger compartment. A sailing pair of legs tumbled through the air, silent testimony to the destructive power of the grenade launcher.

The helicopter lurched violently, wounded by the volcanic blast at its side, and Lyons cursed as the hovering bird slid out of his stream of autofire. Schwarz took up the slack, his .50-caliber carbine smashing out 300-grain tungsten-cored penetrators. A line of half-inch holes exploded along the midline of the windshield, and the enemy chopper suddenly pitched nose-first into the ground. The front of the craft crumpled an instant before the rotor blades bit into hard rock and shattered under the force of the impact, engines ripping out of control.

The sleek transport stood on its face for a moment, then toppled onto its side like a wounded fish, jets of flame and black smoke erupting from where Blancanales scored his deadly hit.

Lyons spotted one of the armored intruders spin and fire his submachine gun. The initial burst cut low, tearing up stone chips at his feet, but the Able Team commander didn't give the killer time to readjust his aim. The Beowulf punched the gunman five times, zippering him up from crotch to throat. The rifle's massive slugs hurled the corpse to the ground after splitting its torso open.

The last of the armored invaders whirled and dropped out of view into a crevasse.

"Get him!" Lyons shouted as he exploded into a running charge after the gunman. He knew that he didn't need to tell his partners, but he was running on pure instinct now. His mouth had a mind of its own, even as his body focused on the task at hand.

A lobbed grenade sailed out of the crevasse and the three Able Team warriors split up, hitting the ground before the minibomb detonated. Shrapnel bounced angrily off stone and equipment, denied the flesh of the men who took cover behind stone and metal.

It took only a single heartbeat for Lyons to find his feet again and continue after the escaping commando, the Beowulf muzzle seeking a target. He skidded to the edge of the crevasse and collapsed. His momentum slid him over the lip and to the bottom of the ditch, right under a slashing line of 6.5 mm armor-piercing bullets.

Lyons rapped off four shots, and his weapon clunked empty. In his rush, he'd reverted to instinct, and assumed that the carbine had the same ammunition capacity as its 5.56 mm counterpart. There was only room in the magazine for twelve fat .50-caliber slugs rather than thirty smaller projectiles.

The armored commando pulled the trigger on his weapon, as well, and received only a click for his efforts.

Even through the black polycarbonate helmet's face shield, Lyons locked eyes with the hardman as the two opponents came to terms with the need for new strategy. Both combatants exploded forward, using their empty guns as clubs.

The Beowulf's tube-steel buttstock glanced off the curved black polycarbonate helmet, but the machine pistol whipped around like a hammer against Lyons's stomach. Hard abdominal muscles and Kevlar armor protected Lyons from serious injury, but the impact slowed the big blond ex-cop. His adversary followed up with a swift stroke of the barrel across Lyons's chin, just missing a solid connection with his mandible, even though the steel tube split skin.

The Able Team leader turned halfway, letting the force of the hardman's pistol whip roll into empty air, then he speared his elbow hard into the joint between the helmet and his foe's shoulder. The blow was dead on, and threw down the marauder, but didn't put him out, not that Lyons waited to see the results. The big ex-cop cut loose with a kick to the ribs that lifted his adversary off the ground a good two feet. Lyons could feel bones crunch against his steel-toed boot, and took another step. He swung his other boot hard, a solid punt connecting with the chin of the helmet's faceplate. Polycarbonate cracked, and even the rampaging Able Team warrior winced as the metal toe guard collapsed under the force of his kick.

Lyons staggered backward, his foot hurting like hell, but the wraith in black lay still, his helmet twisted around, hands twitching in the air. Lyons reversed his Beowulf again and stamped the tube-steel buttstock of his carbine against the dying man's faceplate. One sickening crunch, and it was all over.

Blancanales dropped into the crevasse a moment later. "Carl?"

The Able Team leader breathed heavily, his shoulders rising and falling with each pant. "Did you get a prisoner?"

"No. The wounded guy had a suicide pill," Blancanales replied.

Lyons's eyes narrowed. "Gadgets on the horn to Rogers?"

"Yeah. We've got a medevac for Sarlets," Blancanales stated. "You okay?"

"Nothing a few stitches and a bandage won't take care of," Lyons answered. He limped to the side of the ditch and clambered out.

In the distance, Army helicopters hung like fat bees.

The marauders had left them without a prisoner, and not many clues to go on.

But this wasn't over. Not by a long shot.

Langley, Virginia

GARY MANNING INSTINCTIVELY recognized the slashing thunder of the helicopter's minigun and hit the deck even before the first of the high-powered 7.62 mm bullets tore through a standing remnant of a wall, blasting a fist-size hole.

"Rafe!"

As suddenly as the storm of autofire started, it ended and Manning got to his feet, racing across the bomb-shattered floor, concern for his friend deadening the pain of his injured back. Through the ragged shattered window, he saw the helicopter hovering, not thirty feet out, the door gunner scanning the shadows of the building for any signs of life.

The Canadian pressed against a broken clump of a wall, darkness turning his brawny form into just another mass of rubble.

It made sense. Whoever was inside the building had just wiped out their death squad, an armored, unstoppable group that should have been able to waltz through a building full of paper pushers and keypunchers without so much as a bruise. Instead, their team was incommunicado and the assault gunship had been taken out by two civilians. The commander of the helicopter had to have realized that the men of Phoenix Force would prove to be a relentless enemy if they weren't eliminated.

He looked at the torn office the door gunner had reduced to a wasteland with his minigun, and dread filled Manning again. He'd been there, discovered his friend Rafael Encizo when the Cuban had been shot in the head in France at the climax of a mission. It had been one of the few times in his life that Manning had been reduced to tears, and now he doubted that there had been any way for his friend to have survived the onslaught of the troop ship.

Phoenix Force had suffered losses over the years, two of its members killed fighting for what they believed in, and close allies and friends fallen in other hellish conflicts. Manning wouldn't ever get used to watching a buddy die, but he steeled himself. He pulled the hi-cap 1911 from its holster and checked its load.

If they murdered Encizo, then they wouldn't live much longer. Though he was an expert rifleman, he wasn't nearly as good with a pistol. But the door gunner and his helicopter was a large enough target, even at fifty feet. He snapped around, placed the front sight on the door gunner's helmet and rapped off four quick shots.

The 6.5 mm penetrators exploded across space at close to two thousand feet per second, two missing, but two punching through the faceplate of the marauder's helmet. Polycarbonate shattered and the door gunner convulsed as the tungsten-cored slugs plowed through bone and burrowed deep into his brain.

The helicopter lurched and spun to escape when sparks danced across the side of the troop ship. Smoke billowed out as streams of submachine-gun fire tore into the tail boom of the chopper. This one wasn't equipped with a NOTAR housing, and automatic fire lanced through hydraulics, severing the steering mechanism.

The troop ship climbed frantically as Manning raced forward. As soon as he reached the torn hole in the side of the building, he emptied the hi-cap 1911. Sixteen rounds of 6.5 mm armor-piercing ammunition stitched across the belly of the helicopter toward its nose.

The aircraft jerked and autofire renewed from a shattered window below. Manning's peripheral vision recognized James while Hawkins was still in midreload of the little Uzi-type machine pistol. Manning let the 1911 drop to one side and he pulled out his Desert Eagle and his backup Walther P-5. It wasn't going to be much help, but the Canadian wasn't going to sit out the last of this battle. Bullets ripped from both handguns. It wasn't the most accurate form of gunfire, a pistol in each hand, but against a target as large as a transport helicopter, he didn't need precision fire. He scored hits with all nineteen rounds in his weapons.

He dropped the Walther and reloaded the Desert Eagle.

"C'mon, fall, damn you," Manning swore.

Something lurched in the rubble behind him and the Canadian turned.

Rafael Encizo dragged himself out from under a collapsed piece of ceiling, hauling an injured civilian with him. A cut on his head washed powdered plaster off one side of his swarthy features. "Catch, Gary."

The Cuban lobbed his 6.5 mm pistol over to Manning,

who snatched it out of the air. Desert Eagle and 1911 spoke again, but Manning concentrated on the 1911 first, making sure it was empty before he started on the Desert Eagle. By the third round from his .357 Magnum pistol, the wounded aircraft sputtered and sideslipped into the top floor of another building. Reinforced concrete held against the hurtling weight of the dying bird, rotors and hull crumpling as the helicopter collapsed into it.

The engine mast tore loose from its mooring and the remnants of the rotor sailed through the air like a flying disk. The twisted body of the aircraft tumbled to the courtyard below, erupting into flames.

Manning took aim with the Desert Eagle and hammered out the rest of his magazine into the blazing wreckage, letting the last of his dread and anger fade away in the flash and thunder of Magnum muzzle-blasts.

"I think it's dead," Encizo whispered. "You okay?"

"I thought you were a goner," Manning answered.

"I pushed this guy back under a concrete bar that fell on his back," Encizo replied. "I wasn't able to pull him out because he was pinned in too tight."

The civilian's face was ashen with pain from being battered by the explosion. "But when that monster cannon went off, this guy popped me back under the rebar."

"And at 6000 rpm, that minigun actually broke the concrete over us," Encizo said. "Otherwise we'd never be able to get out."

Manning looked down at the twisted, burning helicopter in the middle of the park. The fuel sparked off in a secondary explosion, but it was far enough away that it only raised a brisk, hot breeze across his face.

"I guess you owe them, then," the Canadian told his friend.

Encizo shrugged. "It balances out. The bastards tried to kill me."

"Let's get this guy some medical help," Manning suggested. "It's going to be a long day."

"What time is it?" Encizo asked.

"About 12:15..." Manning answered.

"I don't suppose you guys get overtime," the battered civilian quipped as they helped him to the stairwell.

"Nope," Encizo answered.

"Whatever they pay you, it sure as hell isn't enough," he said.

Manning felt the ache return in his back, but managed to smile. "Isn't that always the case?"

The civilian nodded slowly. "Thanks, anyway."

The two men of Phoenix Force shared a grin. It wasn't often that they heard gratitude, and even after the hammering they'd taken, they still felt good.

They'd saved lives.

But the enemy was still out there, and the warriors of Stony Man had their work cut out for them.

CHAPTER SEVEN

It was midnight when all eight members of Able Team and Phoenix Force reassembled in Virginia. Hal Brognola looked at his teams, and they seemed as if they had just finished a mission rather than barely having kicked off an investigation into a worldwide crisis.

The right side of Lyons's face was livid under a layer of paper tape and gauze. The bandage protected fresh stitches where a pistol-whipping had lain open his flesh to the bone.

Manning reclined in his chair, the shoulder straps of a back brace visible. Bruises and minor burns covered James, but his clothing made the injuries less obvious. Encizo's black hair was slicked back to provide room for a bandage on his forehead.

Barbara Price took a deep, tentative breath before handing out folders to all present, including David McCarter who had been at the Farm since three in the afternoon.

"We were unable to get anything out of the one survivor we captured," Price announced. "Everyone else died, either killed by our teams or from suicide pills. Whoever assigned these mercenaries was thorough."

"No fingerprints," Lyons said. His speech was slurred thanks to painkillers pumped into his jaw. "They must have removed them with a mild acid."

"Rest that mouth of yours, Carl," Brognola ordered. The Able Team leader glared, but kept silent.

"Inspector Byers filed similar reports," Price stated. She glanced toward McCarter. "The dead men had no fingerprints, and no dental records are on file."

"They sounded American, though," McCarter replied.

"Can you narrow that down?" Manning asked. "They could be Canadian or from the United States. What region?"

"It was just a gut instinct," McCarter said. "When they cursed, they didn't sound British, and they cursed in English. Usually, when you're shocked, your brain reverts to the words you grew up with."

"Okay, that's good enough for now," Price said. "We'll see what we can find from the bodies that have no facial damage. Fortunately, the helmets and uniforms were fireproof."

"Says here that more than a few of the bodies had scar tissue where tattoos were removed." James spoke up. "They were made as anonymous as possible."

"The only things these mystery men had in common were their armor and equipment," Schwarz mused. "And that they were dead-set on causing maximum mayhem."

"Langley is going to be recovering for years," Brognola said. "As it is, a major portion of their computer database has been corrupted."

"Have they started any file recovery?" Schwarz asked.

"Seventy percent of the information technology experts cleared for processing that data were killed," Price stated. "And half of those who weren't murdered are hospitalized."

"Damn," Hawkins murmured. "If we'd only been a little faster…"

"You were pinned down by an assault helicopter," Brognola admonished. "And the doors to the Computer Center were locked down due to the emergency. That you got inside and saved as many as you did was remarkable."

"It doesn't bring anyone back to life," Hawkins added.

"So you hunt down the bastards responsible and make them pay," Brognola stated.

"What does the Bear have for us?" McCarter asked.

"The worm that hit the CIA system slipped into ours," Price explained. "You know we have our own unofficial tap on Langley's database. We ended up in emergency shutdown for several hours while we checked for any remaining virus infection."

"Could we have started out any deeper in the hole?" Blancanales asked.

"Yeah. Rafe could have been turned into a lump of hamburger," Manning exhorted

"And Carl and the others could have been pulverized by artillery rocket fire," Price added.

"Sorry. It's the pain talking," Manning stated. He glanced over at Lyons, whose foot was splinted. "How bad?"

"Dislocated," Lyons said tersely.

"Carl!" Brognola warned.

Lyons rolled his eyes and kept his mouth shut.

"Sorry," Manning apologized.

Brognola sighed. "I know. I've seen all of you in sick bay before. You're a difficult bunch of patients."

"Who's a patient?" Manning asked. "I'm fit enough to handle fieldwork."

"I can walk," Lyons declared. "And my jaw's not broken."

Brognola shook his head in resignation. "Fine, fine."

Lyons looked at Encizo, then gave Blancanales a tap on the arm. The Puerto Rican nodded.

"Rafe," Blancanales began, "you mentioned in your report that you think that this might be similar to an old sparring partner of ours."

"The Fascist International," Encizo answered. "That's right. You fought against them in El Salvador, right?"

"All over," Lyons murmured.

"Yeah. They had a training facility for death squads," Schwarz recollected.

"That was before I started," Price noted. "But I remember reading about that. They were a neo-Nazi movement through Central and South America, right?"

"Pretty much. They were organized to keep the European bloodlines in power south of the border," Blancanales explained. "Of course, the *meztizos* kept wanting representation for their taxation and voting rights…"

"Not to be murdered," Lyons interjected.

"The Fascist International was founded by descendants of old SS agents who escaped to Argentina and Brazil. There are still leftovers across Central and South America," Schwarz noted. "Especially in Brazil."

"Yeah. Those bastards who execute homeless kids in Brazil," Price noted. "You had some dealings with them a while back, too."

"They're still around. We only put a dent in that bunch," Blancanales muttered. Unlike the founder of Stony Man Farm, Mack Bolan, the men of Able Team and Phoenix Force weren't at liberty to pursue their own crusades. They were on the clock, and had enough work cut out for them simply dealing with day-to-day threats to the nation and the world as a whole, rather than to go hunting particular opponents without sanction.

Blancanales took a deep breath and put his anger away.

Sooner or later, a window of opportunity would open up, and the child-murdering death squads of Brazil would cross their paths again. Able Team was lucky enough, so to speak, to have found leftovers from the old Facist International, either in truth or in spirit. Whoever the armored assassins worked for, however, they were part of a career-long crusade against totalitarian thugs that had begun with one of their very first missions as a team. Even if they weren't part of the organization that the Stony Man warriors battled ferociously across several years, they were indicative of the same racist rot that occurred within Latin American society.

The War Room's wall screen suddenly flashed from a world map to displaying Aaron Kurtzman's bearded face. "Guys, we've got some bad news coming in."

A deadly silence filled the room as the Stony Man warriors looked at the smoking skyline of a Middle Eastern city.

Iraq

CAPTAIN DAYTON MEAD was on the career fast track to nowhere, stuck in charge of a U.S. Army Special Forces team in Iraq. At least that's what he'd been told. Mead, however, was devoted to his A-Team. They were his extended family, and the Army high command didn't understand that. Most of them were career men, looking for an office in the Pentagon, rather than doing their duty to their country, taking to the field to make the most of their training.

Mead was different, and he was glad, if not for the work, then for the results and for the people he worked with. The Iraqi citizens were good people, and appreciative of his team's aid, and the smile on children's faces was worth the world to the Special Forces captain, himself a father of three.

Iraq was a hard situation. The media liked to call them insurgents, but Mead knew the truth. It was opportunists from various other Arab countries. He'd even run afoul of some Basque terrorists from Spain. They were terrorists, pure and simple. "Insurgents" implied that they had some sort of legitimate motivation for placing car bombs in the middle of towns where children played and mothers walked to market.

These were terrorists, mad-dog killers. If they weren't from foreign nations, looking to lash out against perceived American imperialism, then they were Baathist party hardliners, struggling to hold on to what little shreds of power they had, never mind who had to die to achieve their goals.

Mead crouched by a low wall and pulled out a

monocular, sweeping a small toolshed where he was informed that there were explosives. His team was spread out, ready to take control of the shed and the small farmhouse where some suspected terrorists had taken refuge. Mead hoped that the family that lived there was all right. He recognized this as Terena's home. Since the "insurgents" showed little regard for the Iraqi people they claimed to fight for, it was possible that Terena, a nine-year-old girl the same age as his eldest daughter, could be orphaned, or even dead.

Mead glanced to Sergeant Lawrence Jacobs, a brawny black man with a thick beard. Jacobs had grown attached to Terena, as well, having a young daughter of his own. There was always the danger that the insurgents would use the people that the Green Berets helped as leverage against them, but the men who signed up for Special Forces duty joined because they cared. Nothing could shut off their hearts, but the soldiers knew how to make those who threatened the people they protected pay.

Jacobs was ready to lead an assault to rescue Terena's family, while Mead made certain that there were no boobytraps in the toolshed. The captain of a Special Forces A-Team was supposed to be an executive, but Mead was a man who believed in true leadership, from the front. He didn't become SOCOM-certified to ride a desk, and he didn't pick a leadership position to send others to do what he wouldn't.

Benmurgy and Schindler accompanied Mead to the shed, while Pepitone, Murphy and Canton were on Jacobs. The rest of the team had control of the perimeter, with Caulfield in a roost a half mile away, controlling the killing box behind the scope of a .50-caliber M-85 Barrett.

"Ready," Jacobs whispered.

"Go," Mead confirmed, and the Special Forces captain, gripping his M-4 tightly, went over the low wall and raced toward the toolshed. The farmhouse doors slammed open and in the distance, stun-shock grenades detonated.

Mead covered the toolshed door while Benmurgy laid a line of det cord along the hinges and door frame. Schindler lit off the det cord, a line of plastic explosives that detonated at only a mere 3800 feet per second. The line acted like a high-speed torch, burning the door off its hinges. As the wood fell away from its frame, Mead caught sight of a plank bouncing off an invisible ledge in the air.

"Hit the dirt!" he ordered.

Benmurgy and Schindler were already at a safe distance and curled up as a wave of nails, bolts and screws hurtled through the air at waist level. A chunk of improvised shrapnel glanced off Mead's helmet. It was a trap.

"Larry!" Mead called out.

"We got nothin'," Jacobs answered.

"Clear out, this is a sucker play," Mead warned.

Mead spotted Pepitone as the SF sergeant smashed out a window. The others slid out of the improvised exit and the four commandos raced back to rendezvous with Mead and the others.

"Cap, we've got company coming." Caulfield spoke up. "Armored vehicles of some sort!"

"Armor?" Mead asked. Confusion colored his words. "We didn't ask for support."

"Not ours," the sniper confirmed. "Three heading your way, more burning toward town!"

"I thought the Iraqi armor was all taken care of," Benmurgy said.

Mead pushed the SF trooper along. There would be time to figure out what was going on later.

Three armored vehicles, shaped like tortoises with scorpion tails, smashed through a wall along the side of the farm.

Baker's M-60 opened up and raked the domelike destroyers with half a belt of 7.62 mm NATO. Mead paused and let one of the vehicles have it with a 4-round burst, but it was like throwing rice.

The rolling monstrosity swiveled its scorpion-like tail, and Mead dived out of the path of twin streams of automatic fire. The arced tail unleashed venomous sprays of death that tore into Benmurgy's back and ripped him in two.

"No!" Mead bellowed. "Get to cover!"

Mead continued to roll as the other two Ankylosaur attack drones spread out and sought the Green Berets. From their over-watch position, other Green Berets cut loose with shoulder-fired rocket launchers. One of the armored marauders erupted as two warheads struck its curved shell. Craters vomited flames and the machine slowed.

The third of the attackers peeled toward the Green Berets with the LAW rockets, its tail booming with a stream of explosive 40 mm shells. The Ankylosaur's automatic grenade launcher hammered the two Special Forces troopers, obliterating them completely.

A fifth of the team was down in only a few moments, and only one of those machines was wounded. Mead moved his finger down to the trigger of his M-4's launcher and punched a 40 mm grenade into the tail boom of the closest killer machine. It was a HE bomb, but the blast didn't tear away the scorpion-like append-age. It did, however, swerve the aim of the Ankylosaur's grenade launcher to pepper the flaming combat drone. A blistering salvo of high explosives slammed into the wounded robot tank, punching through the holes that the LAW rockets made and detonating its vulnerable in-sides. The machine came apart at the seams as it flooded with molten heat.

Caulfield's .50-caliber gun boomed, and the second killer drone jerked as its sensor plate imploded. The A-Team sniper pumped out heavy, 650-grain slugs as fast as he could pull the trigger, and Mead knew that Caulfield's shoulder had to feel like hell from the thun-derous recoil of the rifle. However, the robot tank flailed around blindly, seeking targets. Out of control, it sprayed the farmhouse with cannon fire, bursting apart the walls and windows as if they were made of soft clay. Mead had a glimmer of hope.

"Aim for those sensor plates!" Mead shouted. He spun and ripped off the remainder of his magazine into the low head of the turtle-shaped machine. The 5.56 mm bullets were ineffective against even that relatively vul-nerable spot, but the sparks lit it up for others to target. Baker's M-60 homed in on the last machine and tore 7.62 mm slugs into it.

The Ankylosaur reacted to the GPMG fire and unleashed a shredding salvo of 25 mm cannon shells at Baker's position. Mead watched in numbed horror as his heavy weapons sergeant disappeared in a cloud of stringy flesh and choking smoke.

The flailing, blinded robot seemed to receive instruction from afar and whirled toward Mead. The Special Forces captain rolled out of the path of the machine, just missing being ground beneath the heavy wheels of the robot tank. He shook his head as he finally got a good look at the underside of the Ankylosaur. The killer drone didn't have treads like a conventional tank, but its wheels were heavy, knobbed with steel and looked as though they'd run even when flat. The axle looked far too powerful to disable, even with a 40 mm grenade, which meant that anyone caught in the open would be reduced to ground meat.

"Pull back! Caulfield! Keep up the rocket…" Mead said into his throat mike when the Ankylosaur suddenly whirled to face him directly. It appeared to "hear" him. With a sense of dread, he realized that the deadly machine had the ability to listen to radio signals and home in on them.

The last thing he saw was the bright muzzle-flash of the 25 mm cannon, which burned hotter than the sun.

Then, oblivion.

"WE'RE GETTING SLAUGHTERED here!" Corporal Hector Hojas yelled into his radio. He was at the perimeter of a "green zone" area, where civilian contractors, embedded journalists and military support staff were quartered. Hojas curled up behind the heavy stone pillar as it was hammered by a blistering wave of thunderbolts.

"Keep your ground!" Colonel Jethro Prennial ordered. "We don't have anyone with weapons to hold them off!"

Hojas cursed. "Of course you don't have anyone able to fight, you fucking redneck bastard!"

It was policy among the Army brass to keep their soldiers unarmed when they weren't on active patrol. Rifles were empty, handguns weren't issued, and even pocketknives were forbidden. Not that small arms would have proved worthwhile against the armored juggernauts that rolled into the base.

"Your ass is going on report, Hojas!" Prennial shouted.

"I'll be lucky to live that long," Hojas answered. He was a soldier, and because he was working in supply, he carried only a radio. He was going to die like a lamb in a slaughterhouse. The corporal looked around and saw the skyline of the city throwing up columns of smoke. There had to have been dozens of those things swarming all over the town, laying down destruction wherever they went.

The slap of rotor blades filled the air and Hojas turned to see a helicopter. It was a JetRanger, owned by some oil company executives. What he wouldn't have given for it to be a Kiowa with antitank rockets. He doubted that any Apache gunships would be in the air, since they were rendered useless for city operations by their massive weight and armor and lack of maneuverability.

The oil company geeks were getting away, leaving the soldiers below to face the invulnerable horde. Hojas couldn't really blame them, he'd have loved to sprout wings to escape.

The storm of firepower that chewed at Hojas's position suddenly faded, and the young corporal caught a glimmer of hope, but instead the monstrosity turned its attention on the fleeing helicopter. Flaming lances of explosive shells stabbed into the aircraft and tore it into blazing confetti.

Hojas looked at his pillar, then felt his stomach drop. When he'd crouched behind it, it was four feet wide. Those machines had narrowed it to three feet, and a good two feet had been sawn off the top.

The Ankylosaur whirled and rolled on, seeking out more targets, and Hojas looked down at the radio. He had to have dropped it when he saw the helicopter overhead. Its batteries had been disconnected in the drop, but the hand unit seemed salvageable. He reached for it, then something told him to leave it.

He was in enough trouble. It was time for him to get out of there and hope that when worse came to worst, he'd have the Judge Advocate General to support him when he was put on trial for insubordination. Hojas stood and saw several figures racing through the smoke. He froze—they were dressed all in black.

For a moment he wondered if they were special operations soldiers, but this was broad daylight, and those guys knew how to blend in. Suddenly he spotted one of the wraiths in black pause and fire a machine pistol at a wounded soldier. An explosion of blood erupted from the murdered man, and Hojas realized why the armored machines had passed on.

Here was the mop-up squad, and they weren't going to worry if an American was unarmed or wounded. They were killing everyone they saw.

Hojas clenched his fists. If he had a loaded M-16, he'd be able to do something against them, but there was nothing he could do. The colonel had even confiscated all the folding knives in the company.

"We're not in a combat zone," Prennial had explained.

"This looks like a combat zone now…except we're not combating back, asshole," Hojas growled as he whirled and vaulted over a low wall. Gunfire chased him and he ducked.

If he could make it back to the barracks, he could get the Colt .45 his father had given him before he'd left for Iraq. Hojas wasn't supposed to own a personal handgun, but he'd hidden it well, and he prayed that he'd be able to get to it in time.

Hojas lamented not carrying it under his BDUs, but Prennial had the MPs frisk soldiers at the beginning and ending of every shift. Enough of his buddies in supply had lost personal sidearms and knives to those searches, and Hojas hadn't been willing to lose the pistol his father had carried in Vietnam, also against the rules, and his grandfather had toted through the Korean War.

As if his day couldn't grow any worse, he recognized the whistle of a mortar shell descending from the sky. Hojas threw himself under an overhanging roof and curled up. Instants later, a prefab building twenty yards to his right vaporized into splinters and belching smoke. Hojas felt the ground shake as multiple shells hammered into the Green Zone, and he watched his barracks collapse as it was pounded into oblivion by half a dozen warheads.

So much for getting the .45 and fighting back.

Hojas looked back to see two of the figures in black armor scale the wall. He was about to grab a rock to fight with, when the overhanging roof was jarred loose by a detonation. A slab of the roof collapsed on him. Hojas screamed, then realized that he was safe, there was some space under the slab across him. He kept still, playing dead because he knew his boots were exposed below.

Through the ringing in his ears, he heard the scrunch of boots across the rubble, and clenched his eyes tightly. A machine pistol rattled, and he felt something sting his side. He held his breath and didn't react, even though he felt a growing wet, sticky puddle form under his BDU shirt. Hojas realized that he'd been clipped by a bullet that had punched through the chunk of ceiling atop him. Voices rattled in Arabic, and he heard footsteps fade into the distance.

Hojas took a deep breath and felt a wave of pain slice through him. His fingers reached up, and he found the bullet hole, in the middle of a wet spot the size of a pie plate. The single bullet had glanced off his rib and opened a fissure as long as his thumb. It bled a lot, but the injury wasn't severe. He took a handkerchief and pressed it to the wound to stop the blood flow.

Hojas didn't know when he passed out, but it had to have been right afterward. When he woke up, his side was being sewn shut by a medic, and a bottle of Ringer's solution dripped into an IV tube in his arm.

"What happened?" Hojas asked.

"The attackers pulled back before the Apaches could get in here to fight," the medic explained. "They killed a lot of people."

Hojas took a deep breath. "A building fell on me... and those bastards shot me through the rubble."

"Yeah," the medic explained. "We'll get you to a hospital ship, but they're pretty busy now."

Hojas nodded. "How bad is it?"

"You lost a lot of blood, and you might have a broken rib, but you're okay. That wasn't a million-dollar wound, though."

"Colonel Prennial is going to court-martial me anyway," Hojas mumbled.

"The colonel was killed," the medic explained.

Hojas raised an eyebrow.

"He was trying to get away in his jeep when those things just hammered him. I think he was trying to contact a helicopter by radio, trying to evacuate," the medic said.

"He was on the radio and they shot him?" Hojas asked.

The medic nodded. "We heard the gunfire, then everything went dead."

Hojas suddenly remembered the instinct that kept him from putting the batteries back in his walkie-talkie after he'd dropped it.

"Thank you, God," he prayed.

Hojas drifted back to sleep. He'd need it.

CHAPTER EIGHT

Hal Brognola landed at the White House at 3:45 a.m., and the President welcomed him into the Oval Office.

"You've been burning the midnight oil, too, Hal?" the Man asked.

"We've been covering a related crisis at the Farm," Brognola answered.

Without asking the President poured the head Fed a cup of coffee, then slumped back in his couch. His tie hung on the corner of his leather chair, and his shirt was unbuttoned at the throat. "What do you know about these new armored vehicles, Hal?"

"They were first spotted at Yuma proving grounds," Brognola explained. "We forwarded that report to you earlier this afternoon."

"Yesterday, Hal," the President corrected. He looked at his watch. "They first attacked less than thirty hours ago, on American soil, at one of our most secret military complexes. And only a few hours ago, they struck again, in Iraq. Is it al Qaeda?"

"I don't think so," Brognola answered. "We're under the impression that these things were originally intended for some kind of operation in Central America. El Salvador to be exact."

The President frowned. "I don't buy it, Hal. The attackers in Iraq matched the marauders at Yuma."

"We've managed a partial identification of one of the captured killers. He's an American, with a Christian Identity militia called the Fist of God," Brognola stated.

"Didn't they have ties to an Islamic terrorist organization?" the President asked.

"Yes," Brognola answered.

The President frowned. "I want Stony Man to take care of this. You don't think we're facing a problem in the Middle East?"

"These guys have been striking pretty much around the globe. Our first encounter with these soldiers in body armor was in London," Brognola explained.

The President nodded. "They assassinated a former investigator of ORDEN."

"I think that Iraq was intended to be a case of misdirection," Brognola mused. "To draw attention away from this hemisphere. We have enough intelligence and military assets over there to solve any real problems that pop up."

"I trust your instincts, but I'd rather have Phoenix Force check things out over there."

Brognola took a sip of the coffee. "A couple of my people were hurt in the defense of Langley."

The President steepled his fingers together. "And Able Team?"

"They're better suited to checking out Central America."

"Striker?"

Brognola answered quickly. "He's in the field and we haven't been able to contact him. Once we get through to him, we'll bring him up to speed."

"Where was he last?" the President asked.

"North Africa," Brognola replied.

"So he's in position to lend aid. All right, but how soon will Phoenix Force be back at full strength?"

"Give us forty-eight hours," Brognola requested. "Then if things are still going badly in the Middle East, we'll dispatch them there."

"All right. I'll activate Delta Force and the SEALs in the meantime," the President said. "I've grown so used to having Stony Man at full strength."

"We'll be back at top form soon enough," Brognola promised.

"All right, Hal." He locked eyes with the big Fed. "But somehow I don't think you'll let this crisis last longer than forty-eight hours."

"We're working on it, sir," Brognola said. "We're not miracle workers, but we try."

The President nodded.

Brognola put down his cup of coffee and left the Oval Office.

"YOU WERE RIGHT, it was just a pulled muscle," Barbara Price said to Gary Manning as she reassembled Phoenix Force in the War Room. "How's it feeling?"

"The heating pad's loosened it up," the big Canadian

answered. "And the Farm doctor has me on a mild muscle relaxer that is keeping it comfortable."

"All right. Hal's just called me. He's told the President that you are a lot worse off than you really are," Price explained. "You've got two days to figure out what's going on, and put it away before you get called up to go hunting for these guys in Iraq."

"There can't be more than one freighter load of those machines in Iraq." McCarter spoke up. "According to Kurtzman, the freighter I visited in London had a sister ship that made a delivery to the Middle East."

"Which only supports the notion that our villains have their own manufacturing facilities," Manning mused.

"The last time Able Team encountered the Fist of God and their Islamic counterparts, they were being supplied by a third party," Rafael Encizo stated. "And they had links to a coalition of Filipino extremists. It's not outside the realm of possibilities that whoever is trying to revitalize the Fascist International got their hooks into the Fist of God's contacts."

"That's why Able Team and Jack Grimaldi are going to ground zero, El Salvador, and you guys are stopping off in Mexico," Price explained.

"The port where my freighter made its previous delivery," McCarter noted. "Where they slipped a supply of those Ankylosaurs across the border into the United States."

"It's also where the drilling machine had a number of parts manufactured," Price stated. "They tried to sterilize their machines, but since the driller was expected to be totally destroyed, they got a little sloppy. It took a lot of searching, but we managed to trace some engine parts back to a plant in Mexico."

"Two stops," Hawkins spoke up. "Any chance one of them is Acapulco or Cabo San Lucas?"

"Work on your tan some other time, T.J.," Price snapped. "The factory is an old automobile manufacturer just outside of Mexico City. It was sold to a conglomerate a few years ago."

"And you think they're using the old production lines to build their killer robots," James said.

"Yeah," Price answered. "But we want to make sure first. The port might have more of those Ankylosaurs or body armor suits and submachine pistols. I don't have to tell you how dangerous those could be if they were mass distributed to international terrorists. Most cops, hell, even most SWAT teams don't have the training and firepower to take down bulletproof killers."

"We almost didn't," Hawkins said numbly. "I'm definitely going to carry some full-size firepower with me, even if I am going to work in plainclothes."

"When do we take off? And who's taking us?" Manning asked, getting back to business.

"Charlie Mott," Price answered. "We've got a Learjet at Langley AFB, ready to take you south."

"We'll be able to get our gear through customs?" McCarter added.

"Yeah. We've set it up, and gave you some money from petty cash to grease any palms," Price noted. "It's good we've got a war chest for that sort of thing."

"At least it's money confiscated from drug dealers and terrorists, and not taxpayer money," James commented. "Wonder if we're putting Mexican drug money back into bribing Mexican officials."

"It goes back into the system. It would have gotten to them anyway," Encizo said with resignation. "Back when I was working with the DEA, I ran across money from Irish terrorists and Japanese gangsters going to Mexican customs officials and Colombian judges. It's all one big melting pot of corruption."

"And right now," McCarter stated, "we're supposed to be en route to Mexico. Grab your Glocks and whatever long guns you want, and let's get the ball rolling."

San Luis, El Salvador

THE LANDING WOKE Carl Lyons with a jolt, and instinctively he checked his watch. It was just after dawn. He stretched his broad shoulders. Tendons popped, and he rolled his neck to loosen all the kinks. He glanced over at Hermann Schwarz and Rosario Blancanales who were just stirring, as well. The Able Team leader let his fingertips brush the frame of his sidearm, making certain it was there and at the ready, then got up to check on Jack Grimaldi in the cockpit. He knew immediately that he was at Cuscatlan International Airport. San Salvador itself had a fairly large airport, but there was too much of an opportunity for their enemies to be on alert in their own city. The international airport would give them a screen of bodies, although in the past the Ejercito Secreta Anticomunista— the ESA—never seemed too concerned about untoward collateral damage in their previous battles with Able Team.

"Does it look okay out on the field?" Lyons asked.

"I'd have woken you guys up if I expected trouble. Don't worry, this jet has all kinds of antiradiation and missile-lock avoidance technology," Grimaldi answered, grinning widely.

"Antiradiation," Lyons murmured. "That phrase still makes me think of nuke stuff instead of radar."

"Yeah. That's what I thought when I first heard about it back when I was just a chopper jockey in the Army," Grimaldi admitted. "Still, there's more chance of us running into a radar-guided antiaircraft missile than a nuke."

Lyons snorted in derision. "Only barely."

Blancanales was in the middle of checking on his money roll, and looked up as Lyons joined him.

"Ready?" Lyons asked.

"Yeah. Gadgets is prepping out pistols," Blancanales told him.

Lyons turned and looked at Hermann Schwarz, who was reassembling the handguns after field-stripping.

"Never thought we'd be packing .50s into action," Schwarz said as he handed Lyons his gun. "Now we have something to go with the carbines."

The Able Team leader worked the slide on the Guncrafter Industries GI-50. The pistol looked indistinguishable from a standard Colt .45 autopistol, although Able Team's GI-50s were fitted with night sights. Even the wood-colored, flat aluminum grips were standard issue, though the only change was that instead of firing a .45-caliber bullet, they fired .50-caliber slugs of the same length as the .45 ACP. "We need all the power we can get. How're we loaded?"

"First magazine is standard 300-grain hollowpoints,"

Schwarz stated. "You'll have two spare magazines of combat loads, and two magazines of antipersonal .50 ammo that Cowboy whipped up."

Lyons nodded. "Shame these don't share the same ammo as the Beowulf rifles."

"Cowboy's working on turning some M-4s to .50 GI," Schwarz noted. "It won't have the same penetration as the big .50 Beowulf, but we'll see how much that affects operation."

"I'd rather have the extra thump and range of the Beowulf round," Lyons said. "You wearing your vest?"

"Yeah," Schwarz answered. "Once you get used to sleeping in one, it's like another T-shirt. A stiff, uncomfortable T-shirt that makes you sweat like a pig…"

"I get the point," Lyons stated. "All right. Let's go make sure nobody messes with our airplane."

Lyons slipped the GI-50 into a concealment holster behind his hip. Since the gun was exactly to the same specifics as the Colt .45, it fit the same holsters. It wasn't a big, roaring hunting cartridge like a .50-caliber Desert Eagle. It was designed purely for the purpose of being an effective combat round. Each 300-grain bullet was slower, and gentler, than a .45 ACP bullet, which encouraged quick follow-up shots. Still, the added mass gave it extra oomph, even if it didn't pierce enemy body armor, slowing a foe enough for the members of Able Team to load up a magazine of AP ammo that would tear through anything short of a door gunner's flack jacket.

Lyons hoped that there wouldn't be a need for conflict, but Able Team was back in El Salvador, a place where they had fought some of their deadliest and most vicious battles. Though their enemies didn't know names, or exactly what the Stony Man warriors were, memories were long enough that someone could recognize the unlikely trio and start spreading the word that they were back in town.

Bring it on, Lyons thought grimly, his eyes narrowing. Come and get us, so we can start killing you right back up the chain of command to your rotten leadership. Able Team is back in town...

San Salvador, El Salvador

"I TOLD YOU IT WOULDN'T fall apart," Angela Eosin said as she walked onto the balcony. The sunrise in El Salvador glowed like molten fire, painting the world in shades of gold. The woman's dark eyes glinted alluringly, and Vincenzo Brujo shook his head, trying to fight off the hold her youthful beauty had over him.

Eosin was dressed in a diaphanous robe, barely concealing her full, soft breasts. Brujo couldn't forget the taste of her, even though the aftertaste of the control she wielded over him was bitter ashes. Brujo glanced across the plantation, sunlight reflecting off leaves, making the crops a sea of dark green and glimmering curves.

Her hand brushed across his bare shoulders. Brujo felt the coarseness of her fingers and palms, the only unfeminine thing about her. Eosin's hands looked delicate and feminine, but years of weapon building, welding and tool use, had turned her palms as callused as any laborer's. It only reminded Brujo how weak he was in comparison to her.

Brujo was a big power in El Salvadoran politics, a local warlock who could work magic. He had survived the upheavals of ORDEN and the dissolution of the Secret Anticommunist Army, presenting the image of a progressive politician to hide his allegiances to an international combine of right-wing governments. Anyone who learned about his ownership of a reactionary militia was silenced, either through blackmail or through murder. But he realized that he was simply a large fish in a small pond.

Eosin had come to him, the owner of a high-tech arms manufacturing firm, offering a chance to return El Salvador to its old glory, before the mixed bloods and the natives struggled up through death squads and poverty to claim their rights as human beings, before the time of interference from abroad, before the Army of the Americas came under countless assaults from an unknown force of marauders. She had somehow cut through Brujo's layers of defense, dropping a black raid suit and a helmet on his desktop.

"I give you ultimate power," Angela Eosin had offered, her dark eyes flashing. "An army of unstoppable supermen."

It was a dramatic statement, and Brujo had been tempted to have her thrown out by his bodyguards when she'd pulled a pistol from her trench coat pocket. Brujo'd reacted instantly, grabbing his pistol from underneath his desktop and punching the entire magazine into her chest.

"I was only offering you a light, Vincenzo," Angela'd answered, pulling the trigger, a lighter flickering from the rear of the slide. He'd looked on in disbelief as she was unfazed by nine rounds of .38 Superammo.

She'd lit her cigarette, then put the gun-shaped lighter away. The front of her trench coat had folded open, and Vincenzo could see an identical black uniform stretched across her luxuriant curves. "Granted, without the helmet, you could have killed me with a shot to the head."

He'd swallowed hard.

Eosin had leaned across, pulled the empty gun from Brujo's hand and reloaded the pistol. She'd settled the helmet on the Salvadoran boss's head, then fired five shots, point-blank into the faceplate. Even the Magnum-like power of the .38 Super had been incapable of blemishing the transparent, one-way glass of the helmet. "I have also made remote-controlled armored vehicles that would give you an unprecedented level of power as the new ruler of El Salvador. You will be able to repel any attack with robotic tanks, designed for the terrain of Central America. Nothing in any other arsenal can match your armored forces."

Brujo had known that the moment he removed the black helmet, he'd be totally under her control.

It was a year and a half later, and things were exploding across the globe. Brujo wanted the power that Eosin offered, but the idea that the United States government was being brutally prodded by Eosin's machinations over the past couple of days rested uneasily in his stomach. He was barely sleeping anymore, carried along on a wave of nerves and anxiety.

"Don't worry," Eosin whispered into his ear, her full, sensuous lips brushing his lobe. Electrical sexuality jolted up and down his spine. "The operations in the Middle East went off without a hitch. They lost only two of the drones, and the whole world thinks it was Iraqi insurgents behind the assaults at Yuma and Langley Headquarters. All eyes are pointed across the Atlantic, not at us."

Brujo shook his head, worried. "The London hit…it started the ball rolling. Someone else noticed us, put things together. We lost our freighter…"

"And its records have been lost," Eosin promised. "We're covering our tracks. By the time anyone puts enough together to figure out what we're up to, you'll be sitting in the presidency, and we'll begin returning Latin America to its true conquerors, not these brown little rat-things."

Brujo chewed his lip, wanting so much to believe her, to surrender to her for another morning of fabulous lovemaking, but the phone rang, an urgent alarm slicing through his growing serenity.

Brujo crossed to the phone and picked it up.

"Vincenzo, it's Joaquin."

This wasn't good. Joaquin was one of his allies in San Luis, where the Cuscatlan International Airport was located. Joaquin dropped advice to Brujo whenever strangers arrived who might be with the CIA. The betrayals of the U.S. government in the eighties had hurt ORDEN, the National Democratic Organization, and prosecution of Falange and the White Warriors Union had defanged the relatively small group of wealthy land owners and businessmen who had held their power since the 1800s. The original families that made up ORDEN's elite still had contacts and power throughout the infrastructure of the Salvadoran government, even though they'd been forced to remain incognito in recent years.

"What is it?" Brujo asked.

"A Learjet just landed from America."

Brujo weighed those words, dread filling him. "Who got off?"

"Three men and their pilot."

Brujo closed his eyes. "A blond muscleman?"

"Yes."

"A gray-haired Hispanic?"

"Yes. And a man with a mustache."

Brujo felt his knuckles crack as he gripped the phone. "Keep an eye on them."

"I will. I'm sorry, Vincenzo."

Eosin tilted her head, curiosity coloring her features.

"Your assurances are for nothing. The world may be looking at the Middle East, but someone else is looking at us," Brujo snapped.

Eosin smirked. "Don't worry. I know how to deal with them. I've been wondering when they would show up."

Brujo's eyes widened.

There was no end of surprises from the woman who called herself Fixx.

ANGELA EOSIN WASN'T her real name, but that didn't matter. She had a half dozen identities set up around the globe, and she thought of herself as above normal citizens. She was Fixx, the modern Hephaestus, the weaponsmith of the gods. With her brilliance, she'd shocked the world on several instances, and now, Fixx was getting ready to snap the Americas in two, creating a brand-new world order.

Her partners had suffered setbacks before, and Fixx herself was furious that a plot to pit Israel and Egypt against each other had been defused. A more recent effort to throw the United States into a siege of martial law had also been defanged. But, she had the time, the patience, to sit back and keep working at it. Once the world's governments obliterated one another with petty infighting thanks to the wars their terrorists ignited, Fixx and her allies would swoop in and create a new Utopia. Central America, and the revitalization of its hardcore extremist death squads, was only fuel splashing on the fire. From El Salvador, they would be able to spread through Mexico to Panama and set things up for an international oil crisis.

Venezuela's recent troubles had shown how the world hinged on South American oil. She wished that her partner, Skyline, had done a better job in destabilizing the region, but fortunately, this effort hadn't brought her enemies to her doorstep.

Fixx looked at the photographs that Brujo's men had taken of the new arrivals. They matched the descriptions she'd been given. These were the men who had been previously involved in their North American situation, a brutal conflict that had taken down three of their number. Fixx knew she wasn't a frontline combatant, but she relished the idea of fighting against the mystery commandos who had taken down their deadliest assassins.

Her lips drew into a tight line as she looked at the pilot who had been responsible for killing her friend. The loss of Harpy had hindered their efforts to smuggle supplies around the world, but Fixx had her own means of transport. The pilot had half a dozen phony identities, but there was one thing she was certain of—he was without the magnificent gunship that had bettered her own attack helicopter in Chicago.

A shame, really. Fixx would have liked to have killed the pilot when he was at his strongest, not as a sitting duck on the ground.

Oh, well.

If she remembered correctly, Harpy died in flaming wreckage pinned to the ground.

Fixx would be only too happy to make the rangy pilot burn to death, as well.

Her laptop emitted a barely audible burp, and Fixx turned to it.

"How goes it?" Fixx asked.

Skyline's hard, bronzed face looked back at her from the monitor. "I've got my people on hand."

"Good, because according to past encounters, and the data you've given me, these three are just way too tough for a bunch of white supremacist punks," Fixx explained.

"My ninjas are the finest in the world," Skyline answered. "You have nothing to fear."

"I don't fear, Sky," Fixx retorted. "It's just a shame that they're only going to get to face watered-down versions of my combat armor."

"Depending on who these three are," Skyline remarked, "they've taken down the hired help in that 'watered-down' combat armor."

"New information?" Fixx asked. She was intrigued.

"I had an informant who was still alive after the Yuma fiasco. Those three were at the testing center and part of the hunt for the Ankylosaurs," Skyline explained. "I'm trying to gather more information about the other four who took out another of your gunships."

Fixx frowned. "It was a complete loss? How? It had every form of survival technology on board. They would have needed a rocket launcher to take it down."

"I've checked the footage from Langley," Skyline answered. Fixx didn't doubt that the information broker had his fingers in every pot across the globe. Access to security tapes from CIA Headquarters would have only required minimal effort for him. "Two of them improvised a rocket launcher out of a missile pod your gunship ejected."

"Improvised?" Fixx asked. "Impressive."

Skyline's face darkened with anger. "I had three of my personal guard with the crew we sent to Langley. Only one returned, thanks to your hardware."

"No. Thanks to these mystery men," Fixx stated. "The only things that could have penetrated their battle armor would have been a .50-caliber rifle or the Bofors submachine pistols we supplied. I sold Brujo on the concept that the armor makes anyone wearing it invulnerable, but only my personal armor has that luxury."

"All right, Fixx," Skyline answered. "My men should have been able to wipe out any opposition, and reviewing the tapes, they were against commandos as skilled as they were. They somehow acquired the right firepower, probably after wrestling down one of our team, then were able to expand on their ability to fight back from there. They were resourceful enough to turn an ejected pod into an antiaircraft weapon…"

"I'm sorry about your men, Sky." Fixx was genuine, and Skyline's mood lightened slightly.

"Thanks, babe," the information broker said. "I just hope you're okay."

"What could go wrong?" Fixx asked innocently.

"I don't want anything that Brujo has," Skyline answered.

"I've taken my shots," Fixx replied. "And Brujo... He's been handled."

"Oh, damn. He's shooting blanks?" Skyline asked.

"A little cocktail our favorite chemist whipped up. His sex drive is still in effect, but he's sterile."

"Just as well," Skyline responded. "We don't want that cretin to breed, do we?"

"He's just going to last long enough to make the world a far more interesting place," Fixx answered. "And if the U.S. doesn't take him out with a bunker-busting bomb, he won't last longer than the end of the year."

Skyline smiled.

"There we go. There's that smile I love so much," Fixx cooed.

"You're a heartless bitch," Skyline replied. "No wonder you turn me on."

Fixx grinned widely. "You silver-tongued devil."

CHAPTER NINE

Puerto Peñasco, Mexico

Charlie Mott flew Phoenix Force to Hermosillo airport, landing shortly after sunrise. From there, it was a quick transfer to a helicopter that took them on a 250-mile "hop" to Puerto Peñasco, where McCarter's freighter had offloaded some farm equipment. At the very top edge of the Gulf of California, it was a short distance to the border between Mexico and Arizona. From there, it would have been easy to transfer the Ankylosaurs and their gear via truck to Yuma International Airport. Mexican Highway 2 led to Highway 8, which hooked up with Interstate 95 to Yuma City. There, the marauders' helicopters could have taken the deadly robots across Martinez Lake and over the Chocolate Mountains to launch their operation.

The five men of Phoenix Force prepared to check out the Puerto Peñasco docks. There was a good possibility that the warehouse they spied upon was empty. But there was no guarantee. The deadly battle at the CIA Langley Headquarters had driven home that point like a spear through a rib cage.

"Gary, I want you hanging back," McCarter ordered. "If there's trouble, I want you to give us cover fire."

Manning nodded and pulled out his folding-stock DSA-58 rifle. Based on the classic FN-FAL design, the DSA-58 was small enough to fit into a viola case, but had the power and reach to take down targets at 600 meters in a good rifleman's hands. For the Canadian sniper, however, that envelope of devastation expanded to a full kilometer. "This isn't about my back, is it?"

"This is about my feeling safer with you covering my skinny arse with that FAL of yours, you big sod," McCarter snapped. "If you were up close and personal like me, then I'd say you could come along. As it is, you're our guardian angel."

The Briton looked to James. "Cal, I'll want you a little closer, but toward the end of the dock there. That'll put you in 200 meters. Take your Z-M."

James touched his index finger to his brow as means of a salute, then slipped the folding-stock version of the M-16 into its holder. "A black man, standing on a dock, with a tennis racket case."

"You need an ugly sweater to complete the Bill Cosby look," Hawkins joked.

"Wrong show," James quipped. "Too bad none of you mugs looks like Robert Culp."

Encizo shrugged. "Gary could...if Culp ever got hit by gamma rays."

"Culp smash," Manning said offhandedly as he loaded match ammunition into a magazine.

McCarter shook his head. "I'm surrounded by comedians. I thought I joined Stony Man, not Monty Python. All right. Rafe, you're our point man. T.J. and I will hang back and cover you if there's drama, but I'm hoping you can talk your way past any trouble."

"Does it ever go that easily?" Encizo asked. "Don't answer that."

"I sure won't," Hawkins retorted. He checked the bulge of his Glock G-34 under his windbreaker. "In fact, let me emphasize. Hell, no, I won't answer that. I thought Barbara's name was Price, not Murphy."

"You're answering, T.J.," James gently chided. He looked out to the dock, then down at his folded Z-M rifle. He stared out the back of the van, and had an idea. He popped the magazine from his weapon and placed it in a hollowed-out tool chest. "T.J., run across the street to that hardware store and pick me up a fishing pole and the largest tackle box they have."

Hawkins grinned. "About the size of your folded rifle?"

"Exactly," James answered.

"Brilliant," McCarter replied. "I'm going to go with him. A standard-size tackle box would be just the right size for our P-90s. Good urban camouflage."

"It just hit me," James drawled. "Just a bunch of gringos, fishin' off the docks while on vacation. In fact, I'm going to hit the convenience store for some beer and ice to fill a cooler. Gary, feel like a short walk?"

"Hell, why not?" Manning answered. "Pop in a bottle of Mescal, too…"

"I wouldn't recommend it mixed with those muscle relaxers," James interjected.

"For show," Manning responded. "Just as easy to spill some out of the bottle as to drink it. Some salt, a little lime…"

Encizo slid behind the wheel and turned the key just enough to activate the battery. He turned on the radio and listened to a Latin songstress do a pop-style rap and bobbed his head. "Oh…I like her…"

"Don't get too into the music," McCarter chided, popping him on the shoulder softly. "Catch you later, mate."

THE STONY MAN warriors regrouped at the van later. Manning had placed his DSA-58, folded and wrapped in a plastic garbage bag, at the bottom of the ice- and liquor-filled cooler. He lifted it effortlessly, and knew that his muscle relaxants and twelve hours of resting had helped to improve his condition. His forearms swelled only slightly at the weight of the large cooler and its contents, while James carried a pair of fishing poles, and his assault rifle-filled tackle box. A plastic bag with sandwiches and bags of pork rinds hung between the Canadian's hand and the handle of the cooler. Wearing loose, colorful silk shirts that concealed their Kevlar vests, Glock pistols, knives and backup guns, they completed their image as tourists with a pair of souvenir Mexican baseball caps and sunglasses.

McCarter and Hawkins were similarly attired, but each carried his own tackle box. Inside, their two-foot-long FN P-90 machine pistols lay with spare magazines. The only one who went without a fishing pole or container was Encizo, who put his autoweapon into a battered old duffel bag. He'd switched to a slightly over-size white shirt, open halfway down the chest, and topped his look with a straw cowboy hat. The traditional attire of Mexican laborers was baggy enough to hide a high-capacity autopistol and a pair of combat knives.

Manning and James separated at the dock, James taking a closer overwatch, while Manning went to the far end, giving the two riflemen a wide spread of coverage for their partners. Once the two were in position, Encizo trundled along, sipping from a bottle of cheap beer that he'd filled with water. Already, the sun made his dark skin glisten with sweat, and he felt sorry for the others who were suffering the added insulation of their Kevlar vests. His disguise had made the vest impractical, and he realized that if there was anyone in the warehouse, and they were armed with the deadly Bofors autoweapons, concealable body armor wouldn't provide much security against the tungsten-cored 6.5 mm flesh rippers.

McCarter and Hawkins hung back, walking lazily among the warehouses, pretending to look for prime fishing spots, unused by other fishermen. Half a dozen tourists and about twenty locals walked along the piers, taking advantage of the crystal-blue waters, and others wandered among the warehouses, to and from the rails over Bahia de San Jorge to the store where Phoenix Force had bought their snacks and beers.

"You know, it may not be Acapulco, but it ain't that bad, either," Hawkins noted, making conversation.

"Stick with me, lad," McCarter answered. "I know

all the choice vacation spots. Oman, Hong Kong, the Philippines…"

"Yeah, but you didn't vacation there," Hawkins replied.

"Well, at least I had a laugh or two," McCarter quipped.

"Can't argue with that. Then again, you're crazy," Hawkins concluded.

McCarter shrugged. "All part of the charm."

Hawkins chuckled, then paid attention as Encizo closed in on the warehouse. The Southerner wished his partner luck, and kept his gun hand empty, ready for a fast draw.

ENCIZO LOOKED the warehouse over, his machine pistol bouncing lightly against his back as he walked. A man wearing a light-tan security guard uniform sat near the doorway, the brim of his straw cowboy hat shadowing his face. Mirrored sunglasses hid his gaze. The only thing that broke the illusion that he was an innocuous security guard was the gun in his holster.

Even police officers in Mexico favored carrying Colt 1911s stuffed into their waistbands, or large-frame revolvers if they couldn't get them. If they did carry holsters, they were ornate, beautiful designs, akin to a cowboy's quick-draw rig. This security guard had a modern Kydex belt and holster. Kydex was a high-tech polymer. The belt was a professional model, with spare magazines and pouches for several accessories that wouldn't be out of place, even for a low-paid rent-a-cop in the United States. He also carried a Glock in his rig.

Mexican law prevented civilians from carrying

weapons chambered for military calibers, so 9 mm or .45 ACP was strictly forbidden. Most Mexican Colt autos were .38 Super, a macho, manly round that duplicated the power of a .357 Magnum. It was possible that the Glock was a .40 caliber, allowed in Mexico because it was a civilian and police round like the .38 Super, but the .40 Smith & Wesson round in a dull, plastic pistol went against Mexican sensibilities. And Glock didn't make anything in .38 Super.

The "security guard" turned his head, almost imperceptibly. He'd noticed Encizo's interest in his setup. One tanned hand slipped from the middle of his chest to his belt buckle, coming to rest within easy access of the Glock in its holster.

"*Hola*," Encizo said, walking closer to the rent-a-cop. "*Que pasa?*"

The guard froze for a moment, then answered. "Nothing much."

"It happens," Encizo replied. He handed over a spare bottle of beer. "Any word on hiring around here?"

The security guard kept his hand on his belt buckle as he accepted the bottle. The gunman looked at it, then shrugged. "Not at this warehouse. I think there's one a couple blocks over that needs someone."

Encizo nodded. The man was used to workers drifting in, bribing him with a cool drink to find out about job opportunities. It happened all to often in economically depressed Mexico. The sentry loosened his grip on his belt buckle and rested his palm on his stomach.

"Have an orange," the guard said.

"*Gracias,*" Encizo replied. He bent and picked up a

ripe fruit and tore off the skin. Citric acid erupted in a volcano of pungent juices, and he bit right into the hole he tore. It was delicious. Encizo slipped into a nonchalant stance. "I'd be willing to do anything to get some money in my pocket."

"I hear what you're saying," the guard told him. "But let me give you a hint. Don't take a security job."

"I don't know… They give you some nice equipment," Encizo answered.

The sentry looked at his belt. "Yeah, but it's boring."

Encizo smirked. "Being paid for being bored is a lot easier than not being paid and having nothing to do."

"You got me there," the guard answered. "Pedro."

"Rafael," Encizo responded. They shook hands.

"Thanks for the beer," Pedro said. "Sorry that I didn't have any good news for you."

"You've got good enough news," Encizo responded.

Pedro cocked his head. "What's that?"

"That someone thinks this warehouse is worth protecting," the Cuban replied. He hooked his foot around the leg of the guard's chair and yanked the man's seat out from under him. Before Pedro could recover, the Phoenix Force warrior stepped on his wrist and ripped the Glock out of its holster. He stuffed the muzzle behind the guard's ear, and that killed the fight in him.

"Move in," Encizo whispered. From the feel, he could tell that the plastic pistol was a 9 mm framed gun. He tilted his head, and sure enough, it was a Glock 17. "Word of advice, your toys are too pretty for a Mexican rent-a-cop in the armpit of the Sonora province."

"All right, all right. You got me…don't shoot," Pedro pleaded.

Encizo pressed the Glock tighter against the base of the man's head. "Shush."

Pedro closed his mouth, and Encizo frisked him. He pulled the guard's radio from his belt and looked at it. It wasn't transmitting, but Pedro might have tried to activate it, letting his backup listen in on the conversation. Encizo pocketed the radio as Hawkins and McCarter showed up.

"Pretty pistol for a security guard," McCarter noted. He grabbed the gunman's free wrist and slipped a nylon cable tie around his hands. Hawkins stuffed a do-rag into Pedro's mouth and held it in place with a piece of duct tape.

"That's what I told him," Encizo replied. "Might as well have put up a neon sign that read 'top secret bad guys hiding here.'"

"Probably going to be installed next week," Hawkins quipped. The Southerner threw Pedro over his shoulder and hauled him off to the cover of a garbage bin.

"Nobody's paying attention to you," Calvin James announced over the radio.

"There are cameras at the other sides of the building," Gary Manning added. "Nothing watching the front where the security guard was sitting."

"Security cameras," Encizo said with a sigh. "This place is loaded with bad news."

"Bad news is still good news to us," McCarter stated. The Briton pulled his P-90 from its tackle box. Hawkins and Encizo withdrew their weapons and affixed sound suppressors to the muzzles. "We still incognito?"

"Yeah. These old guys are more interested in their bottles than anything you've got going," James replied. "Hell, it doesn't even look like anyone has any fish on hand."

Hawkins snorted. "Cal, how many times you been fishing?"

McCarter grinned. "It's cooler in a bar, T.J."

"Yeah, but at least you look like you're doing something, and you stop off at the market to pick up dinner," the Southerner answered.

"Right. Back to business," McCarter ordered. The Briton sized up the door and tested the handle. It moved easily, unlocked, and he slipped in first. Encizo took up the rear as Hawkins followed McCarter in. The trio paused only to take off their sunglasses, the shades having allowed them to immediately acclimate to the dimmer interior of the warehouse. Rows of crates filled the storage area, and boxes piled five high loomed over their heads.

Encizo gave one of the boxes a rap. "Hollow."

Hawkins flicked on his flashlight and looked between two slats in another crate. "Yup. This one's loaded with straw."

"Making things look more crowded than normal. The goodies will be hidden deeper inside," McCarter responded.

Encizo listened on Pedro's radio before clicking it off. "No communication. They haven't missed him yet."

"Good," McCarter replied. "I wouldn't want any of those fishermen caught in the crossfire."

Hawkins peered through a crack in the door. "One of the fishermen is walking with a purpose."

"Gary, you hear that?" McCarter inquired.

"Yeah. He looked back at the warehouse, then set down his fishing gear. He might be going to the bathroom," Manning responded.

"Shit," James interjected. "Another of our fishing buddies just touched an earpiece."

"Have you been made yet?" McCarter asked.

"No, their attention seems more on the warehouse. I count three more guards who'd been acting like fishermen," Manning responded.

"Their back door," McCarter said. "One that they'll try to slam on us."

"Gary and I can handle it," James replied. "I've marked my targets. Gary, confirm with me your hostiles."

"Gotcha. Switching over," Manning answered.

"T.J., prepare a warm welcome for our visitor," McCarter ordered. "Rafe, on me."

"Right," Encizo said.

The Briton and Cuban slipped through a gap between rows of crates similar to the empty ones that crowded the entrance. Almost immediately, both men paused as they looked at the opening that led into the depths of the warehouse, their instincts firing wildly.

"Trap," Encizo whispered.

McCarter nodded in agreement, frowning. He felt his pockets, and remembered his fishing pole. He snatched Encizo's hat off his head. McCarter unscrewed the halves of the fishing pole and hefted them. After he slid the sling of his submachine gun over his shoulder, he hooked the straw cowboy hat over the top of one of the halves of the pole, then put his baseball cap over the other.

"What're you doing?" Encizo asked.

"Faking out the bad guy." He looked toward the ceiling. Crisscrossing walkways hung overhead, but nobody was visible.

It didn't matter. The sentries outside would undoubtedly be in communication with the forces inside. McCarter nodded to Encizo, who set up his P-90 for a long-distance shot. The Phoenix Force leader crouchwalked out, holding the hats at head level. A burst of automatic rifle fire tore Encizo's hat to strips of straw, and the Cuban avenged his head wear instantly.

A stream of 5.7 mm tumblers connected with the sniper in the catwalk, zippering him from crotch to throat. Instantly dead, the gunman toppled over the rail and crashed through a crate twenty feet beneath him.

A second defender cut loose with a wild blast at where he assumed Encizo had fired from, but the Cuban had ducked behind cover.

The chatter of automatic rifles had made the guard approaching the warehouse reckless, and he burst through the door, pistol drawn. Hawkins lurched out of the shadows and snapped the toe of his boot into the newcomer's groin. The blow lifted the man a foot off the ground, and he fell to the concrete floor, his pistol forgotten as he clutched his ravaged testicles. Hawkins stomped his heel against the poor bastard's jaw, knocking him out instantly.

Back inside, McCarter exploded from the cover of a crate. His Browning Hi-Power ripped out three quick shots that caught the second of the mystery gunmen just above his navel. The 9 mm rounds didn't have the authority of the P-90, but the pistol was the fastest weapon that the Briton could draw. It still was sufficient for the rifle-armed killer in the catwalk as he forgot shooting and simply hung on for dear life, his blood boiling out of his guts in a flood tide.

McCarter was going to grant the guard a reprieve from his suffering with a follow-up shot to the head, but another gunman's slugs sprayed in a wild dance in front of his feet, skidding him to a halt. Encizo caught this maniac with a swarm of hypervelocity 5.7 mm bullets that smashed through the thug's head and neck. Skull reduced to a pulp, the hardman dropped into a lifeless heap.

"Trouble," Manning mentioned over the radio.

"Report," McCarter ordered.

"Fishermen are scrambling like crazy to get out of the way. We have hostiles making for the warehouse, and there's a chance all this noise is going to bring the local authorities," the Canadian explained.

McCarter transitioned to his FN machine pistol after holstering his Browning. "Can you even the odds?"

"I'm hurt that you have to ask," Manning stated.

"If any cops show up…"

"I'll keep their heads down."

"Good man," McCarter replied.

Hawkins joined the party as he appeared between a row of crates. McCarter had lost sight of Encizo, but knew that his partner was looking for more trouble throughout the warehouse.

"T.J., cover me," McCarter ordered.

"Got you," Hawkins answered.

McCarter crossed the open floor to a tractor trailer

container, one of a dozen parked just inside a set of rolling cargo doors. The container was locked, and Mc-Carter aimed his P-90, angling the shot so his bullets wouldn't bounce back at him when they struck the locking mechanism. A pull of the trigger and armor-piercing bullets tore through the lock as if it were a clump of wet clay. Kicking the remnants away, he tore open the rear door and shone his flashlight inside, looking down the barrels of two .50-caliber machine guns.

The SAS veteran took a deep breath and realized that the Ankylosaur combat drone hadn't been activated. He crawled into the container and looked deeper. The trailer was long enough to fit three of the stubby robot tanks, and he looked back at the rest of the parked containers.

"Thirty-six of these things," McCarter mused.

"Shit," Hawkins muttered. "That's enough armor to take out an entire city."

"Not only that, but there's room for twice as many of these containers," McCarter mentioned. "Someone took at least thirty more of the Ankylosaurs out of this warehouse."

"There were only five in Arizona," Hawkins mentioned. "David…"

McCarter glanced back at the open doors. "What is it?"

"Didn't you hear Calvin?"

McCarter shook his head and poked his head out of the back of the container. Suddenly he heard Calvin James's voice.

"…arrived. Gary took out two of their cars, and they pulled back," James reported. "What's wrong, David?"

McCarter looked at the interior of the container and shone his light on the interior walls. "These containers are insulated. I'm getting radio interference."

The frontmost combat drone suddenly lurched to life beneath the Briton.

"Aw, hell," McCarter cursed as he tumbled off the back of the deadly robot. Hawkins dived out of the path of the killer machine. "These things are awake!"

The Ankylosaur rolled forward, vaulting from the back of the container. Its machine guns ripped out deadly bursts that barely missed the Southerner as he dived for cover.

"The radios!" Hawkins snapped. He tore the transceiver off his ear and armor as the murder bot whirled toward him. The little plastic communicator sailed through the air for a heartbeat before the lethal drone blew it apart with a firestorm of 25 mm slugs.

McCarter realized that their secure frequency, while encrypted for privacy, was still a beacon that could be picked up by the sensitive "ears" of the brutal robot. The robot would be attracted by Encizo's communicator unless he turned it off, and with a jolt of dread, he realized that the Mexican police cars were putting out transmissions. One of these lethal robots tearing through Puerto Peñasco would be a nightmare as it homed in on any radio communications it picked up. The sensors had to have been primed to activate, in case the highway patrol pulled over one of their transport trucks. Any cops who discovered the Ankylosaurs in transport would be blown to shreds as they tried to figure out what they were looking at. Or to turn the warehouse into a kill zone in case anyone uncovered the hidden cache of superrobots.

The Briton leaped out of the container and wrapped his arms around the robot's arched scorpion tail.

With a violent twist, the robot whirled as if it were a ballerina performing a pirouette. McCarter hung on, centrifugal force throwing his feet out behind him. The Ankylosaur spun again, and the Phoenix Force commander realized that it was looking for his radio transmitter.

McCarter pumped his feet, running along the side of a container as the compact robot tank swung him effortlessly, searching for the source of the maddening radio transmission. He kicked off a rail and tucked himself into a ball, rolling to the top of the drone as the swinging tail tore the wall off another container. The robot had no room to maneuver, but that didn't slow it down. Its strength was enough to bend steel, and its armor prevented the tail from being torn off on impact.

Through the gap in the side of the other container, the Phoenix Force leader saw another Ankylosaur whirl to life, its head cannons poking out like feelers. He blanched at the sight, but rolled frantically off the back of his bucking bronco. Heavy streams of slugs smashed into the back of the free killer, tearing gashes in its roof.

The Ankylosaur reacted to the flaring heat of the head guns and swiveled its "stinger" toward the cargo container. Rocket-propelled grenades sliced into the hole, and McCarter scrambled for safety as multiple detonations melted together into a single awesome shock wave. The lean Briton knifed beneath the cover of another trailer, shrapnel pinwheeling to his left and right.

"T.J.! Rafe!" McCarter called loudly.

The Ankylosaur rolled toward the Phoenix Force leader, and McCarter leaped behind a concrete support pillar before twin lances of machine gun fire homed in on him.

As it was, the blistering fusillade of autofire wasn't letting up.

The hammering guns chipped away more concrete, getting closer to killing him when the support pillar finally gave way.

CHAPTER TEN

San Luis, El Salvador

Rosario Blancanales returned, shaking his head. He glanced back toward the customs officials he'd dealt with. Carl Lyons knew immediately there was trouble.

"What's wrong?" Lyons asked.

"They settled on a price too easily," Blancanales answered.

"Maybe you're just good at haggling with them," Schwarz interjected.

"No. We've been down here too many times. I know what it takes to get past customs, and those guys are too eager to have us out of this airport," Blancanales stated. "We've been made, and they know we're trouble."

"You think our armory tipped them off?" Lyons asked.

"Irony isn't your strong suit, Carl," Pol retorted. "We've had enough conflicts with the White Warrior Union and Flange to have built up a reputation in this country."

"Hell, on this continent," Lyons growled. "It's not our fault we have to come down here so often to kick their racist asses."

Schwarz waved to the customs officials, then looked back at Blancanales. "Are they on to us, or did someone else tell them to wave us through?"

"Those guys wouldn't have known us from the Dave Matthews Band," Blancanales said. "They're airport rent-a-cops, and they don't give a damn about who's coming through here. They just have a glad hand out for anyone not on the up and up, and an eye permanently cocked in the opposite direction."

"Makes you wonder why we even bring fake IDs down south," Schwarz quipped.

"Never know when we'll go somewhere with real security," Lyons mentioned.

"We usually go over the back fence in those places," Schwarz replied.

"You got me there," Lyons admitted. "All right. I'll let Jack know he has to cover his ass here."

"Right. I'll get us some wheels," Blancanales responded. "Gadgets…"

"I'll keep an eye out for surveillance," Schwarz said.

"Think Stone Age, too," Lyons told the electronics genius.

"Stone spears and bearskins," Schwarz replied. "Just like your momma used to make."

"Remind me to laugh later," Lyons mocked. "Just keep your eyes peeled."

Schwarz nodded. "Sure thing."

The men of Able Team split up, not needing to acknowledge that they were back in the fire again.

JACK GRIMALDI ACCEPTED the news from Carl Lyons and made certain that he had one of the Stony Man GI-50s in his holster when they left. He shouldered his flight bag and headed for the nearest hotel. Grimaldi hadn't been in Central America for a while, but Huntington Wethers back at the Farm had set up accommodations for him under the name Jack Griswold, supplying him with an appropriate credit card.

As he checked in, he was aware that he was under the eye of a stalker, but his years of working as a Sensitive Operations Group pilot and sometimes field agent allowed him to keep his cool. He'd learned all too recently the danger of taking any place for granted. His girlfriend had been murdered by a conspiracy, recently, when he'd been on vacation in the Caribbean. Grimaldi hadn't expected to run into a team of trained assassins in the middle of an idyllic pleasure trip, and he paid for it with a short hospital stay and the loss of the woman he loved.

With grim resolve, the ace pilot kept his eyes forward, thankful for the mirror behind the desk clerk at the hotel.

There were two of them, and while they were tanned and dark-haired, the blue eyes of one of the pair marked him as of "pure" Spanish blood, not a *mestizo*—someone of mixed European and Indian blood. That was enough to make the hairs on the back of Grimaldi's neck stand up, but he kept the anxiety from his face. He smiled and accepted his room key and gave his bag to a bellhop.

The Stony Man pilot made as if he were going to board the elevator, then turned, just as the doors opened, and went to the hotel gift shop instead. This threw the two strangers off their course and Blue Eyes stumbled into his partner. The pilot suppressed a grin and picked up a couple of bottles of diet soda and a bag of snacks.

Grimaldi was killing time, playing his shadows on a leash. He'd already tipped the bellhop, so he could spend all afternoon in the lobby. He steered toward an oak table and took a seat, setting up his little improvised picnic. Blue Eyes and his partner spoke to each other in hushed, angry tones. They had planned to follow him up to his floor and barge in on him when he was just settling into his hotel room. Now they needed a new course of action, but Grimaldi simply lounged, sipping a cold, refreshing drink and popping fried pork skins into his mouth. Even though he looked totally relaxed, he still paid attention to the mirrors around him in the hotel lobby, observing his stalkers. Blue Eyes looked up at the reflection of Grimaldi as he ate, and the pilot simply turned his glance slightly, avoiding eye contact.

He spotted Hermann Schwarz and Rosario Blancanales as they entered the lobby. He recognized them, even though Blancanales had hastily colored his hair a dark brown and both men were wearing white, untucked shirts and khaki pants, the unofficial uniform of Central America. Schwarz was well-tanned, brown-eyed and dark-haired so that he could pass for Latino, especially of strong Spanish blood.

Grimaldi kept from laughing at the pair of shadows who were oblivious to the men who had put their masters on alert.

The Able Team commandos stepped away from the two and continued deeper into the hotel. Carl Lyons, with a camera, flowered shirt, mirrored sunglasses, shorts and a straw tourist hat appeared at the entrance, talking loudly in English to the bellhop who smiled and nodded weakly. Grimaldi felt sorry for the young *mestizo* carrying the Ironman's bags as the poor kid obviously couldn't understand the big ugly American that well, but was getting an earful at full volume.

Blue Eyes and his buddy cast their gaze toward Lyons, but the big man's shirt hung loosely, the full sleeves hanging to cover his elbows. The Able Team leader had bulked up his belly somehow, and Grimaldi assumed it was a load-bearing vest and loaded pouches under the flowered shirt. The two goons shook their head and returned their attention to the pilot.

Lyons may not have known enough Spanish to blend into Central America like a native, as Blancanales and Schwarz did, but he knew how to look like the perfect tourist. He checked in and handed the bellhop a fifty-peso bill, thanking the kid crudely by saying, "Grassy ass."

Grimaldi managed a snicker and shook his head in disbelief. The big blond ex-cop made his way to the elevators, and the pilot returned his attention to his shadows. Blue Eyes appeared to be on edge now, and was talking to his friend. Lyons had ignited the tail's instincts, and Grimaldi finished the last swallow of his pop. He got up and headed for his room, leaving the two snoopers to decide whether to alert their boss that something wasn't right, or to follow him.

Their orders won out, even though the smaller man flipped open his cell phone to call his boss. Grimaldi stood a few feet behind Lyons at the elevator doors, and both Americans looked at the El Salvadoran men in the reflection of the brass doors. The little spy with the cell phone gave it a couple of whacks, frustration clearly showing in his face as the thing was dead. Others throughout the lobby also started to complain that their phones were on the fritz.

Grimaldi grinned. Able Team had just closed the back door on their trap, although he didn't see where Blancanales and Schwarz had disappeared to.

He realized that the two commandos were still hanging back, waiting to see if Grimaldi had any more tails than the two most obvious ones. It could have been that there were more skilled hunters at the hotel, and they were also checking to make sure *they* weren't being followed. It wouldn't do to have more bad guys pop up while all their attention was turned toward grabbing the two death-squad flunkies.

The smaller hunter put his phone away and shrugged, and Blue Eyes waved off any further explanation. The elevator doors opened and all five of them, Lyons, his bellhop, Grimaldi and the Salvadoran thugs, piled in.

Lyons kept up his nonstop, bellowing rap to the poor kid carrying his bags, and Grimaldi winced at the volume that he was capable of within the enclosed space of the elevator.

In the middle of a sentence, Lyons broke out of character. "Now, Jack."

Grimaldi almost missed the transition as Lyons stabbed his finger into the elevator stop button. Blue Eyes and his friend were caught off guard by the sudden change in Lyons's tone, and didn't even have time to flinch as the Able Team leader spun and smashed the smaller one in the nose with his elbow. The Salvadoran's head snapped back violently, his black hair splaying against the wall of the elevator. The air filled with a cloud of misty blood.

Grimaldi pivoted and launched a savate knee strike to Blue Eyes's groin. Lyons followed up with a ham-size fist that crashed into the base of the remaining stalker's neck. The bellhop looked on, frozen in horror, and Lyons turned and spoke softly and gently to him, his Spanish suddenly better than he'd displayed in the lobby.

It took a few sentences, eye contact, and a reassuring hand on the boy's shoulder to get him back out of shock.

"Jack, keep the kid calm. He understands enough English. Keep telling him that it's all right. I'll get our buddies," Lyons told him. The big ex-cop scooped up both of the Salvadorans, one over each of his brawny shoulders, then poked the stop control again. The elevator returned to its rise and when the car stopped, the door opened to reveal Blancanales and Schwarz.

"Souvenir shopping already?" Schwarz quipped.

"They're such an adorable matched set," Lyons muttered. "Here."

He unloaded the smaller one between his teammates, who bracketed the unconscious man as they hauled him down the hallway. Grimaldi kept talking with the bellhop, who had grown more nervous.

"Jack, you help Gadgets with this guy. I'll take over," Blancanales ordered.

The pilot was all too ready to hand over the bellhop and hooked a hand under the stalker's armpit. Blancanales went to work, soothing the rattled young man's nerves with a stream of Spanish that Grimaldi couldn't hope to follow.

When they reached his hotel room, Lyons pulled out his key card and swiped it through the lock, holding the door open for the others. Blancanales dismissed the bellhop with a sizable tip, then disappeared into Lyons's room.

MARIO COSTA, THE MAN Grimaldi had labeled Blue Eyes, woke up, his neck aching where someone had dropped a sledgehammer on it. At least that's what it felt like. He couldn't see, and for a moment, he wondered how long he'd been out, but then he felt the constricting presence of a blindfold keeping his eyes shut. He squirmed, but his wrists were too firmly tied behind his back, and his ankles were bound to the legs of the chair he sat in.

He could speak, though.

He heard the report of a suppressed gunshot inches from his head, and jerked away from the sound.

"Get the blindfold off the other bastard," Lyons growled. "Let him see what we did to his buddy."

Costa's spine shivered at the grim anger in that voice. His hair was yanked back hard, and the blindfold twisted roughly off his head. The man who gripped him released him with a hard shove that made his chin bounce off his chest. The whole chair shook with the force of the shove, but it didn't topple.

"Do you speak English?" Rosario Blancanales asked him, giving his cheek a slap.

"Y-yes," Costa replied. As he adjusted to the light, he looked over to Gomez, who slumped in his chair. The man's hair was slicked down with blood that dripped over his shirt. Ugly red holes in Gomez's pants told him that these men had shot him multiple times in the legs before killing him.

"Gomez didn't say a word to us," Blancanales explained as Costa looked on in horror.

"Fucking waste of ammunition," Lyons snarled. He snapped another magazine into his pistol and stuffed it into his waistband. "Get my ax."

Costa's eyes widened. "Ax?"

"Listen, Mr. Stone, you know how much trouble the boss gave you the last time you interrogated someone," Schwarz said nervously.

"Can it, Tinker," Lyons barked. "These guys don't squeal when we pump bullets into them, then they'll talk when I do my wood chipper impersonation."

"Oh, God…" Costa began as he saw the gleaming hatchet handed over to Lyons. Nausea slashed through him and he struggled to pull out of his bindings. Blood trickled from his wrists where nylon straps cut into his skin, and he knew that wouldn't be the first blood staining his flesh by the time this was finished. Terror sliced through his heart. "You wouldn't!"

Lyons broke into a broad, twisted smile and smacked the handle of his hatchet against his palm. "I'll start with the toes. By the time I get to his thumbs, he'll believe I could."

Costa trembled in horror. "No, wait…"

"I know, I know. If you talk, they'll kill you," Lyons replied cynically. "And if you don't talk, I won't kill you."

"What does that mean?" Costa asked.

Blancanales sighed, and explained in Spanish. "It means he'll stop after we've put tourniquets on your shoulders and hips…and cauterized your genitals. You'll live, without a tongue, eyes, nose, lips, limbs…"

"But you'll have ears," Schwarz butted in, also in Spanish. "Stone is sick. He wants you to hear the horrified reactions to the lump he leaves behind."

Costa vomited instantly, coating his shirt against his chest, and he bounced wildly in the chair. His head thrashed and he bumped against Gomez's chair so hard that it toppled to the carpet. He started to wail in Spanish, but Blancanales shoved a rag into his mouth to shut him up.

"He's lost it," Blancanales said with a sigh. "Just pop a bullet in his head and we'll be done with this."

"Nah. I'm all hyped to cut this punk up like lunch meat," Lyons answered. He stepped over to the chair and pressed his knee to Costa's chest. The hatchet's cold blade pressed against the side of the Salvadoran's nose, and he obviously remembered Schwarz's description of Lyons's mutilation plans.

He became very still and spit the rag out of his mouth with a herculean effort. "Wait. Wait! I can tell you who sent me."

Lyons glanced to Blancanales. "Think we can trust him?"

"Please, for the love of God…" Tears poured down

Costa's cheeks. Gomez was slumping on the floor, a puddle of dark, sticky redness soaking into the carpet under his head. More bile blocked his throat and he spit it up, letting it dribble down his chin. "I was sent by Joaquin Malina."

"Joaquin Malina?" Schwarz asked. "Sounds like a made-up name. Shit. This punk got blood all over the floor before I could put some plastic down."

"It's just a fucking hotel room," Lyons snarled. "Neat freak."

"We're supposed to be low-profile, Stone," Blancanales snapped.

"Colonel Malina was part of ANEP," Costa cut in.

"Shut the fuck up," Lyons growled, pressing the hatchet blade against his nose. "I don't want your spit all over me, bitch!"

"Colonel Malina?" Schwarz asked. "He was the director for Asociacion Nacional de Empresa Privada in La Paz province."

"Yes…" Costa said. His stomach heaved again, but only acid flashed in the back of his throat. He coughed and sputtered, and Lyons stepped back in disgust.

"La Paz? Where's that?" Lyons asked.

"This is La Paz. From the coast to Lago de Ilipongo," Costa muttered. "Malina's retired. He's been retired for years."

"So he's a nobody…" Lyons stated. "He's feeding U.S. useless shit!"

"No, no, no!" Costa interrupted. "He's officially retired, but he still has his people watching things in the province."

"So why was he watching our pilot?" Blancanales asked.

"Because security noticed the three of you. Malina was around, he'd heard of you. He told us to be careful," Costa answered. "God, we weren't careful enough."

Lyons shrugged. "Your funeral, punk. Can I fuck him up now?"

"Put a cap on it, Stone," Blancanales ordered. "He's starting to be useful."

"You're as bad as these shits," Schwarz interjected.

"They kill nuns and reporters," Lyons answered. "This bitch here, he was armed, and he was going to kidnap our pilot. If he's willing to fight, then he's fair game for me."

"No…please…I was just ordered to watch him and report in if he contacted you," Costa answered. "There was another team."

Blancanales nodded. "How many?"

"I don't know. They're not even part of the UGB," Costa whimpered.

"The White Warriors?" Schwarz prodded.

"Yes," Costa answered.

"See? He's a baby Nazi. Nobody's gonna care about his rights," Lyons attested as he took a step forward.

Costa felt his bladder release, and his pants and the chair became warm and wet. "I don't want to die."

"Neither did the people you bastards murdered over the past three decades," Blancanales admonished. "Who're the other team if they're not White Warriors? Are they Falange? FDN? ORDEN?"

"I don't know," Costa answered. "I don't know."

Costa broke down in tears, knowing he'd reached the end of his usefulness. He couldn't tell these three maniacs what they wanted to know, and the blond freak with the ax was going to take out his frustrations on their sole remaining prisoner.

Lyons turned and put the hatchet back in its suitcase.

"Pick Gomez up, but don't get any of the fake blood on you," Lyons ordered. "It's a bitch to wash out."

Fake blood? Costa looked over and saw his fallen friend breathing.

Blancanales lifted up the unconscious Gomez.

"If you call for help, I really will kill you," Lyons told Costa. "Just be glad that we're not scumbags who torture unarmed enemies."

Costa shuddered.

The three Able Team commandos left Costa and Gomez in the hotel room, locking the door behind them. It was nearly twenty-four hours before a family of tourists came in and discovered the exhausted, bound UGB thugs in residence in the room they had just rented.

Costa, parched and hungry, counted himself lucky to be alive.

"OUTSIDE CONTRACTORS," Blancanales mused as he went over what they'd gotten from their two prisoners. They had drugged both of the captured Salvadoran death-squad members with Thorazine and interrogated them one at a time, making it look like they'd killed the other in both instances. It had been a risky business and a time-consuming process, eating up three hours of preparation, but with a bottle of fake blood concentrate and a spray that duplicated the coppery smell of hemoglobin and the stink of voided bowels and bladders, they'd set up the situation perfectly.

It wasn't a neat way of doing it, and Blancanales wondered when Lyons's hand would be forced in such an interrogation session. The Able Team leader, in emergencies, had ripped the answers out of captured foes, sometimes along with chunks of flesh. Lyons hated it, but with the clock running down in those instances, and innocent lives at stake, the ex-cop could live with the guilt later. Blancanales hoped that their mind games would keep Lyons from living with more guilt on his conscience in the future.

"It's nothing new," Lyons replied. "Remember Colonel Gunther?"

"Yeah, the guy was KGB who'd infiltrated the Guerros Blancos," Schwarz recalled. "And he tried to make you Unomundo's puppet."

Lyons nodded. Blancanales could feel the storm brewing in the back of his friend's mind. The Fascist International had tortured him and tried to brainwash him. Those same racist bastards had killed Lyons's lover, Flor Trujillo, a fact that provided an anchor of fury that steeled him against Colonel Gunther's torture and brainwashing. Only the efforts of Blancanales, Schwarz and Phoenix Force's Rafael Encizo had rescued Lyons from the International's clutches, and crushed the leadership of Miguel Unomundo's Reich of the Americas. Fighting against rightwing death squads in Central and South America was a personal issue for the men of Able

Team. They'd severed the main head of the hydra, but there were hundreds of thousands of true believers still spread across the continent, fomenting new plans and schemes.

"These guys are looking for anything to give them a leg up. Gunther disguised himself as a South African neo-Nazi," Lyons said. "And his team was welcomed into the International with open arms."

"So we're dealing with ex-KGB, calling on old alliances?" Blancanales asked.

"It's easier to make money selling nerve gas and nuclear weapons on the black market," Lyons said dismissively. "No, I think someone else has their own reason for getting the band back together."

"They weren't that fun to listen to in the first place," Schwarz commented.

"That's why we're going to nip this reunion tour in the bud," Lyons stated. He walked to the window and looked out over the hotel's grounds. Schwarz had gone over the hotel room and its hallway with his electronic detectors. He'd also taped a watch to the window, the ticking sending vibrations through the glass to prevent a laser microphone from picking up their conversations. This hotel room was relatively safe, but Lyons wasn't interested in staying cozy and comfortable.

Someone was setting the stage for El Salvador to turn into a bastion of fascism, and they had the firepower and technology to make the country impregnable to an invasion. The death squads were a difficult enough enemy back when they were ex-cops and former soldiers armed with U.S.-supplied M-16s and helicopters.

The thought of bulletproof storm troopers backed up by squadrons of remote-controlled tanks clawed at him.

Lyons's jaw locked as he pressed his hand to the glass. He'd lost too many friends to those who wanted to set up a citadel of racial purity in Central and South America. Every one of their number he exterminated was another enemy sacrificed to the thousands murdered, crying out for blood. He took a deep breath and let his berserker rage submerge back beneath the surface. Now was not the time to feed it, to let it roam free. He'd need that focus, that adrenaline later, when he was fighting for his life. Now, he needed his mind clear.

"Delivery truck," Lyons said out loud.

"What?" Schwarz asked.

"Delivery truck," the Able Team leader said. He checked his watch. "We're getting company."

Blancanales and Schwarz opened their cases and brought out their Beowulf carbines.

Lyons's Spanish might have been lacking, but he had spent countless weeks south of the border, so he knew the timing and feel of things.

It was the middle of siesta, the heat of the day when most of the people who toiled took a break. Delivery vans wouldn't be out and about, because nobody would be there to receive whatever packages they dropped off.

That meant that the "outside contractors" Costa and Gomez mentioned had figured out Able Team's location. Lyons hated the thought of starting a firefight in the hotel, but there was no time to get noncombatants out of the way, barring a miracle. He looked over at Schwarz.

"Got a way to clear out the hotel to give us some clear fields of fire?" Lyons asked.

Schwarz nodded and climbed onto the bed. The hotel was new enough to have sprinklers installed. Schwarz's knife pried out a section of ceiling and he found a pair of wires connected to the sensor in the sprinkler. He knelt and opened his laptop, hooking a wire between the computer and the sprinkler wires. "Give me two minutes."

"You've got thirty seconds," Lyons ordered as he rammed a magazine of .50-caliber slugs into his Beowulf. "They just reached the entrance."

"Working on it," Schwarz answered. His fingers flew across the keyboard, and a bar grew across the center of the screen. "Cracked the fire control system for the hotel."

Lyons smiled mirthlessly. "Set off the alarms and sprinklers in every room but ours, but don't send a signal out to emergency services."

"Got it," Schwarz replied. "One panicked throng coming up."

Out in the hall and through the walls, the jangle of alarm bells split the air. Lyons heard doors open and the hallway fill with stamping feet. He looked through the peephole and saw that the sprinklers in the ceiling sprayed water over confused hotel guests.

Satisfied that the way was being cleared for a conflict with the death squad, he looked at Schwarz again. "Tap into the hotel's security systems."

"Already on it," Schwarz replied.

Lyons pulled out a duffel bag, and stuffed his Beowulf carbine into it. "Keep in contact with me. I'm going along with the crowd."

"Have a nice walk," Blancanales said, looking over Schwarz's shoulder.

Lyons left the hotel room and was instantly drenched to the skin, even through his shirt and concealed body armor. He'd traded the load-bearing gear that made him look like a fat man for the lightweight, concealed vest after taking the two White Warrior Union thugs captive. Behind his hips were nestled the GI-50 and three spare 7-round magazines for the authoritative handgun. If he had to shoot, he'd start the festivities with that. His assault rifle bounced against his back in its duffel bag, well hidden from the preoccupied hotel guests. The sight of an automatic weapon would only create worse panic, getting noncombatants hurt as they scrambled to safety.

The only ones Lyons wanted screaming in terror and pain were the mysterious allies of the death squads. These monsters helped arrange for the deaths of almost two hundred American soldiers over the past couple of days, and while he and the other Stony Man warriors had inflicted some damage on them, that didn't satisfy the Able Team leader.

However much they suffered, it was never enough.

But he was going to make up for it with sheer volume of carnage.

The crowd milled around the stairwells, starting to push and shove. Lyons plucked a child out of the path of a clumsy adult who would have stepped on her, then glared at the frightened evacuee. "Watch it."

The man nodded and gave Lyons a wide berth.

"Carl, I've got these fools in the main elevators,"

Schwarz said over his earpiece. "Hell, they've got control keys for the cars."

Lyons looked at the intersection in the hallway ahead. One leg branched off to the right, leading to the elevators. Too many civilians were in the way for him to plow through, at least without hurting some of them.

"Can you slow them down?" he asked.

"The keys give them override," Schwarz stated. "They'll be on this floor in thirty seconds."

"Kill the power," Lyons ordered.

"If I do that, the crowd is going to go nuts, and anyone in the stairwells could get hurt. Wet steps and no lights… Someone could die," Schwarz answered.

"Right. Can you kill the lights in this hallway?"

As if on cue, the hallway was plunged into darkness and Lyons ducked into a doorway. People screamed and children cried, but the crowd continued to move toward the stairwell. The little alcove that fed into two adjacent hotel rooms would give him cover and concealment from the hall.

"They're here," Schwarz announced.

"They'll have to fight through the evacuees," Lyons whispered. "Set up a greeting for them."

"Pol's across the hallway. I gave him a universal key," Schwarz answered.

"You get out of the way, too," Lyons ordered.

"As soon as the doors opened, I found my retreat," Schwarz replied. He sounded as if he were speaking in an echo chamber.

In the darkness, he spotted a group of men cut past him against the flow of evacuees. Lyons tensed and observed their shadowy forms, the GI-50 in his fist. The attackers lined up outside the door stacked to breach the hotel room in an explosive entry.

"Gadgets…"

"Who's there?" he heard Schwarz shout at the end of the hall.

The commandos kicked down the door and automatic weapons fire filled the air.

Lyons burst into the hall, leveling his .50-caliber handgun at the rearmost assassin.

As he did, he prayed that Schwarz was all right.

CHAPTER ELEVEN

Puerto Peñasco, Mexico

As soon as the Ankylosaur paused, Rafael Encizo leaped off the top of one of the trailer containers and landed on its battle-ravaged back. The machines had the same firepower, capable of obliterating each other if they focused. Even the .50-caliber head guns were able to shred armor plating, which was no surprise to the Cuban. These were drones meant to be expendable. If an enemy force took control of them, the owners wanted to be able to stop them. Their survivability came from their agility and compact size, hard to target and difficult to track in combat.

Standard small arms would be insufficient against the robot tank, and Encizo knew he had to think of something before the hellish creation tore David McCarter to ribbons. He landed on his stomach and gripped a strip of furrowed armor. Using the clump of metal, Encizo hauled himself forward, his P-90 bouncing on the roof of the turtle-shaped robot. The tail boom swiveled up into position to lock on the concrete pillar that Mc-Carter hid behind.

Encizo kicked down hard, his boot striking the base of the tail boom. The grenade launcher at the tip lurched backward violently, spraying a salvo of 40 mm grenades against the loading dock doors. Corrugated aluminum blew out, flakes of jagged metal riding a growing cloud of orange flame.

If Encizo's radio were on, he'd probably hear Manning or James calling for help, but he'd turned off his unit to keep the radio-sensitive combat drone from homing in on him. Encizo twisted and looked at the pillar. Half of the concrete had been chewed away by a torrent of heavy-caliber slugs before the head guns stopped. Encizo's stomach dropped, and he worried that McCarter had been hit, but he saw the Briton poke his head around to see him.

The Ankylosaur paused, then pivoted toward the ragged doors.

It had heard the people outside now that McCarter was no longer a beacon attracting its rage. Encizo grimaced and dragged himself toward a larger hole in the top of the machine.

McCarter leaped up and grabbed the robot by the tail again.

"Rafe…"

"You okay?" Encizo asked.

"I'll live. Got any plans on how to take this thing out?" McCarter asked.

"I was going to stuff my P-90 down a hole and hold down the trigger until I destroyed something," Encizo answered.

"A good plan," McCarter replied.

Encizo stuffed his machine pistol into a rent in the armor and burned off the remains of his 50-round magazine. High-velocity slugs banged around inside, but the Ankylosaur showed no signs of slowing. He peered into the interior and couldn't see a thing as the deadly robot closed in on the dock doors. "No good!"

"Crap. I'm going to draw its fire again," McCarter answered as he dropped off the tail.

"David!" Encizo called out, but the remote drone beneath him lurched violently and nearly dislodged him. McCarter had turned on his communicator again, and the Ankylosaur whirled like a shark smelling blood in the water.

McCarter killed his signal and dived for cover before a firestorm of heavy bullets chewed up the floor behind him. He'd bought the Cuban some time to stop the robot tank from slaughtering their partners and the Puerto Peñasco policemen outside.

Encizo pulled himself back to the largest hole and plunged his arm deep inside. He drew his fingers away from grinding pistons and reached for his knife.

That's when McCarter and Encizo spotted T.J. Hawkins running out into the open with a boom box. Confusion filled the two Phoenix Force veterans before the Southerner turned on the radio. Latin music blared loudly, and the Ankylosaur whirled violently and raced toward the source of radio signals.

"Rafe! Get off of that thing!" Hawkins shouted out.

Encizo didn't have to be told twice and he rolled off the robot's back.

The heavy head guns opened fire at once, turning the radio into a cloud of shattered plastic and electronics. The annoying radio frequencies eliminated, it turned its attention back toward the dock doors.

Hawkins, bruised, singed and bleeding from a cut on his cheek, stepped out of an office with a massive rifle. The weapon was nearly as tall as the Phoenix Force commando, and he rested the barrel on a crate. When Hawkins pulled the trigger, it sounded as if a grenade had gone off, as a single armor-piercing .50-caliber rifle round punched into the side of the remote combat drone. Sparks flew inside, and Hawkins leaned into the rifle, pumping out six more shots as fast as he could pull the trigger. The killer tank jerked and spasmed as each 750-grain penetrator plowed into its engine works.

"Die," Encizo growled as he reloaded his P-90 and dropped to the ground. The four sets of tires beneath it were visible, and he milked the trigger, slicing twenty-five rounds into one axle. Tires shredded, and chunks of rubber blew free. The relentless robot continued, but it was slow, its engine damaged. Encizo ripped apart another axle with his subsequent, magazine-draining burst, and McCarter dropped to the floor next to him, targeting the wheels of the rolling killer.

"Those are damned good wheels," McCarter stated as one tire rolled free, and the Ankylosaur ground along on the heavy metal wheelbase. "T.J.! Aim for the base of the tail!"

"Got it!" Hawkins answered, and he adjusted his aim with the heavy .50-caliber Barrett.

The monster rifle roared again, metallic beast attacking metallic beast. Hawkins's shot had to have struck a live grenade in the Ankylosaur's magazine, because a single explosion erupted. That started a chain reaction that severed the tail boom in a sheet of fire and disintegrating steel. Explosive gases blew through the interior of the machine, spewing out in jets through the "wounds" in its back.

Finally the robot tank lurched to a halt, smoke and fire pouring from multiple holes in its armor. The blazing tank sat like a lump, blocking the loading dock doors.

The three Phoenix Force warriors staggered toward the bonfire, then looked back at the trailer containers. More of those robots waited inside, like time bombs. Any searchers who opened them up, wearing their communicators, would unleash the wrath of the killer machines all over again. McCarter turned on his communicator, keeping an eye on the containers, making sure none of the Ankylosaurs stirred to life.

"Gary, are you okay out there? We need your help. Badly."

MANNING LOOKED through his Bushnell scope when he heard McCarter's voice. He'd done a good job of putting 7.62 mm bullets through engines and tires. Any Puerto Peñasco police officer who stepped forward rapidly retreated as a bullet sparked a fender or windshield near enough by to make him think twice.

"What's the problem?" Manning asked. "What woke up the drones?"

"Radio sensors," McCarter replied. "The containers were insulated, but if they were opened…"

"Police officers wearing their radios would instantly activate them and they would be killed before they could report in that these bastards were smuggling robot tanks," Manning concluded. "You need a way to take out the Ankylosaurs without waking them up."

"It would be nice," McCarter answered.

"Any vehicles in there?" Manning asked.

"There's no way we could haul them all out together with that little forklift," McCarter said. "Not before police snipers get one of us."

"Yeah. I'm worried when the cops start to realize that we're not aiming to kill them," Manning confessed. "Maybe if I shot a gun out of one of their hands, or knocked a hat off…"

"Can you make a hit like that?" McCarter asked.

Manning took a deep breath, then sighed. "Not with the muscle relaxants in my system. I could hit an object the size of an apple at this range, but I couldn't guarantee I'd pull the shot and not hurt someone."

"All right. Don't risk it," McCarter said.

"Maybe Calvin might have something," Manning offered.

"I'll ask, just keep thinking about a solution."

Manning returned his attention to the policemen, feeling dread and uselessness engulf him like a swirling flood tide.

"Let me talk with Rafe," Calvin James requested of David McCarter.

"Right," the Briton answered. He motioned for Encizo to turn on his radio, then killed his own unit, so as not to tempt the sleeping robots in their containers.

"I want to see if the warehouse you're in is over water," James asked.

"Hey! That sounds promising. Gary can knock a hole in the floor, or set it up so the whole warehouse collapses into the Gulf of California. If we dunk the lot, the Ankylosaurs won't be able to fight under water," Encizo agreed.

"We hope," James interjected.

"Either way, if they're at the bottom of the bay, Mexico will request a U.S. Navy salvage team to take them out," Encizo added.

"Check the warehouse floor, see how their drainage ditches are set up," James answered. "T.J. and David are going to have to check out what evidence we can find before we pull this off."

"I'm on it," Encizo said.

The Cuban quickly filled his partners in on James's plan, and McCarter agreed.

"We'll find the office and do what we can. Just be careful, we never made sure this place was empty," McCarter warned. "We only encountered three gunmen here."

"And more were outside," Hawkins said. "Maybe they were going stir crazy."

"Or maybe someone's destroying the evidence while we're chin-wagging here," McCarter snapped. He reloaded his P-90 and made his way toward the office, Hawkins on his heels, ready for anything.

The men of Phoenix Force were running out of time,

and they needed to work a miracle to get out of Puerto Peñasco alive, let alone without causing an international incident.

San Luis, El Salvador

AUTOMATIC WEAPONS FIRE blew the door to splinters as soon as Hermann Schwarz called out, confusion slurring his speech. It was an award-winning performance, and he was rewarded with high-caliber autofire as he watched from his hiding spot. The television in the room disintegrated into flames as a stream of bullets sliced through its tube. The louvered closet doors exploded into toothpicks as the deadly gunmen directed concentrated fury against it, hoping to slaughter anyone hidden within.

The bathroom door was riddled with slugs that punched clean through it and pulverized the tiles over the bathtub. The gunman anticipated his target taking cover inside the tub, and his weapon chopped viciously through porcelain, tattered flakes of the shower curtain filling the air like blue plastic snow.

The killers who'd concentrated on the closet moved to the pair of beds, reloading with precision and speed that impressed Schwarz. They fired through the mattress, walking streams of fire through the beds to kill anyone cowering beneath them before they stepped back. Two more of the gunmen flipped the beds aside, looking for anyone underneath.

The assassins transitioned from their assault weapons to handguns, firing into the bunched curtains over the windows, firing systematically from floor level to the ceiling.

Schwarz couldn't count the sheer volume of ammunition that the intruders had expended, but it had to have easily been a thousand rounds in the space of ten seconds, and they'd ripped apart every inch of hiding space that they could imagine, even the top shelf of the closet. They'd gotten everywhere, except for the crawlspace in the ceiling of the bathroom.

"They cleared out," one of the gunmen said.

The man at the bathroom entrance stepped in, the remnants of the door swinging shut behind him. He scanned below, and even stooped to look under the sink. He wasn't wearing any armor, but Schwarz was glad for the suppressed GI-50 in his hand anyway. He stuck it down through the hatch and triggered a 300-grain hollowpoint into the base of the stooped assassin's neck. The .50-caliber bullet, no louder than a sneeze, exploded through the killer's throat and he toppled to the floor. Chunks of vertebrae and pulped flesh flew everywhere.

"What was that?" someone asked.

"The bathroom!" came the answer, and two gunmen appeared at the shattered door.

They didn't dare to enter, ripping off the full loads of their weapons through the shredded door, spraying the walls and the mirror.

Schwarz backed up, made sure the duct tape around his grenade was secure, then crawled to the neighboring bathroom's ceiling hatch. He kicked it open, then dropped into the room, pulling the length of fishing wire he'd placed around the pin. As his feet hit the tile, a nerve-shattering explosion detonated in the next room, its roar rumbling through the crawlspace, all of its fury and shrapnel vented through the tunnel in a straight line.

"Now!" he whispered.

Blancanales and Lyons, their .50-caliber carbines blazing, cut loose through the walls and doors of their old hotel room. The thunder of the twin automatic weapons filled the air as tungsten-cored bullets punched through drywall and wood. Able Team had set the trap, Schwarz acting as bait, then let the enemy spring it. With the same ruthless precision as the hit squad displayed, they ripped into the enemy, then fell back.

Schwarz pulled his rifle out of the crawlspace and raced to the back of the room. He used the buttstock of his weapon to hammer out the glass and crawled onto the small ledge. The remaining assassins, shielded by multiple walls, had the same idea for an escape and threw coils of rope over the windowsill.

When the first hit man poked his head out, Schwarz ripped it off with a salvo of heavyweight hollowpoint rounds. Decapitated, the lifeless assassin dropped out of the window, tumbling to the front of the hotel below. The crowd of evacuees shrieked in horror as the headless corpse smacked onto the driveway.

The last killer poked his rifle around the corner and cut loose. Bullets bounced off the wall and slid into space, as he didn't expose more than his hand.

Lyons charged into the room and before the gunman could haul his weapon back in the window, the Able Team leader slammed into him with all two hundred pounds of his muscular frame. Sandwiched between the windowsill and Lyons, the assassin was battered into unconsciousness. Lyons grabbed him before he, too, could be lost through the window and threw the insensate murderer over his shoulder.

Schwarz opened the door and met his partners in the hall.

"Grab the gear," Lyons ordered. "I'll take our prisoner downstairs."

"Jack, we'll meet you in the lot," Blancanales called into his radio. "Get the van ready."

"I'm on it," Grimaldi answered. As soon as the alarms rang, he was already halfway to the lobby, ready to assist Able Team in its retreat.

Stony Man Farm, Virginia

"ANY WORD FROM OUR field teams?" Hal Brognola asked, walking into the War Room.

Barbara Price glanced up from her monitor, and the look on her face said it all. Her blond hair was all over the place, and her lower lip showed signs of being vigorously chewed. She'd been getting reports, and Brognola sighed. The big Fed pulled a cigar and chomped on it. He didn't like it, but the spongy cylinder gave him something to work on without grinding his teeth or lips down to nubs.

"Able Team?" Brognola asked.

"We're not sure yet. The hotel that they checked into just dropped off the grid, their telephones knocked out," Price announced. "So, maybe they're raising hell in San Luis."

Brognola groaned. "They probably drew the attention of the death squads already."

"It was part of their plan," Price admitted. She looked at Brognola and shrugged. "You never can tell with Lyons. He seems to think we don't have a rule book."

"He does have a rule book," Brognola answered. "It has one page with one sentence on it."

"Yeah?" Price asked.

"Don't get noncombatants killed and don't shoot our allies, unless they're on the take," Brognola replied. "I think he gave you a copy of it."

"He might have, I usually don't read and keep my fortune cookies."

Brognola laughed. "What about Phoenix Force?"

"The Puerto Peñasco police department reported a shooting down at the docks. They've called for the fire brigade, but they can't get close to the warehouse where a fire broke out," Price responded. "It seems as if a sniper is keeping them at bay."

"Manning," Brognola mused.

"That's what we think, too," Price answered. "I think it's safe to say that Phoenix Force has just uncovered where the enemy stored some of its hardware."

"I'll get on the horn to the Mexican department of Justice, but I don't think I can pull off a miracle in time to pull their fat out of that fire," Brognola stated. "They're on their own in looking for a back door to that place."

"I know. They're limiting their radio communications," Price said. "We're out of touch with them for the time being."

Brognola frowned. "I know they don't have to keep in touch with us every minute of the day, but why are they forcing radio silence?"

"Bear thinks it might be something that General Rogers mentioned," Price suggested. "The combat drones, Ankylosaurs, as we call them, are sensitive to radio reception. We think that's what happened with the fire at the warehouse."

"They could be activated by radio signals?" Brognola asked.

"A sort of automatic pilot-targeting program, similar to antiradiation missiles used by the Wild Weasel aircraft in the Air Force and Navy," Price noted. "The Ankylosaurs might be on standby, for all intents and purposes powered down, but if their radio transceivers pick up radio communications, even encrypted signals like our teams utilize, they could come online and attack the source of those signals."

"Diabolic," Brognola exclaimed. "Not only could that make any lawman investigating one of their transport containers a walking target, but if they were left at certain roadsides, they could be left behind camouflage until a convoy passed by and with the firepower that they have…"

"I know," Price answered. "You wouldn't need many of them to control major roads or rail routes around a small country…say El Salvador."

"Have Bear run a projection on how many would be needed for that scenario," Brognola suggested.

"We're adjusting our figures based on this new theory," Price said.

"If that's the case," Kurtzman interjected, "they'll only need two-thirds of our projected estimates to set up an effective perimeter defense around El Salvador."

"How many?" Brognola asked.

"Call it four hundred of the machines. Judging from our estimates, they only require slightly more material than a standard Humvee to produce, and they're nearly as small as a Volkswagen Beetle," Kurtzman explained. "You'd need only 120 standard trailers like eighteen-wheelers haul. A cargo ship, loaded to the gills, could carry four times that many."

"Five hundred containers… Fifteen hundred of these killer tanks?" Brognola asked. "That's practically battalion strength. It's more armor than we sent into Kuwait in the first Gulf War!"

"They're small and expendable," Price commented. "An M-1 tank could knock out a dozen of them if it wanted to, but in the jungles, it couldn't maneuver after them. The Ankylosaurs, being smaller, could easily flank one. Only one in those twelve has to get lucky, and with their sensor and automatic-fire control systems, they could give as good as they got."

"So if they get a toehold in El Salvador," Brognola began, "it'll make the Soviets in Afghanistan seem like a picnic."

"Pretty much," Price answered. "I suggest you talk to the President about giving us some form of air support options."

"Between disaster relief efforts and the Iraq mess, we don't have enough force to dedicate to this. Besides, hc's fully focused on the Middle East, and he wants us over there," Brognola explained. "We're on our own. They faked out the government too well."

Price looked down at her monitor, trying to hide the look of dread on her face.

"Barbara," Brognola cut in, "how could they have made more than a thousand of these things?"

"They must have a factory at work on it," Price replied. "The National Reconnaissance Office is scoping things out from China to Germany, but there're no tank production facilities that aren't unaccounted for."

"Fifteen hundred tanks the size of a Volkswagen…"

"What was that?" Price asked.

"Fifteen hundred tanks."

"No—the size of a Volkswagen. I mentioned that before…" Price mused. "Someone bought the old Volkswagen plant in Mexico after it closed down a few years ago."

"So?" Brognola asked.

"They're producing relatively cheap farm vehicles and shipping them across the world," Price replied. "Farm vehicles."

Brognola winced. "The Soviet Union used to transport tanks and other armored vehicles around the world to their puppet nations, claiming that they were farm equipment."

"Bear!" Price called out. "Does the NRO have an eye in the sky over Mexico?"

"No. It's mostly watching over Venezuela and Colombia," Kurtzman responded. "There have been new tensions arising on the border between the FARC and the two armies, and their governments are each blaming the other side for letting these maniacs run free."

"What kind of tensions?" Brognola asked. "Wait I remember the daily threat matrix reading. It appears that some judges were assassinated. They were involved in the case of some oil field saboteurs."

"After the crisis with the presidency that would be more than enough to destabilize Venezuela, and Colombia would love to add oil production to its exports," Price observed. "A breakdown of government, and the Colombians only have to cross a couple hundred miles to get their very own oil field."

"And with the 'war on terror,'" Brognola interjected, "our resources are spread just a little too thin to do more than issue a stern warning to Bogotá."

"It might be factoring into our enemy's plan," Price said. "A destabilized northern South America, it's practically in El Salvador's backyard."

"Nicaragua and Panama are in the way," Brognola noted.

"Nicaragua and Panama are rotten with the same kind of thugs who made up the Fascist International. Remember Manuel Noriega's Dignity Battalions?" Kurtzman asked. "After Unomundo was squashed, we found allegations that he had been secretly funding the Dignity Battalions. If the International's leadership hadn't been taken out by Able Team, things might have gotten much worse when we moved in on Panama."

Brognola shook his head slowly and poured himself a cup of Kurtzman's coffee. Even its thick, putrid viscosity did little to drive the thoughts racing though his mind away, and when he had trouble noticing how nasty Kurtzman's coffee was, he knew full well that things were going to hell in a handbasket. "I'm going to go to the White House. I need to tell the President about this."

"Can we get that extra backup?" Price asked.

"I doubt it, but the map of Central and South America is going to be changing drastically if we can't pull a miracle out of our asses," Brognola conceded. "God have mercy on us if we can't find the engineer behind this mess and shut him down."

CHAPTER TWELVE

Puerto Peñasco, Mexico

Rafael Encizo pulled himself out of the hatchway and looked at David McCarter and T.J. Hawkins, who were covered in soot. "I take it you don't have good news for me."

"Sorta," Hawkins said. "The last of the guards for the warehouse has been accounted for."

"And we recovered most of a ledger," McCarter added, holding up a smoking book. "He was burning records, just as we thought."

"So we burned him," Hawkins stated.

"Do you have any good news?" McCarter asked.

"Yes," Encizo answered. "Maybe not so good all around, but we can make a dent in this warehouse and their supplies."

McCarter took a deep breath, then activated his communicator. "Gary, Calvin, fall back to the warehouse.

We'll provide cover fire. T.J., got a spare magazine and maybe a spare Barrett?"

"I found a crate of five," Hawkins answered. "Grab one and we'll put some real fear into the cops."

McCarter nodded and followed Hawkins to where he'd found a crate full of the heavy-caliber Barretts. The five-foot-long rifle was a massive bar of steel with a bolt assembly milled from a solid billet of cast iron. It was a big, strong weapon, but that was necessary. Twenty-five pounds of metal was required to contain the awesome forces of the .50-caliber bullets the gun fired. It had enough power to punch through armor plating at one mile.

"Might be a bit much. Make sure of your backstop," McCarter mentioned. "I don't want to put a bullet through a bus full of schoolkids."

"Yeah…" Hawkins agreed. "Think the cars will be enough to slow down a Ma Deuce round?"

"Better be," McCarter replied. "We don't have time to go searching for something lighter."

"It'll only be a few shots," Hawkins offered as they hauled the massive rifles and spare magazines to the loading dock.

In the distance they could see the ring of squad cars had grown in size.

Hawkins extended the bipod on his Barrett and lay on the ground. McCarter did likewise and made sure his magazine was fully seated. He pulled back the bolt on the big semi-auto to chamber a round. The recoil spring made the effort similar to arm wrestling with a grown gorilla, but he jacked a massive 750-grain slug into the breech and focused on the axle of a police car.

"We've got you covered. Come inside," McCarter said into his radio. He triggered his bullet and the wheel of the parked police car detonated as the antimateriel bullet smashed through it. The vehicle collapsed onto its nose, fender crumpling as gravity plowed it into concrete. Puerto Peñasco policemen raced wildly away from the collapsed squad car, screaming as the Phoenix Force warriors unleashed fresh madness into the equation.

James and Manning, their spare gear dragged behind them, raced to the warehouse. McCarter regretted having positioned them out at the end of the pier to cover them, but the two Phoenix Force riflemen had halved the distance they needed to scramble as the Mexican authorities arrived. As the cops ran for cover, Hawkins blew out the engine of a Mexican army truck. Panicked soldiers who had been dispatched to the scene hadn't even gotten the opportunity to load their own weapons. McCarter blew off the rear wheel of the army truck, then pivoted and fired four rapid shots into the grille of a second truck.

"So much for U.S.-Mexico relations," Hawkins muttered as Manning and James raced into the shattered dock doors.

"After all we did during the Mexican presidential crisis, too," McCarter groaned. "Ah, well, at least they're going home safe tonight."

"Oooh, big rifle," Manning said as he set down his cooler. He hadn't brought the container along because he wanted to carry beers. Indeed, it had been emptied of nonessentials. The only things that remained were magazines for his folding FAL carbine and blocks of plastic explosives. "Oh…a Barrett. I've shot that."

"Want to take it with you?" McCarter asked.

"I have my McMillan folding-stock Fifty," Manning answered.

"We could still use one for Hawkins," McCarter mentioned. "He's been doing really well with his."

"Can I?" Hawkins asked.

"Don't go complaining to Barbara if you shoot your eye out," Manning countered. "Rafe?"

"Yeah, the hatch is this way," Encizo directed, getting them back to business. "There's a latticework of support beams under the warehouse, a crawlspace for maintenance work, and then there's a slope beneath leading right into the water."

"Then I might be able to do something without crippling Puerto Peñasco's shipping and storage facilities for a year," Manning noted. "Take me to it."

"Got it," Encizo replied, and the two Phoenix Force veterans raced off.

McCarter looked at James. "How did he look out there?"

"He ran fine, but I kept pace with him too easily," James said. "Gary's usually fast for a big man."

"Yeah, he runs marathons to relax," Hawkins added.

McCarter nodded. "He wasn't winded, though. That's a good sign. And he was hauling around a load of ammo and explosives."

"True," James said. "Hard to run fast with a cooler in your hands."

"Just check him out after we get out of this mess,"

McCarter requested. "If he's too under the weather…"

"It'll be damned hard making him sit things out," James said. "Especially if we need to demolish more caches of these things."

"Hard on us or hard on him?" McCarter asked.

"It'll be hard to keep him sitting down. Granted, now he's only stronger than two of us, instead of three," James stated. "He can still put you in your place."

McCarter grinned. "That's all I have to hear. Just take care of him. If he goes on sick leave, I'll have to start annoying someone else on the team."

"Aw hell," James said, eyes widened in almost mock fear. "You're kidding, right?"

"I could always take you driving with me," McCarter said ominously.

James took a deep breath. "I'll go see how Gary and Rafe are doing with setting their charges."

McCarter winked and James rushed off.

"Hell, I don't see what's wrong with your driving," Hawkins said as he continued to watch the Puerto Peñasco cops and soldiers.

"Yeah, but you come from a region where *The Dukes of Hazzard* was required viewing in driver's education," McCarter answered.

The Southerner chuckled. "That was Georgia. I consider myself a Texas boy."

"Close enough. They have NASCAR in those states, right?" McCarter asked.

"Too-shay, monsieur poosec-cat," Hawkins quipped.

"How's the line?" McCarter asked.

"Doesn't look too bad," Hawkins replied. "After we trashed the trucks, everyone decided to pull back just that much farther down the road."

"Just so they're not trying to come up on our blind side," McCarter said. "I'm going to get some altitude and check the flanks."

"All right," Hawkins answered. "I'll hold down the fort here for now. Be careful."

McCarter left Hawkins to his post and raced for the nearest catwalk.

IT TOOK TWO MINUTES of examination for Gary Manning to get a feel for the structure of the warehouse. He looked down through slats and saw the bay beneath him, only four feet below. Thick support struts centered on stress points, but branching smaller arms enabled large sections of floor to stand freely.

"How long do you think it'll take to do your voodoo?" Encizo asked.

"If I have a couple extra pairs of hands…" Manning said.

"I'm here," James interjected. The lean ex-SEAL slipped through the hole in the floor.

"Great," Manning replied with a grin. "Okay. See this joint structure?"

"Yeah. Looks like a sea urchin made out of rebar."

"There's about twelve of these spots which, if we place our charges right, will collapse the floor beneath this warehouse and dump everything into the Gulf of California," Manning explained.

"They all look like this?" James asked.

"Yeah. Pick four and put a kilo apiece around the main strut—this one." Manning pointed it out, illuminating the strut with his flashlight. He tamped the pliant explosives around the beam in a demonstration, then inserted a radio detonator. He handed both Encizo and James four detonators and four blocks of explosive each. "I have these keyed in."

"You brought twenty-five pounds of this stuff along with your assault rifle?" Encizo asked.

"Yeah," Manning replied. "I packed light because of my aching back."

The Cuban rolled his eyes. "Packs light. And people say he has no sense of humor."

"We just don't get those crazy Canucks," James replied, climbing off through the crawlspace. "How're we getting out of here?"

"Through a hole I'm going to open," Manning said. "We're swimming out. You're going to have to lead the way."

"We can handle it," Encizo replied. "Can you keep up?"

"Well, I won't be swimming around with twelve kilos of plastic explosives and detonators," Manning responded. "I should make it."

"Good," James agreed. "I definitely do not want to end up in a Mexican jail, or have to shoot past a bunch of cops and soldiers."

Manning nodded. "We just have to take care of the Ankylosaurs first."

"Hell, we've got you on our side, Gary. They're as good as scrap," Encizo commented.

Manning sighed. "The man. The myth. The legend in my own mind."

He set to work on the other three struts.

IT TOOK FIVE MINUTES before all five members of Phoenix Force reassembled at the hatch.

"We heard some shooting," Encizo said as he crawled up into the warehouse.

"I spotted a team of operators trying to creep up our rear," McCarter advised. "I cut loose with the Barrett and my FN. Lots of bullets, no hits. Never thought I'd be so glad to miss."

"It bought us some time," Manning noted. "We've got this entire section of the warehouse wired and ready to take a big dunking. But we're going to need to get some distance first. If the floor and the containers collapse while we're still underneath the dock, we're going to get caught in their undertow."

"We're good swimmers, but not that good," James stated.

"Yeah. If we drown, Hal's going to have to promote some blacksuits," McCarter griped.

"So glad your priorities are straight," Hawkins quipped.

"It's a talent," McCarter said. "All right. I say we've got about a minute and a half. Gary…your detonator is waterproof, right?"

"To fifty meters," Manning answered. "It'll fire under water, too."

"Good. Cal, Rafe, how does the swim look?" McCarter asked.

"We've got enough headroom so that we can surface swim to the edge of the docks proper. There's some space under the piers, and then open water, but I don't think we're going to have to go that route," Encizo explained.

"I'm going to get Charlie to pick us up. We're going to head over to a support pillar about a hundred yards away. It's a clean swim, and we've got places to hold on to if there's a major current caused by all that matériel that Gary's going to flush," James added.

"Did you call him yet?" McCarter asked.

"Already did. He's going to rent a fishing charter and bring along some changes of clothes for us," James said. "He'll pick us up in about two hours."

"You can wade that long?" McCarter asked Manning.

"You should see it under there. We could wait on the sand in the shadows under the pier," Manning explained. "In case you didn't notice…"

McCarter looked at the cut-off pants James, Encizo and Manning now sported. "Those won't pass muster as swim trunks."

"Close enough," Encizo said. "And we're not going to be out in the open."

"I've got the waterproof bags I kept my magazines and rifle in," Manning stated. "We put our pistols and knives in them. We'll have to leave the longer guns behind. That means your Barrett, too, T.J."

"Shucks," Hawkins muttered with mock disappointment. "Hell, I didn't want to take a swim with this boat anchor anyway."

"All right," McCarter said, "let's get to the water. The cops might be gearing up for another crack at us."

Manning frowned.

"What's wrong?" McCarter asked him.

"Someone is going to have to stay behind to hold them off," Manning stated. "And that means swimming through the aftermath of the landslide."

McCarter shook his head. "No way."

"If we leave the warehouse empty, they'll move in, and we'll end up drowning dozens of cops when I knock the floor out of this place."

McCarter looked back at the containers. "Not necessarily."

"What?" Manning asked.

"T.J., keep their heads down," McCarter ordered. "We're going to improvise. Calvin, cut loose some insulation from that damaged container there. Enough to shelter its sensors. Rafe, you're small enough. Slide into the container and get to the front and see where the radio pickups are at. Gary, you have any explosives left over? We're going to hobble the wheels. I'll get the forklift."

"We're going to use that to hold them off?" James asked incredulously.

"It could work," Manning said. "We could even see if we can find dummy ammunition for the head guns. Plastic training sabots that rapidly destabilize in air. It could break an arm, if it hits, or snap your neck, but it won't tear you to pieces."

"Right. If you can, see if you can disable its grenade launcher, Calvin," McCarter instructed. "As it is, we're cutting it close with those head guns if you can't find the training belts."

"The Barrett should be enough to give them second thoughts," Hawkins stated.

"All right," McCarter replied. "Let's do this. We've got bad guys to take down."

PUERTO PEÑASCO POLICE Captain Luis Garza considered himself lucky that none of the psychopaths who started their "gang war" on his docks had killed any civilians, and seemed to be shooting to miss the soldiers and cops he'd sent to root them out. He didn't relish being in the middle of a war zone, and even though his men were alive, he'd lost four squad cars and the army lost two transport trucks in the melee.

But sooner or later, he was going to have to make his move. The docks had been shut down for an hour by this mess, and businesses were going to be screaming to have their warehouses freed up.

Garza shook his head.

"Captain, there hasn't been any fire from the warehouse for the past five minutes," one of his men said.

"Have we fired a few shots across the dock doors to see if they're still awake?" Garza asked.

"Yes. No return fire," the lieutenant stated. "We were going to ask for a swim team, but we don't have any equipment ready for such an endeavor. Our best estimate is that we'll have another half hour."

"Sir!" someone else called. Garza walked over to the burned-out hulk of a police car and watched as a forklift pushed a foil-covered object into the open, just behind the bulk of the strange machine that had been destroyed forty-five minutes earlier.

Garza lifted a bullhorn to his lips. "Throw down your weapons! You're surrounded! We promise fair treatment if you surrender!"

"Bollocks to you!" a British-accented voice called out.

Suddenly the foil was ripped off the lump, and the thing lurched on the horns of the forklift. A scorpion-like tail snapped up, swiveling at the line of police cars. It seemed to want to project a stream of destruction from that appendage, and when it couldn't, the low-set head swung up. Muzzle-flashes split the air and Garza ducked. The squad car he hid behind shuddered as it was slammed by twin streams of autofire.

"Open fire! Open fire!" Garza ordered. Those soldiers who could hear him and his police officers poked their weapons around corners and wrecked vehicles, cutting loose with a storm of lead that hammered wildy at the warehouse. He wasn't sure if anyone could hit anything, but whatever that monstrosity was, it wouldn't be able to last for long against the concentrated fire of dozens of cops and troopers.

Garza was proved wrong. The hammer storm from the squat, pinioned tank continued for two minutes. He had used up all the ammunition in his pistol, firing under the frame of a wrecked squad car, but the thing still kept shooting. For some reason, though, the machine guns on this hellish beast weren't penetrating the wrecked vehicles.

Finally the guns went silent.

It had been two and a half minutes since the foil was removed from the squat tank. Garza took a step out from behind the squad car, and a policeman grabbed his wrist to pull him back to cover. Garza paused, then looked at a piece of blue, flattened plastic on the ground. He stooped and picked it up, finding it still hot. There was an inscription, in English, on a disk-shaped circle on the other side.

"It's .50 BMG training round, plastic sabot," he read out loud. He looked back at the car he had been crouched behind, and though hundreds of pieces of plastic were imbedded in the sheet metal from fender to fender, none had penetrated. The car looked as if it'd been assaulted by a thousand hammers, dented and crumpled on the one side, but the plastic didn't have the density to punch through the frame of the car.

"They were holding us off, they didn't want to hurt us," Garza said softly.

He turned back to the warehouse as the others, emboldened by their captain standing untouched in the enemy's field of fire, got up.

Garza took two steps toward the warehouse when the entire structure shook mightily. Within moments, a section of the building's roof collapsed, as if an invisible fist had punched through the top of a cardboard box. The warehouse's shaking continued, but was soon accompanied by a rush of boiling water underneath the pier. He and dozens of others raced to the railing and watched as chunks of concrete and rebar, mixed with tractor-trailer containers, washed out into the bay. A couple of the strange tanks popped to the surface, guns spitting wildly into empty air before gravity took over and sucked them under. More than a few corpses bobbed in the whitewater before they, too, were sucked underneath.

Garza took a deep breath and looked at his men.

"They killed themselves," Garza stated. "They knew that we had them beat, and they chose to destroy themselves and whatever hellish contraband they were protecting."

"You think so?" Colonel Rodrigo Mendez of the Mexican Army asked. His soldiers scratched their heads as the floodtide of rubble and debris settled under the frothing waters.

"It's the only logical explanation," Garza answered. "There was no other way out. We had the pier locked under wraps."

"What a shame," Mendez replied. "Now we'll never know what this was all about."

Garza frowned. "No we won't. But in the long run, what matters most is that none of our people were hurt, and it looks like thousands of illegal weapons have been destroyed."

Mendez smiled weakly. "Do you really think they killed themselves?"

"It makes the paperwork go more easily," Garza stated. "If those men wanted to kill us, they had the weaponry to blow their way through an armored battalion."

Mendez looked as the last corpse turned in the water, then sunk below the surface. The bay looked beautiful again, as smooth as glass, golden light reflecting off the calm waters. "We'll ask for the U.S. Coast Guard or the U.S. Navy to send a salvage operation to clean up the bodies and weapons. Pretty soon, it'll be afe to fish here again."

"You actually catch fish here?" Garza asked. "I just come for the breeze, the view, with a six-pack of beer."

Mendez chuckled. "If that's the case, when can I take you up on the invitation?"

Garza smiled and the two men walked back to their vehicles. "Tomorrow all right for you?"

"I'll be there. First six-pack is on me," Mendez offered.

"Good. Wait until you try my wife's tamales…"

SOAKED TO THE SKIN, their clothes and gear wrapped in plastic bags, the men of Phoenix Force sat on the beach in the shadow of the pier, sharing Manning's bottle of tequila in small sips, waiting for Charlie Mott. Splitting the bottle among the five of them, and not drinking deeply, they were still sober when Mott pulled up in a motorboat ten minutes later.

"A party?" Mott asked.

McCarter handed him the three-quarters-full bottle as Encizo took the controls of the launch. "A celebration of getting out of a sticky situation."

"And role camouflage," Manning added. "Just looking like a bunch of vacationing fools getting drunk on a Mexican beach."

"Did you?" Mott asked.

"Just a little bit of a buzz," James answered. "We've still got work to do."

Encizo nodded. "We'll save the real partying for when we get back."

"Yeah," Hawkins concluded. "I may like you guys a lot, but I'd rather have some girls and barbecue to go along with my tequila."

"All right, but let David pick the music," Mott warned. "Country-western just isn't my cup of tea."

McCarter sighed. "We'll have time enough to plan the victory celebration once we've achieved our victory, gentlemen."

The crisis was far from over.

CHAPTER THIRTEEN

San Luis, El Salvador

Carl Lyons poked the groggy hit man with the point of his knife. "Wake up."

The marauder looked down where the blade tip had pierced his shirt and drawn a drop of blood after stinging his skin. He looked, blurry-eyed, at the Able Team leader and frowned. "You're not going to get anything out of me."

Lyons sighed. "Looking for your pill?" A small white tablet was pinched between Lyons's blunt fingertips. "We found your cyanide capsule."

"So you got my suicide pill. You're still not going to get any information out of me," the assassin stated. "I know all the tricks. I'm not some Central American bumpkin with a gun, a badge and a hard-on for Communists."

Lyons went nose-to-nose with the assassin. "We figured that. I also figured you'd be smart enough to know that we'll pull out all the stops when it comes to learning what we need to know."

"Torture?" the assassin asked. "Do you have it in you?"

Lyons nodded. "Do you have anything in you worth doing it for?"

"Try me, big man," the assassin taunted. "Otherwise, go home and let these Third World bastards kill one another."

"Wrong answer," Lyons said. He didn't hide his disappointment or sadness. He hated to be brutal to an unarmed captive.

Two hours later, a Justice Department clean-up team retrieved the bloody assassin. Lyons had his answer.

COLONEL JOAQUIN MALINA hadn't heard anything from the men he'd sent to shadow the American pilot. Though they had reported that he was at a hotel, by the time he arranged for a follow-up team to check in, the hotel had been through a small-scale shooting war. His spies had disappeared, and a mysterious group of men, armed with automatic weapons, had been discovered dead in one of the hotel rooms.

Things were spiraling out of control. He'd heard stories of the mysterious death squad that hunted death squads. Years ago, when he was a young man in ORDEN, he had been scheduled to go to one of their training facilities to be instructed in counterinsurgency operations. His training was canceled—the facility had been attacked by the unknown killers, dozens of representatives from different right-wing anti-communist squads left dead or crippled in the wake of a savage assault. All that was known was that three North Americans had been responsible.

Three men pitted themselves against the cream of white El Salvador.

It should have been no contest, and unfortunately, it was.

ORDEN and the Ejercito Secreta Anticomunista—ESA—hadn't recovered from the blazing assault. Malina poured himself a small glass of brandy and sat at his couch, thoughts racing around his skull like suicidal motorcyclists in a steel sphere.

He should be well protected. Malina had some of the finest bodyguards in all of Central America. They had been trained by ODESSA Nazis in Argentina, and he'd equipped them with the best in body armor and assault weapons.

If anyone tried to break into his estate, they would run into a wall of burning lead.

"Let them try to come here," Malina said as he took another swallow from his tumbler. The liquor burned in his chest, and felt the beginning stages of arousal burning at the base of his flaccid manhood. Idly, he wondered which of his mistresses he should call up. His wife, old and fat, was no good for an alcohol-fueled state of excitement like this.

Maybe he would use it on his wife's hairdresser, Consuela, with long flowing black hair that fell to the middle of her back, a shimmering curtain of black silk that drew his eyes to her fine, round buttocks. He buzzed his secretary's desk and he answered.

"Send Consuela up here," Malina said. "I'm in need of some of her styling."

Pedro cleared his throat. "Certainly, sir."

Malina grinned. His estate was on full alert, and he felt invulnerable, brandy granting him liquid courage and an erection that demanded the ministrations of a nubile young beauty. He walked over to his desk and slid it open, looking at the massive Colt .45 in the drawer. He wrapped his fingers around its wooden stocks and held it up. His fingertip brushed the trigger and the cocked pistol exploded, chewing a divot of plaster out of the ceiling.

A heartbeat later, two armed guards and his secretary, Pedro, raced in. "Sir?"

Malina smiled. "Just celebrating being alive. Where's Consuela?"

"She's on her way, sir," Pedro answered, looking away from the master of the estate. "I'll send her in."

"Good," Malina said. He took another drink of the brandy, then thumbed the hammer down on the Colt. A second shot erupted from the muzzle, smashing a marble statue of a Greek goddess just above her naked navel. Malina winced and set down his brandy, lowering the hammer again with both hands, careful not to cap off another shot. The Salvadoran picked up his glass and walked over to the statue. He smirked.

The Greek goddess now looked like she was sporting a brand-new body piercing, the shiny base of his lead bullet glimmering like a navel ring in the sculpted woman's belly.

"Perfect shot," Malina slurred. He smirked and took another sip. "Any North Americans who want to come into my house and mess with me…they'll get a navel piercing, too."

He laughed, finding himself funny, then turned to the window. His smile disappeared as he saw it being opened by a broad, powerful man with cold blue eyes. Malina dropped his glass and raced toward the pistol on the desktop.

Carl Lyons scooped up the weapon by its barrel and crashed the steel butt across Malina's jaw. The blow rocked the colonel onto his rear end, the small of his back bouncing against a coffee table. Malina opened his mouth to speak, but a brawny hand clamped over his mouth.

"Say a word, and I'll twist your head off your shoulders," Lyons growled.

Malina felt his pants grow wet and hot, his bladder draining. As the big American squeezed his jaw, blinding pain knifed up his mandible.

"Do you understand?" Lyons asked.

Malina nodded, no matter how badly the motion of his head moving against his tormentor's hand made his jaw ache.

Lyons let him go and stepped back. He pressed an earplug he wore and whispered softly, "Do it, Gadgets."

Hollow thumps rumbled outside and the night sky suddenly flashed to brilliant life. Flares filled the air and the mansion shook as a grenade detonated just outside the window that Lyons had come through. Malina crawled backward, toward the presumed safety of the depths of his office. Lyons speared him with a withering glare.

"Did I say you were allowed to move?" Lyons stormed.

"Please..." Malina begged.

"I'm the one who's going to ask you for things," Lyons snapped. "You forced me to hunt an unarmed, helpless human being today. I don't like torturing people."

Malina looked confused. "So you're not going to torture me?"

"I said I don't like it," Lyons answered. He threw something on the floor between Malina's legs. It took a moment for him to realize that the spiderlike brown thing looked to be a human hand. Malina howled in fear and backed up rapidly, sliding over the top of his coffee table. Its legs didn't have the strength to hold his weight, and the table collapsed to the floor in a crash of splintering wood.

The office door kicked open as the two security men raced through, and Lyons brought up his GI-50. Before the Salvadoran bodyguards could react to the Able Team leader, he pumped two shots into each of the gunmen. Half-inch entry wounds exploded into grapefruit-size craters in their backs, their corpses collapsing into messy heaps on the floor.

Consuela, standing in the doorway, looked on, her brown eyes wide with horror.

"Take a hike, sister," Lyons ordered. "Your sugar daddy and I have to talk."

The young beauty glanced at Malina, reduced to a cowering animal, then spun and disappeared.

Malina looked back at Lyons, who reloaded and leveled his pistol at the Salvadoran's nose.

"This is a .50-caliber pistol," Lyons explained. "If I pull the trigger now, it'll take everything from your nose to the top of your head off."

Malina trembled. "What do you want?"

Outside, explosions rocked the grounds, and security men fired wildly into the darkness. Malina thought this man had to have brought an entire army with him. Memories cut through his fears, the description of the mysterious blond American who lead the death squad that hunted the ESA killers and destroyed the training facility he had been scheduled to visit. "You're the North American death squad leader."

Lyons smirked. "It's good to have a rep down here."

"Why…"

"Because I don't like bastards like you calling yourselves 'right.' Because I want your kind to be extinct."

"Oh, God," Malina whimpered.

"He's not going to answer you. Not when He sent me to throw you down to hell," Lyons replied. The .50-caliber pistol pressed against Malina's nose.

"If you shoot me, you won't—"

"I won't what? I won't listen to you sell out your buddy?" Lyons asked. "The one who put you up to spying on me and my partners?"

Malina froze.

"All I have to do is phone my headquarters. Their computers will track your last week's worth of calls, and let us know exactly who you spoke with, who called you, and who you called," Lyons answered.

Malina looked around the office. A table leg lay within reach. It wasn't much, but it could be used as a weapon. Suddenly the length of wood detonated, split in two and blasted into splinters by Lyons' big fifty-caliber handgun.

"Please…pick up a weapon so I don't have to feel bad about putting a slug in your skull," Lyons asked.

"Vincenzo Brujo is the one who told me to keep an eye on you," Malina said. "But I wasn't to do anything."

"Who's Brujo working with?" Lyons asked.

"I don't know," Malina replied.

"You expect me to believe that?" Lyons prodded. "You're Colonel Joaquin Malina. You're the greatest true believer in the La Paz province."

"You know me…" Malina said.

Lyons smiled. "I just missed you at the party I held at the ESA's little kill school. Glad I finally caught up with you, though. I figured you could pay me back for putting you in charge of this little corner of El Salvador."

Malina's eyes widened.

The destruction of the ESA's training facility had cleared out the ranks of ORDEN, putting Malina on the fast track to promotions and political power. Malina didn't know that Lyons had confirmed with Stony Man Farm the history of the Salvadoran strongman. Able Team's campaign against the Fascist International had inadvertently given Malina a free ride to the top of the food chain.

Well, almost to the top.

As big a predator as Malina was, there stalked a deadlier carnivore in the wilderness.

Lyons was that big cat, the ultimate hunter.

Malina closed his eyes, tears flowing down his cheeks. "All Brujo told me was that he was working on a deal to give us Salvador on a silver platter."

"What have you been contributing?" Lyons asked.

Malina's lips trembled as he opened his eyes, staring down the cavernous barrel of Lyons's pistol. "I had local commanders send some of their best soldiers to a staging area."

"Where?"

"Metapan."

Lyons went over his mental map of El Salvador. "Major international highway juncture and one of the main railroads between Guatemala and El Salvador cuts through there."

Malina nodded.

"Anywhere else?"

"Atiquizaya," Malina responded.

"Cutting off all entry to El Salvador to the west. You know if Brujo asked anyone else to send his buddies to Perquin or Pasaquina?" Lyons asked.

"He's been keeping me in the dark," Malina replied.

"What about La Herradura? Any new equipment protecting the coastline there?" Lyons continued.

"We received some equipment and assembly teams, but they're still in port at La Herradura," Malina answered. "We're not supposed to set them up yet."

Lyons nodded. "Probably have other teams at La Libertad, Acajutla and La Union. Shore-based missile launchers to keep the Pacific fleet from coming in too close."

Malina shook. "The Pacific fleet?"

"You think when Brujo makes his move, the U.S. is just going to look the other way?" Lyons asked. "Why do you think he's garrisoning troops at the major choke points along your western borders?"

Malina shrugged.

"Yeah. I don't know why I'm asking you." Lyons raised his pistol's sights to eye level. "Goodbye."

"Wait!" Malina pleaded.

Lyons held his fire. "Give me a reason why I should."

Malina looked at the carpet. "I'm unarmed. And I promise…"

Lyons nodded and lowered his pistol. He leaned in close. "You promise not to warn Brujo about us?"

Malina nodded. His mouth was dry, and his jaw throbbed painfully. Every time he touched his teeth together, it felt like a dagger of fire plunged into his brain.

"See, but that's the thing. I want you to phone up Vincenzo. Tell him we're on our way to say hello to him," Lyons told him. "I want him to pull out all the stops and put up the fight of his life."

Malina looked on in disbelief. "Why?"

"Because," Lyons said, "I don't want to spend a lot of time rooting through this country looking for Brujo's co-conspirators. And knowing you *macho* bastards, Brujo is going to face us, not go into hiding."

"You're insane," Malina whimpered.

"I've been told that before," Lyons replied. "But I'm alive, and they're maggot food now. So make the phone call, before I send you to the big ORDEN reunion picnic down below."

Malina got up and moved to his desk. Despite the explosions rocking his mansion's grounds outside, he still got a dial tone when he picked up the receiver. He dialed swiftly, feeling the hairs on his neck rise.

"Vincenzo," came the answer on the other end.

"It's Joaquin."

"What now?"

"I have a visitor…" Malina replied.

He glanced back and Lyons plucked the handset from his numbed fingers.

"Hi, there, Vincenzo."

"You're a dead man," Brujo snapped into the phone. "You and that little traitor!"

"You can kill me in person, Vinnie," Lyons taunted. "My friends and I, we're sorry that we didn't pay a visit to you all those years ago. But good news…"

"You're coming after me," Brujo answered.

"Bingo. Tell your weapons supplier, Fixx, and your intel guy, Skyline, that the Cowboy Jihad is coming to town," Lyons growled, dropping the names Lyons had pulled out of the death squad goon. Fixx had been rumored to have started out in South America, but had been elusive enough to stay off the Farm's direct hit list. The intel from Lyons's prisoner had confirmed what Lyons and the Farm had suspected.

"I will," Brujo replied. "Tell Joaquin that he's a dead man when I get through with him."

"He's going to live a long time if he plays his cards right, Vinnie," Lyons answered.

"Vincenzo."

"Vinnie. Vincenzo. Racist piece of shit. Dead fucker. All those names sound the same to me."

"Tough talk, American," Brujo answered. He wasn't frightened.

"I talk the talk, but I walk the walk. See you later, dead meat."

Lyons hung up the phone.

Malina stood, racked with nervous tics.

"I suggest you take a trip somewhere," Lyons told him. "Go someplace safe."

"Where?"

"Iraq. Afghanistan. Jakarta. Some place where I'm not killing everything with a tie to a death squad," Lyons suggested. "Who knows? You could even turn yourself in to the authorities and hope that Vincenzo can't hire someone to shove a shank in your back before tomorrow night. I don't care. Confess. Hide. If I see you again, I'm going to forget that I owe you one."

Malina nodded and Lyons threw open the window.

"Goodbye, Joaquin."

And then the blond warrior disappeared into the night.

The explosions stopped. The flares hanging in the sky burned out. Here and there, jumpy sentries fired their weapons at shadows, but the *norteamericanos* were gone. They were finished.

Malina dropped to his knees and swore he would make things right. God had given him a second chance, and he wasn't going to let it lay.

The shadow of death cleared from his eyes and the world, though still scary, was a whole new place.

Then again, that was how it usually went when Able Team came to your doorstep and you lived to tell the tale.

Stony Man Farm, Virginia

BARBARA PRICE RUBBED her brow.

"You're going to get wrinkles, Barb," Hermann Schwarz teased.

"Don't worry about it," Price told him. "You're certain that El Salvador is preparing to fend off a possible invasion?"

"We don't have all the information, but according to Colonel Malina, Brujo's got the La Paz province set to repel any naval forces. We figure it's either Tomahawk or Harpoon missiles," Schwarz explained. "Brujo's also been sending Malina's reinforcements to Ahuachapan, Atiquizaya and Metapan."

"Those are all connected by rail and a major highway," Price noted. "According to the Bear, those robot tanks, having control of that road, could blunt any ground force trying to cut through."

"It just keeps getting better with the missile launchers though," Schwarz replied. "Especially if they're anything like what we encountered in the Chocolate Mountains."

"You survived," Price commented.

"We had a mountain to hide under," Schwarz corrected. "There's nothing an aircraft carrier can hide behind, except a destroyer. And in that case..."

"One crew of sailors dies instead of another," Price said. "The missile launchers also make things tough for ground forces, since you said they were used for artillery barrages."

"Yeah," Schwarz confirmed. "If they set up batteries at strategic locations, nothing is getting through."

"Even against concentrated air strikes?" Price asked.

"Antiaircraft defenses," Schwarz noted. "We were lucky. But consider a screen of such equipment."

"El Salvador will be sewn up as tight as a drum," Price agreed. "Moreover, we don't have enough for a full-strength expeditionary force to go into Central America."

"That's why we're here, Barb," Carl Lyons interjected.

"How's your jaw?" Price asked.

"Feels better."

"Healing?" Price asked.

"No, but I broke the jaw of one of those right-wing bastards," Lyons stated.

"Nothing helps Ironman's pain like spreading it around," Schwarz quipped.

"That explains Bear's coffee," Price muttered.

"I heard that," Kurtzman called.

"You were meant to," Price retorted. "We're adjusting the situation based on your observations of the artillery missiles."

Lyons spoke up. "There isn't much need for an evaluation on our end."

"What is your evaluation?" Price asked.

"We've got a lot of bastards to kill," Lyons answered.

"Why am I not surprised?" Price asked. "What about this hit team that came after you?"

"Malina was tight-lipped, but I got information out of my death squad goon that there are two players pushing the pieces around," Lyons explained. "There's a weapons designer known as Fixx, and an information broker who goes by the name of Skyline."

"Information broker?" Price said. "More like a master assassin. He's like smoke."

"Well, he's the one running these armored ninja death squads," Lyons explained. "Actually, only a small portion of these squads works directly for Skyline. The rest is hired muscle—displaced Christian Identity militiamen."

"We were afraid of that. You lost track of a couple of extremist groups awhile back," Price said. "The Hand of God, an Islamic group, and the Fist of God, white supremacists."

"I was in the hospital at the time, remember?" Lyons asked. "I missed out on the knockouts for these groups, and the guy in charge of the Fist, a guy calling himself Logan, skipped out."

"A small-change three-time loser kicked out of the Rangers for abusing minority soldiers under his command," Price said. "We've had an open file on him for a while."

"I know. I memorized it," Lyons answered. "He's not getting away a second time."

"It must be the Hand of God who was working the diversion in Iraq," Price mused.

"Once we're done in El Salvador, we'll give Phoenix Force a break," Lyons stated.

"I am not dropping you three into Iraq," Price commented. "It's hectic enough for our boys over there."

"Offer remains open," Lyons said. "You know our record in the Middle East."

"Yeah. I'd like for the President not to shut us down because of that," Price told him.

Lyons shrugged.

"I have Hunt and Akira trying to track down Logan while Carmen's trying to crack what we know of the machines' command codes," Price explained. "If we can somehow hijack their programming, we might be able to stop the tanks from rampaging without firing a shot."

"There's still the brains behind this," Lyons replied. "Until they're dead, they'll simply pick up their toys and move to a new playpen. There are enough hot spots out there for them to find plenty of cheap muscle."

"That's a cheering thought," Price responded.

"I wasn't hired to be Pollyanna. I was hired to be the stark fist of removal," Lyons said. "And I am a most jealous fist indeed."

"And you're going to show Logan and his Fists of God, right?" Price asked.

"If I have to explain, then it loses its punch," Lyons quipped.

"Please, enough with the puns," Price begged.

"Sounds like she's knuckling under," Schwarz joined in.

"Goodbye, Able," Price mumbled, killing the connection. She shook her head. Able Team didn't know when to give up.

That applied to joking around, and it especially applied to hunting down mass murderers.

Too bad for Fixx and Skyline, she thought.

CHAPTER FOURTEEN

Mexico City

From Hermosillo, Charlie Mott flew Phoenix Force down to Benito Juarez International Airport. The scanner on the Stony Man jet read the damaged pages of the ledger that McCarter and Manning fed into it, and it took Aaron Kurtzman's computer systems only an hour to reconstruct the smoke-obscured writings within. Translator programs and Spanish-speaking blacksuits double-checked the contents of the enhanced reproductions of the ruined ledger, giving them an idea of the extent of transportation from the Puerto Peñasco warehouse to the rest of the world.

It was nearly midnight when Phoenix Force touched down in Mexico City, and Barbara Price got back to them.

"You sound frustrated, Barbara," McCarter said when she showed up on the Web cam. "You must have been talking with Able Team."

"Yeah," Price answered. "I swear. It's like being a kindergarten teacher for the Munsters."

"Raising hell in El Salvador, I take it?" McCarter asked.

"Hand over fi—" Price began before she winced. "Now they've got me making hand puns. I'm warning you…"

McCarter raised his hand. "Scout's honor, Barb."

"You were never a Boy Scout," Price retorted.

"Shit, you saw through my loophole," McCarter cursed.

Price grinned. "I'm faxing over the transcriptions of the reconstituted ledger pages, as well as the original enhancements of the scans, just so Rafe can confirm our translations."

"Right," McCarter said. "Got a quick summary for me?"

"There's bastards to kill," Price replied.

"Okay…not simple enough for Lyons to understand," McCarter prodded.

"Fixx and Skyline are involved."

"Those names are a bad mix," McCarter said. "They've been on Stony Man's most-wanted list for a while. Let me guess. The Hand of God and the Fist of God are involved, judging from your ban on puns?"

"Right the first time," Price congratulated. "Actually, we're aware of only the Fist operating in Central America. I'm pretty sure the Hand, or their allies, are at work in the Middle East, raising the ruckus with our peacekeeping forces over there."

"Stony Man could probably clean them out in a month," McCarter stated.

"Yeah. Ironman offered to do that once he's done in El Salvador."

"Oh, hence the gray hairs and wrinkles," McCarter quipped.

Price narrowed her eyes. "I'll chalk that up to blowing off some steam, old man."

McCarter winked. "Sorry, Barb."

"Never mind," Price replied. "There's nothing concrete on the warehouse ledger, no smoking gun about X number of tanks or rocket launchers…"

"They've been spreading automated missile launchers?" McCarter asked. "So that's how they intended to fortify against the Navy. They probably could be used either as artillery or antimaritime targeting missiles."

"I thought I was updating you."

McCarter shrugged. "Sorry. I just like thinking a few steps ahead of the opposition. Didn't mean to cut you off, too."

Price rolled her eyes. "Yeah. That's how we're reconstructing it, unless the launchers themselves are modular in terms of what they fire and what targeting systems they use."

"That's another possibility," McCarter agreed. "It would have been nice if Able Team had taken the one used in Arizona in one piece."

"Yeah. Well, it would have been nice if you had captured one of those armored assassins alive so we could have grilled them," Price answered.

"The next time I run afoul of bulletproof murderers, I'll make a mental note to not go so rough on him," McCarter promised.

Price sighed. "No, just do what you have to do. We'll figure it out afterward."

McCarter grinned. "You sure?"

Price glared at the Web cam lens.

McCarter whistled and looked at the printer. "Well, we've got the pages printing up over here. I'll take them to Rafe and we'll cross check to make sure everything's in order, then set up our battle plan."

Price still wore a mask of irritation, and remained silent.

McCarter grimaced. "Okay, take care, love. Talk to you soon." He killed the connection, then fought off a shiver at the base of his spine.

"Barb's mad," Manning noted.

"Did the not-blinking and not-speaking clue you in, Sherlock?" McCarter asked.

"Elementary, Watson," Manning answered. "Want me to talk to her next time?"

"Yeah. I don't think she'll want to deal with someone with a sense of humor for the next week or so," McCarter stated.

Manning rolled his eyes.

"See? You're perfect for the job," McCarter continued with a grin.

"You should have gone into show business as a comedian," Manning commented.

"But if I did, I wouldn't have met my favorite straight man," McCarter joked.

"I'm touched," Manning muttered. "Then again, so're you."

McCarter chuckled and the two Phoenix Force warriors gathered up the printout and went to confer with the rest of their team.

CALVIN JAMES CAME UP from the lobby and T.J. Hawkins came down from the roof to their hotel suite where Encizo, Manning and McCarter were poring over the printouts.

"Any sign of surveillance?" McCarter asked as soon as they entered.

"I made the rounds a couple of times through the lobby, the bar and the restaurant. Nothing that I could see," James said.

"T.J.?" McCarter asked.

"I took some pictures of a few repair crews," Hawkins answered, handing over his digital camera. "This the intel from the ledger?"

McCarter nodded as he plugged the digital camera into the laptop. Kurtzman's image enhancement software blew up the small image to a 9x9 photo. Using a mouse, McCarter magnified the writing on the side of the first of the repair vehicles. Clicking on the sharpen toolbox, he made the insignia readable, then turned the monitor to Rafael Encizo, who looked it over. While McCarter was no slouch when it came to Spanish, it was Encizo's native language, and he knew it forward and backward, and was idiomatically familiar with dozens of Spanish dialects.

"Look legit?" McCarter asked.

"At first glance," Encizo replied. "Let me look through the other images."

"Feel free," McCarter offered. "Tired of reading spreadsheets?"

"I'm going loco," Encizo answered. "At least checking photographs is a change of pace."

"Have fun," McCarter told his Cuban friend.

"Only if T.J.'s been taking snapshots of *señoritas* in bikinis and tight jeans…"

Hawkins grinned. "I was bored, but not that bored."

"You let me down, son," Encizo answered, then went to work.

Hawkins chuckled and went back to studying the ledgers.

It was a few minutes of crosstalk where the team analyzed the shipping schedules when Encizo said, "It could be a typographical error, but the delivery van at the gas station across the street is all wrong," Encizo replied. "And check this."

He swiveled the laptop and displayed a repairman by the back of the van.

"I don't think that's a power drill," James commented.

"Able Team had some visitors before, too," McCarter said. "These blighters must be on full alert for us. Gary, the window!"

The phone warbled and McCarter snatched it up. "Shoot."

"This is Hunt. We've been keeping a close eye on the hotel's computer systems. Someone's hacked into it and has been looking for you. We're blunting the search on our end, but the resistance we're supplying is drawing some heat," Huntington Wethers said on the other end of the line. "I'm going to give you guys a minute or two to get ready…"

"We're already on full alert. Let 'em in," McCarter told him. "We'll arrange a handy surprise."

"All right," Wethers replied. "Letting their search through."

Moments later the lights went out and the sprinklers in the ceiling erupted, spraying the room with water. Flashlights clicked on instantly.

"We're the only floor affected by the power outage!" Manning called out. The Canadian had opened the window and looked outside.

"They closed in on us quickly," McCarter replied. "Did you hear that, Hunt?"

"Yeah," Wethers answered. "We're keeping an eye on the system, and all the elevators and phone systems have been knocked out."

"Cellular reception hasn't been interrupted," McCarter commented. "Then again, this and the laptop have satellite hookups."

"Right," Wethers replied. "Try a conventional cell."

"On it. I've got zilch," James announced.

"Same here," Encizo said.

"They're isolating us, expecting us to try to leave the hotel," McCarter mused. "They're pulling the maneuver that Able Team did."

"Hitting us with our own tactics," Wethers added.

"We're not Able," McCarter answered.

"I've got your laptop hooked up to view the elevators. Chances are they might try to take the stairs, but just in case," Wethers responded.

"Thanks for keeping us up to date," McCarter answered. "I'll talk to you after we say hello to our visitors."

"Rafe and I've got most of our gear, except for the laptop, stowed away," Hawkins announced.

"Right, keep an eye on the monitor," McCarter ordered. "Gary?"

"The van's moved," Manning answered. "Pulled behind the hotel."

"They'll be here shortly," McCarter stated. "All right, Calvin, you've got hallway duty, left side. Grab your night vision."

James nodded and opened his gear bag and took out a set of light-amplification goggles and a Fabrique Nationale P-90 with several spare magazines. He opened the door to the hall and noticed the throng of guests clearing out. The black ex-SEAL waited until the bulk of them passed, then slipped into the hallway.

"Gary, get on the ledge and go right," McCarter ordered. "Rafe, cover the front entrance. You've got elevator monitor watch."

Encizo grabbed the weather-resistant laptop and crouched to one side of the suite's wet bar. The Cuban touched a control on the monitor and lowered the glare so as not to betray his position.

"Calvin, Gary, comm check," McCarter called as he led Hawkins to the bathroom.

"Static and crackles, but I hear you," James answered.

"Same here," Manning said over pops and hisses on the line. "They must be trying to jam us."

"Okay," McCarter answered. "T.J., get the maintenance hatch."

Hawkins leaped up and braced himself between the sink and the steel curtain rod, using his multipurpose tool to pry open the painted-over bolts to the maintenance hatch. It took him moments, but he had the hatchway open. "Which way, boss?"

"Left. I've got right," McCarter announced. "Rafe?"

"Elevator cars are moving now. We've got half a minute," Encizo answered.

"Cutting it close," McCarter said. "One bathroom down, T.J. No need to be neat about it."

"Got it," Hawkins replied. He disappeared down the crawlspace and McCarter launched himself up, going the other way.

It took twenty seconds for McCarter to snake through the crawlspace and batter down the hatch in the other bathroom. As soon as he landed, he braced himself, able to watch both the door to the room and the crawlspace he'd just exited, just in case the enemy tried to come through earlier.

"They stopped one floor short," Encizo announced over the communicators. "They must be letting off people to crawl into the vent systems."

"If they've been able to shut down the power on this floor and set off the sprinklers," McCarter said, "then they must have seen that the elevator shafts provide access to the maintenance crawlspaces."

"Oh, joy," Encizo answered. "These guys are good."

"They got jumped on by Able Team once," Manning said. "They don't want to be screwed the same way again."

"That's okay," James replied. "We've got our own style, baby."

"Right, Cal. Now kill the chatter," McCarter ordered. "T.J., I'll stay low here, but you be ready to go up."

"Already braced," Hawkins answered.

McCarter knew that he was on the side of Phoenix Force's suite that was closest to the elevator bank. If the assassins were coming through the shaft into the tunnels, then they'd see that the bathroom he'd dropped into was open to the crawlspace.

He braced, knowing that the assassins wouldn't take any chances. He kept his P-90 leveled at the open hatchway.

"Moving aga…" Encizo said before a wave of static overwhelmed even their encrypted signal.

McCarter tensed. That's when he heard the grenade roll into the crawlspace. The Briton leaped out of the bathroom and tumbled over the side of the bed in the next room. As he rolled across the squishy comforter and mattress, he was glad that the enemy had cleared out this floor of the hotel. The grenade landed a heartbeat later and detonated. The shock wave knocked the pictures and thermostat cover off the wall.

McCarter whirled and started for the bathroom entrance when a sheet of flame splashed outward. He whirled aside as a tongue of fire singed his arm. Even despite being soaked, his skin felt sore and cracked under his sleeve. Whatever the enemy followed up with, it was a strong enough accelerant to keep the blaze roaring amid the sprinklers' output. A quick glance at the bathroom ceiling showed that the enemy had placed a sheet of something over the hatchway. McCarter triggered his machine pistol, 5.7 mm slugs ripping out of the barrel and into the plaster over his head. The roar of autofire rumbled through the ceiling, indicating that Hawkins had just started in on the fight.

McCarter pivoted and pumped a burst into the sheet over the hatchway, but his bullets bounced off the plate. It had to have been a reinforced version of the armor that the assassins wore in England. The Phoenix Force leader whirled, reloaded on the run and blew out the hotel room's window with an extended burst. He leaped onto the sill, hooked the window frame and swung out onto the ledge.

"Rafe!"

No answer except static, so McCarter charged along the ledge, hoping that Encizo was holding his own for now. The detonation of the grenade in the bathroom would have given the Cuban some warning that the enemy was packing high explosives. He leveled the muzzle of his machine pistol at the window to the suite and blew it out with a pull of the trigger, leaping through shattered glass like a panther. He hit the soaked carpet and rolled, coming up behind the sofa next to Encizo.

"What kept you?" Encizo asked as he aimed around one side of the couch and fired a burst at the doorway.

"Traffic," McCarter grumbled as he poked his P-90 over the top of the sofa in a "Hail Mary" shot, not aiming, just pulling the trigger to empty the weapon. "The laptop?"

"Trashed," Encizo replied. "But Hunt pulled the information we added off the drive."

McCarter shrugged as he reloaded. "Shame to lose a nice machine like that."

"Life goes on," Encizo answered as he transitioned to his Glock.

McCarter poked his head up and saw a lake of fire between the door and the sofa. Only the drenched carpet had slowed the spread of the gel accelerant. He dropped down as the back cushions exploded under a hail of bullets. "They seem cross."

"You technician, you," Encizo mocked. He fed the P-90. "They have enough of an angle to keep us from retreating to the ledge."

"And we're cut off by the fire," McCarter replied. "Any word from the others?"

"Nope."

"Let's give them a minute," McCarter suggested as he popped off a salvo of 5.7 mm slugs toward the doorway. Encizo swung around and cut loose with both the Glock and his FN. The concentrated storm of armor-piercing chewed the door to splinters.

The Phoenix Force veterans hoped that the flames engulfing the suite's common area wouldn't reduce them to ashes.

CALVIN JAMES PUSHED another magazine into the well of his P-90 as he ducked into the hotel doorway. Enemy bullets chopped at his cover, and static popped and hissed in his communicator's earphone. The assassins were well-coordinated. Their body armor was good, but the 5.7 mm FN rounds had wounded one of the killers before he took cover.

James nudged the stubby muzzle of the machine pistol around the corner and fanned the hallway with slugs. He poked his head out and glimpsed Manning, firing from the cover of the window frame. The Canadian had his DSA-58 carbine, the compact .30-caliber rifle responsible for shattering the helmet of one of the black-clad wraiths, dumping his corpse in the center of the hall. Blood poured from the crater in the head armor, running into the swampy hall carpet.

If the sprinklers kept this up, James would need a swamp boat to get up and down the hallway. "Gary, are you readin' me?"

Nothing. The enemy had them jammed too well. He looked over to see Hawkins across the hall, looking a little singed.

"Fireball," Hawkins explained. "Where's the rest of the team?"

"Gary's got them pinned down from his end. And they're really cutting loose into the suite, so maybe David hooked up with Rafe," James explained. "But it's a standoff."

"We'd better get moving," Hawkins said. "It's been a full minute for this firefight. The police will be on our backs any moment now."

James nodded. "Cover me. I'm coming over."

Hawkins swung around and let his P-90 burp for an extended 40-round burst that kept the armored marauders pinned down. James leaped across the hall to Hawkins's alcove.

"Keep 'em busy here," James told him. "I'm going to check on David and Rafe."

"Be careful out there," Hawkins said. "Your boots are

soaking wet. We don't need you doing a header off the side of the hotel."

James cut through the hotel room and smashed out the window with the hard polymer butt of his FN. Clearing a hole large enough for himself, he crawled out onto the ledge. The smooth stone looked treacherous, but his wet hands and soaked slacks gripped it firmly. He decided against standing up and crawled along, looking down six stories.

He glanced up and saw the ragged hole in the window of their suite and grinned. McCarter had to have cut across, and he perched at the side of the window, peering around. He saw his partners huddled behind the sofa, then ducked back in time to avoid a face full of shattering glass as 6.5 mm armor-piercing bullets slashed at him. James aimed his muzzle around the corner and cut loose with an extended burst at chest level. He drew his weapon back as bullets crashed into the corner. Concrete exploded into dust as the high-velocity enemy slugs ricocheted off of them.

"David! Rafe!" he shouted.

"We can't reach the window," Encizo answered.

Manning appeared at the far corner, and James waved him back. The sniper nodded and returned to his post on the ledge.

"Cal! Think outside the box!" McCarter called out.

That was all James had to hear, and he headed back for the hotel room. He started for the bathroom and the ceiling hatch when he remembered Hawkins's soot-covered face and scorched hair.

"T.J.?" James asked at the door. He jerked his thumb at the bathroom.

"The bathroom is a firestorm," Hawkins answered. "Luckily the metal door contained it."

"I'm going across the hall," James told him.

"Have fun," Hawkins replied. "I'll need another magazine if you need the cover fire."

"I'm thinking outside the box," James answered. He headed back to the window.

James stepped onto the ledge and his sole skidded slightly. Only his grasp on the ledge kept him from losing balance, and he remembered to be careful. Just to be certain he'd have a clear path, he crawled along the ledge for another two rooms, then punched out the window with the stock of his machine pistol. He crawled through and made his way to the bathroom. His G-96 Jet Aer dagger pried open the maintenance hatch and he slipped his slender frame through the hole. The crawlspace down to his right glowed with angry amber flames licking through those open accesses. He turned on his flashlight and saw that the crawlspace stretched wider than the hall. He pushed himself along, making certain that he was on a support beam, and reached the opposite bank of hotel rooms. The crawlspace was fully supported here, and he scurried on his hands and knees until he was across the hall from the pair of glowing hatchways.

He would be right across the hall from the entrenched gunmen. It was possible that they would have retreated to use the room he was perched over as a temporary firebase. James took a deep breath and hammered his heel through the hatch, slipping down as if he were on a slide. As soon as his feet hit the bathroom's tiled floor, he spotted an armored assassin whirl in reaction to his arrival. James triggered his FN, the 5.7 mm bullets penetrating the enemy's protective uniform. The gunman gurgled painfully as he slumped against the wall.

"Dammit!" a voice cursed in English, and James hit the bathroom doorway quickly, ripping out another burst of armor-defeating FN rounds. Two assassins perched in the entrance to the hotel room jerked and spasmed under James's hellish assault, and he ducked back as the .50-round reservoir of the P-90 emptied.

The gunman perched in the doorway of Phoenix Force's suite cut loose with a salvo of 6.5 mm tungsten-cored bullets that stitched along the wall. The shower tiles exploded as the hypervelocity penetrators expended the last of their energy trying to break through. James fed his weapon a fresh magazine, realizing it was his last.

"Okay, gang, time to do your thing!" James called out.

Manning's DSA-58 boomed in the hallway as McCarter and Encizo focused their weapons on the doorway of the suite. Hawkins's P-90 ripped out elongated bursts and James swung around.

The last assassin danced bonelessly, shredded by five streams of fire. His corpse folded to the soggy carpet, and the firefight for the hotel was over.

James stepped into the hall, wary of any unaccounted-for marauders, but it was clear. Encizo and McCarter appeared from the hotel room that Hawkins had perched at, and Manning came down from his window, his big feet squishing the blood- and water-soaked carpet.

"No prisoners?" McCarter asked, holding half of Phoenix Force's gear bags in his hands.

"Nope," Manning answered, not passing by the elevator bank.

"I counted only six," James said.

"The cars," Hawkins noted.

Encizo nodded and set down the other half of the Stony Man warriors' luggage and opened a case. "Flash-bangs."

Hawkins took one grenade and McCarter took the other. They gave each other room to throw, pulled their pins and let fly. The two men bounced the stun-shock bombs off the far corner of the intersection to the elevators, and both blasters erupted in unison. James and Manning swept down that subhall, but found only closed elevator doors.

Manning let his rifle hang on its sling and pried one set of doors open. James looked down the shaft, his flashlight slicing into the darkness.

"They moved the cars down one floor," James announced.

"We're on it," McCarter and Encizo called, making for the stairwell.

"Get your rappelling gloves on," James warned. "Those elevator cables will tear the flesh off your hands if you're not careful."

"Good idea," Manning agreed, pulling them off his load-bearing vest. Hawkins and James put theirs on, too.

Hawkins extended the stock of one of the enemy's

machine pistols and jammed it between the open elevator doors, giving Manning a reprieve. The three Phoenix Force warriors descended into the shaft, one at a time.

Manning leveled his Glock at the maintenance hatch on the car as Hawkins crouched to open it.

A salvo of autofire ripped through the trap door and Hawkins nearly tumbled off the car. James grabbed a handful of the Southerner's shirt with one hand, ripping off a burst from his P-90 in the other. Manning cut loose with his Glock, as well.

The elevator car lurched.

"Shit…" Manning said.

"What…" James began, but suddenly a burst of autofire inspired him to step back. The motor in the center of the car erupted in sparks as 6.5 mm tungsten-cored slugs destroyed it.

"Jump!" Hawkins yelled. The Southerner grabbed the other elevator car, his legs dangling in space.

James dropped his flashlight and threw himself onto the support cable. Even through his rappelling gloves, he could feel the steel splinters stab into his palms, and then momentum took over as the cable yanked his wiry frame upward. Thinking quickly, James let go the second he felt pulled toward the roof, twisting in midair. Instants later, he grabbed on to the center strut of the elevator door, the jolt jarring his shoulders, but he was alive, hanging on as his feet dangled into the shaft below.

The torch whirled into the darkness below as the car accelerated away. A thunderous crash resounded as the elevator hit the bottom of the shaft.

"Gary!" James bellowed. He couldn't see the big Canadian in the darkness. "T.J., do you see him?"

"No!" Hawkins answered, crawling to a more secure handhold on the side of the other elevator car.

"I'm here!" Manning answered. His voice sounded weak with exertion. "Cal, there are ladder rungs just to your right."

A flashlight clicked on in the darkness below and illuminated the rungs, just where Manning said they would be. James kicked off the side of the remaining elevator car and swung to the maintenance ladder. He gripped the metal rail, then climbed onto it. "Gary?"

"I'm fine," Manning answered.

"Cal? Gary? T.J.?" McCarter called from the top of the car that Hawkins clung to.

"We're fine!" James replied. "I think."

"Give me a hand, David," Hawkins requested. McCarter leaned over the side and grabbed the Southerner's hand and hauled the ex-Ranger onto the roof of the elevator.

"Cal?" McCarter asked.

"I've got a ladder," James answered.

"And Gary?" McCarter asked.

"I'm okay," Manning replied. He didn't sound like it. A light split into the shaft as the Canadian opened a door below. "We'll meet you downstairs."

"Right. Rendezvous Beta," McCarter announced.

James climbed down to where Manning had exited the shaft, and crawled through the propped-open doors. Manning sat, drenched. His left arm was folded across his stomach, and his eyes were closed.

"Were you hit?" James asked.

"No, but hitting the ladder as fast as I did wasn't good for my back," Manning answered.

"And your hand?" James continued, kneeling by him.

"I can move my fingers without pain," Manning told him. "It's sprained."

"Can you walk?"

"Yeah," Manning replied. "We can wait to wrap me up."

James nodded and helped haul the burly Phoenix Force veteran back to his feet. "This just isn't your week, Gary."

Manning nodded. "I'm still breathing, though. It can't be too bad."

"No," James replied. "But it still sucks to be you."

"Anyone ever tell you that you've got a wonderful bedside manner?" Manning asked.

"Not really," James said.

"You won't hear it from me, either."

James smiled. If he could joke through the pain, then Manning'd be okay after a few minutes.

James hoped so. Phoenix Force needed to be at full strength if it was going to survive any more battles with Skyline's trained assassins.

CHAPTER FIFTEEN

San Salvador, El Salvador

Otomo Golgo frowned as he took a sip from his juice. Across the table, Angela Eosin smiled prettily and puffed on a cigarette.

"I sent two teams of my best people after the groups the Americans pitted against us," Golgo stated.

"Sky," Eosin said, sighing. "it happened. It's over. We've learned our lesson."

"I thought your armor was supposed to turn assassins into invulnerable warriors, Fixx," Golgo replied, not keeping the disdain from his voice. "Instead, those American super-soldiers have chopped through everything we've thrown at them."

"What is it you always say?" Eosin asked. She took a puff on her cigarette.

"There is no knowledge that is not power," the man called Skyline answered. "So you're saying that they were prepared for invulnerable killing machines."

"The 6.5 mm Bofors machine pistols were designed to be able to punch through the mass production armor," Eosin explained. "So are the FN P-90 and the Heckler and Koch MP-7 5.7 mm and 4.85 mm rounds. Anything that can defeat a Kevlar helmet can defeat our current production."

"But your personal armor and mine can still deflect that?" Golgo asked.

"Of course," Eosin answered. She let out a lungful of smoke, letting it hang in the air between them. "Of course, our personal armor suits are too good to let just anyone have."

Golgo nodded. "There is that. It would make things difficult if we couldn't control our enemies."

"That's why I calibrated the formula to allow the current crop of PDW ammunition to cut through it. Only truly special forces would normally have access to such weaponry, or whomever we supplied with the armor," Eosin said. "If there was no fear of reprisal from their commanding officers, most forces would be tempted toward insubordination."

"Point taken," Golgo answered. He waved a tendril of smoke from his face, then took another sip of his juice. "What does Brujo think of all this?"

Fixx sighed. "You know how these petty little despots are."

"The first signs of trouble, they're paranoid," Golgo replied. He shrugged. "I'm sure you can keep him in line."

"He's upset, but I told him that I have a team on the case," Eosin explained.

Golgo smirked as he felt her toes slide up his thigh.

The ninja master raised an eyebrow. The restaurant was abandoned, and the wait staff had been retired to another room while the pair ate. He felt his loins stir. "Your confidence knows no bounds."

Fixx chuckled. "I just like seeing how far I can push your buttons."

Skyline sighed and placed his hand over her instep, holding her toes against his aroused manhood. "That's not a button."

Eosin threw her head back and laughed. "Sky, you slay me."

"Just be careful that I don't have to," Golgo warned. He gave her foot a squeeze and she sat upright, pulling it out of his hand.

"No, that's not a button. More like a stick shift," Fixx taunted, the smile still flashing sensuously on her lips.

She leaned over the table and brushed her fingertips along his jaw. Golgo tasted her lips, a kiss with a hint of strawberry. Eosin stood, then pulled out her compact to check her lipstick. "You must be made of iron, Sky."

"No. I just know that you'll come back to me," Golgo answered. "There's no one in the world as dangerous as I am."

"Not a little bit egotistical?" Fixx asked.

"Maybe just a bit of pride," Golgo returned with a grin.

"So you'll make sure that Brujo doesn't get too uptight?"

The master ninja nodded. "Consider it taken care of. I'd say it was fixed."

"But that's my specialty," Eosin answered with a broad smile. "Get the check, please."

Golgo nodded as the weapons designer left the restaurant. He sighed and walked over to the next table and took the cover off of a platter to reveal a sound suppressed SIG-Sauer. He picked it up and walked to the next room where his bodyguards had gathered the restaurant staff. When they saw the gun in his hand, the men and women released gasps and whimpers of fear.

"Thank you for a wonderful meal," Skyline told the captives.

It took only eight shots to kill them all, but he reloaded and gave each corpse a "tip" in the form of an extra bullet.

EOSIN SHOOK HER HEAD as she entered Brujo's office. A half-empty tumbler of liquor sat next to him on the desktop, and the Salvadoran boss's eyes were red-rimmed. He was starting to come to pieces. It was only eight in the morning, and he was well past his first drink of the day, if he'd even stopped drinking since she left him last night for the early morning rendezvous with Skyline.

"Vincenzo?"

"Hi, Angelita..." Brujo answered. His smile was crooked, his speech slurred. "Sorry. I've been busy this morning."

"Did you go to sleep at all?" Eosin asked.

Brujo rested his chin in the palm of his hand, his curly black hair poking up all around his head. "I got a call last night after you left. They called you by name."

"Who did?" Eosin asked.

"The *norteamericanos,*" Brujo explained. His red-rimmed eyes flashed with anger and, explosively, he swept the half-empty glass off the desktop. It shattered against a bookcase, spraying leather bindings with alcohol. "They called you by name!"

"What name?" Eosin asked.

"Fixx," Brujo huffed. "They know you're here!"

"If they did, then the whole might of the United States armed forces would come slamming down on our necks," Fixx replied coolly.

"They turned Joaquin against me. He served me up like a lunch platter!" Brujo bellowed. He slammed one powerful fist into the desktop. The impact toppled the bottle of booze and bounced his penholder to the floor. "I've been listening to reports all morning long about how la casa Malina had been attacked by terrorists last night. Terrorists, armed with mortars. Lots of corpses, but no Joaquin."

"So he's still alive?" Fixx asked.

"He phoned me personally and let me talk to one of them," Brujo said. He was red-faced, apoplectic. "They said that you should expect the Cowboy Jihad. Does that mean anything?"

"Not a thing. It's just big talk from a small group of loose cannons, Vincenzo," Eosin cooed. She stepped closer to him.

"A small group?" Brujo asked.

"If they had any significant force, they would have snatched Malina without leaving you a hint of his disappearance," she answered. "They hit his home with a big, flashy, violent display of force, typical tactics for a small special forces unit behind enemy lines. It's called force multiplication. You've been trained in counterinsurgency. Set up a big, loud diversion, then slip in the back way and do your job."

Brujo looked around the office.

"The United States Navy is not parked off our coast, the Air Force is not thundering overhead in bombers, and no Airborne Rangers are dropping on your home," Fixx continued. "You're safe and secure. No one can touch you."

"They struck with impunity," Brujo said, uncertain.

"Because you've been shifting your forces around. The country isn't under martial law, at least not yet," Fixx explained. She stepped behind him and ran her hands over his broad shoulders. She ran her tongue up his neck and felt him loosen, a small moan escaping his lips. "They can go where they want, make it look like they're phantoms, but that's only because you have the country off balance, to keep the liberals from finding out what you're up to."

Brujo rested his head against hers. "I'm sorry I lost my temper."

Fixx stroked his inner thigh. "You haven't slept all night, Vincenzo."

"I'm so tired. I wish I could sleep," he murmured.

Fixx kissed his cheek. "Rest easy, Vincenzo. I'll take care of everything."

Fixx went to the door, snapped her fingers and a couple of Brujo's men entered the office and helped him to his bedroom. They'd put him under the covers and let him recover.

In the meantime, she had business to conduct.
She picked up the phone.

Stony Man Farm, Virginia

"WE'RE PICKING UP something from Brujo's home phone," Akira Tokaido announced. "He's calling out."

"Put a trace," Barbara Price ordered, knowing that the Stony Man cyber team was already on the case.

Price had been busy through the night coordinating the teams. She'd only just received word that Phoenix Force had evaded an attack by Skyline's assassination team in its hotel suite. Gary Manning had sprained his wrist and aggravated his pulled muscles, but using the medical supplies on the charter jet, he was recovering well enough to go into action by later that evening.

Both teams had experienced their fair share of injuries over the years, so she wasn't overly concerned. They were only human, no matter how many times they had fended off war and disaster utilizing their considerable physical and mental abilities. Lyons had dislocated his toe in snapping the neck of an armored assassin in Arizona, but the stubborn ex-cop splinted the digit and worked through the pain. Manning had fallen down an elevator shaft and ended up with a sprained wrist for his trouble. Only the fact that the Stony Man warriors were in top physical condition enabled them to snap back from injuries that would sideline professional athletes for weeks. It was a proved scientific fact that those who engaged in intense regular exercise avoided serious injury better, and when they did get hurt, their systems recovered more quickly.

No, they weren't supermen, and they bled and limped like other men. But with the fate of nations and millions of civilians hanging in the balance, whatever aches and pains they suffered were shrugged off as they continued to do their jobs.

Price looked around at the cyberteam. They had been operating on only small snatches of sleep and copious amounts of caffeine from Aaron Kurtzman's sludge-dispensing coffeepot. Through it all, their minds remained razor-sharp, their concentration as focused as lasers on the tasks at hand. Though the computer experts didn't have to submit themselves to hails of bullets and escaping from dive-bombing gunships and artillery missiles, they still put themselves through mental and physical gymnastics on the same daily basis.

Hunt Wethers would never be confused with a football player, and Aaron Kurtzman's stomach was hardly flat and cut like a bodybuilder, but both men demonstrated remarkable endurance and stamina. The same went for Akira Tokaido and Carmen Delahunt. The fact that all four of the cyberwarriors were able to program, juggling advanced mathematic equations with only short periods of sleep was all the more impressive.

"Fixx sent a phone call through to Mexico City," Tokaido finally announced.

"Where?" Price asked.

"We're still tracking the call. But the area code and prefix are unmistakable," Tokaido told her.

"Keep on it," Price told him. It was like telling the young Japanese-American hacker to breathe, or to put on his earbuds and blast out heavy metal to focus his brilliant, if hyperactive mind. But it was something to do, until she could coordinate again with the NRO later that morning.

"We've got a call coming in to the factory." Carmen Delahunt spoke up. "San Salvadoran area code!"

"Contact," Price said. "Good job, team."

"I don't like this," Kurtzman noted. "Carl told us that he dropped the bug in Brujo's ear that he knew about Fixx. We've wanted this witch for a long time, but she's stayed ahead of us by being careful."

Price frowned. The cybercrew had linked the arms designer and her compatriots to several large-scale terrorist incidents around the world. The Executioner and Able Team had blunted an effort by Fixx's allies a while ago, and there was an indication that Stony Man had nibbled around the edges of other conspiracies set into motion by the death merchant and her friends. They knew her by her title, but until now, they had no real clues as to who she was or where she operated.

Because she was careful, just like Kurtzman said. Now, she was drawing a direct line between Vincenzo Brujo's estate and her factory in Mexico.

"She's suckering us into a trap," Price said. "You're right. Dammit, Carl."

"Don't blame him," said Hal Brognola from where he stood over Tokaido's shoulder. "He's just going by what's worked in the past. Rattling cages, shaking up the enemy, hoping to spook them out into the open."

"Fixx isn't spooked, though," Price observed. She turned to regard the head Fed, who hadn't changed his suit for the past thirty-six hours. "How long until our deadline?"

"Twenty hours before the President wants us to deploy Phoenix Force and Able Team to Iraq to mop up the Ankylosaurs," Brognola stated.

"It's a tight window," Price commented.

"We've had tighter," Brognola replied.

"Is he going to send any support our way on this one?" Price asked.

"We've got an aircraft carrier out of San Francisco steaming toward Panama. If something happens in El Salvador, the Navy will divert it," Brognola explained. "Other than that, nothing official. We've also got a couple Coast Guard ships in the Gulf of California, cleaning up the mess Phoenix Force dumped in it."

"Not a lot, then," Price concluded. Her shoulders slumped. "Aaron calculated that if Fixx's artillery launchers were modular, they'd have the capability to provide defense against both strike fighters and warships off the coast."

Brognola chewed on his cigar. "Fixx has whipped up some pretty impressive designs. I don't doubt that she's made her missile launchers modular enough to cover all bases against reprisal. Based on Gadgets's reports about the barrage one unit could deliver…"

"One aircraft carrier group isn't going to be enough," Price replied. "Not to mention that there's no way we could get a major mechanized infantry force through Guatemala or Honduras, even if we did have anything to spare in this hemisphere."

"Which is why Fixx and Skyline picked that little corner of the world," Brognola conceded. "Enough divisive politics and disenfranchised radicals to supply the raw muscle, and just one man willing to sell it all to them."

"From there, they've all of Central America to spread out into. Sympathetic coups from fellow purists," Kurtzman explained. "You couldn't have picked a better ground zero for this nightmare."

"Well, there is the Chinese presence in Panama," Price said.

"Fascists on one side, Communists on the other." Brognola groaned. "As if this situation wasn't depressing enough."

"If anything, they'll slow down the Dignity Battalions if they should make a bid to come back to power," Price offered. "So that's good news."

"Very little," Brognola answered. "Fixx could set it up so that Panama will get all the firepower it needs to set that country straight. Once the Canal falls into Fascist hands…"

Price nodded.

Things looked desperate.

But that was when Stony Man's heroes shone their brightest.

EOSIN HUNG UP the phone, then got out her cell.

"What's up, angel?" Golgo asked.

"It's on," she replied, then hung up.

It was all she needed to say, a quick coded message that let Skyline know that the enemy who had countered them at several turns was on hand. Golgo didn't know exactly who they were, only possessing hints and code names like Able Team and Phoenix Force, mysterious vigilante groups who slipped through the shadowy back streets of the world hunting down terrorists, gangsters and conspirators.

Eosin dialed her personal bodyguards, the Iron Guard, and their leader, Euclide Potts answered.

"Boss?"

"In the zone."

"We're ready," Potts replied.

Eosin hung up. The short cell phone calls wouldn't give the enemy much to track, unlike her phone call to Mexico. But that was to give them the location of her factory. Situated in the Mexico City metropolitan area, it would be difficult for the U.S. Government to condone or sanction an air strike, and if they did, it would only make the world look upon any accusations by the presidential administration seem more suspect. No, the way she had it set up, it would have to be the covert operations groups that had been dogging them that would have to finish the job, to keep America's face clean of egg.

Potts and the Iron Guard and Skyline's ninjas were forewarned and equipped with her absolute finest equipment. Anyone who came up against them expecting things to flow as easily as it had been when taking on the Fist of God wrapped in inferior protection would come face-to-face with a truly irresistible force.

Eosin smiled, spun a chair and plopped in it.

All she had to do was to wait for all the pieces to fall into place.

CHAPTER SIXTEEN

El Salvador

Carl Lyons grinned slightly as Rosario Blancanales checked out his splinted foot. "Tell me the truth, Doc, will I ever tap dance again?"

"Nope, it appears someone replaced your legs with those of a troglodyte," Blancanales quipped. "Seriously, I think you're okay. But don't get punched in the jaw."

Lyons nodded. "If it's a choice between not chewing for a while or getting my windpipe crushed by a punch, I'll shut up and enjoy my energy drinks."

"Okay…within reason, then," Blancanales replied. "It was only a hairline fracture anyway."

"Still hurt like a son of a bitch," Lyons grumbled.

"So why'd you keep talking at the briefing the other day?" Blancanales asked.

"When I have something to say, I say it," Lyons replied.

Blancanales chuckled. "Yeah. You're cute when you're stubborn, big guy."

"Just got offline with Barb," Schwarz interrupted. "Phoenix Force had a busy night."

He described how the hit squad sent after their counterparts had adjusted their tactics after a similar defeat at the hands of Able Team.

"Sounds like it came close for David and the boys," Lyons answered. "Which means the next time we run into Skyline's assassins, we're going to be in for a hell of a scrap."

"Cripes." Blancanales spoke up. "Even when we were fighting Unomundo, or the Aryan Right Coalition, they never adapted to our tactics."

"This is the same bunch that laid me up in the hospital," Lyons noted. "They're pretty damn good."

"So are we," Blancanales reminded him. "We took down the guys who knocked you out of action."

Lyons frowned. "They never identified his body."

"That's because it was packed into a car that blew a parking lot into a blast crater," Schwarz replied. "Teeth were found ninety feet from the epicenter."

Lyons locked eyes with Schwarz. "He's still out there. And I intend to be ready for him next time."

Schwarz and Blancanales went silent. Few foes in Able Team's history had so readily defeated the Ironman in one-on-one combat. Even the Executioner had met his match in the deadly assassin, and Bolan himself expressed similar doubts as to Dark's ultimate defeat.

"When we nail down Skyline and Fixx, I'm personally going to put a fifty in each of their faces and make damn sure that they're dead," Lyons told them. "None of this 'no one could have survived that' shit."

"All right, Carl," Blancanales said. When Lyons put his mind to something, almost nothing could stop him.

"Barb also said that we only have twenty hours left on the clock before the President pulls us back to take on the Ankylosaurs overseas," Schwarz warned.

"Are they still raising hell in the Sandbox?" Lyons asked.

"Yeah. So, by four tomorrow morning, we either have to have Fixx wrapped up, or find a control command sequence that will disable them completely," Schwarz replied. "I'll bet that Fixx is a completist, and that she will have a way to disable this stuff under her own command."

Lyons nodded in agreement. "Good luck in getting it out of her."

"You don't think she'll go down easily, do you?" Blancanales asked.

"Fixx and her compatriots have been doing their damnedest to rip the world's governments apart and set up their own puppets," Lyons explained. "I suspect she sees herself as a goddess in a new global pantheon, and people with that kind of megalomania will go down fighting with all their might."

"Speaking of might," Grimaldi called from the next room, "check the surveillance camera that Gadgets put to watch the street."

Able Team, having finished in San Luis at Joaquin Malina's residence, had moved to a safehouse that the CIA had stationed in San Salvador, the capital of El Salvador. That was where Vincenzo Brujo had made his headquarters, and it was a good place to start to hunt down not only the ex-ORDEN strongman, but to home in on Fixx, who undoubtedly was staying close to her patsy.

The safehouse was a second-story home on a crowded street in the middle of a slum at the rim of the city proper. Central America, like South America, was set up so that the most affluent lived in either the hearts of the cities or deep in the countryside on their own plantations. The poorer classes clung to the edges of these estates, like peasants in medieval Europe who'd set their homes in the shadows of castles. The same old world sensibilities carried over to the new world. The "slum" placement was ideal for the Stony Man team because even security forces didn't make their presence known in the dirty back streets of the poor.

If such an official presence did show up, then the surveillance cameras that Schwarz put in a ring around the safehouse would spot them a mile away.

Four men appeared in the street, having stepped out of the back of a delivery truck. They were men, but they looked like robotic monstrosities out of a science-fiction movie. They were tall, covered in gleaming chrome, and carrying large, impressive-looking rifles. Civilians in the street looked on in awe and horror at these metallic juggernauts as they walked toward the safehouse.

"Get the carbines," Lyons ordered the rest of his team. "Jack, take cover and put on your heavy armor."

Lyons threw on his armored load-bearing vest, as did Blancanales and Schwarz. The vests were kept close at hand, and were a mix of not only Kevlar and ceramic trauma plates, but also a sandwiched layer of high-tensile polymer chain mail. After having faced the armored marauders in Arizona, the trio realized that they would need the maximum protection if they were going to survive against the conspiracy. The heavy armor was similar to their older protection, back when they faced renegade bikers and South American thugs armed with top-of-the-line assault rifles. Back then, they used actual metal chain mail, sandwiched between layers of Kevlar and ceramic trauma plates. The polymer replacement made the vests lighter to wear, without sacrificing defensive durability.

"Get the ammo we packed for taking down the Ankylosaurs," Lyons added as an afterthought.

"You think they're that well-armored?" Blancanales asked.

"They're not even bothering to hide," Schwarz replied. "They remind me of the juggernauts that Mack took on."

Lyons charged a round into the chamber and moved toward the window.

"Carl!" Schwarz called. "Down!"

Lyons didn't even process the warning. He just hit the floor. In the same heartbeat, the window he'd approached disappeared in an explosive cloud. He glanced up, but the room was full of smoke and fluttering debris. He winced and pulled a two-inch-long splinter out of his forearm. "Guys?"

"So much for the computer," Schwarz muttered as he crawled under the choking cloud. He flipped the broken device out of his path. "I'm alive."

"I'm fine," Blancanales keyed in.

"What in the hell was that?" Grimaldi asked from the cover of a dresser.

"A grenade launcher," Schwarz replied.

The floor erupted as bullets tore through the wood at an angle. Lyons, Schwarz and Blancanales rolled out of the center of the room as splintered craters marked the passage of hundreds of high-powered bullets through the hardwood. Grimaldi scrambled into another room instants before the dresser he'd used for cover exploded under the assault of the heavy-caliber rounds.

Lyons pressed against the wall, then looked at the perforated floor. "They're going to chew us to pieces if we don't do something."

"Like what?" Schwarz snapped. "We've got good armor, but…"

Lyons suddenly disappeared. His motto was "Nut up and do it," and when he said that, it was usually just before bursting into action that pushed his luck to the limit. This time, Lyons dived like an Olympic swimmer through the weakened floor. The juggernauts' fire had subsided, and their weapons had devastated the wood. Lyons's two hundred pounds of bronzed muscle and fifty-odd pounds of battle gear shattered the splintered floor beneath him and he dropped to the level below.

Blancanales and Schwarz didn't even exchange a look of incredulity, instead leaping after their leader before another wave of enemy gunfire slashed into the apartment.

The men of Able Team landed in a crouch, saw Lyons huddled against a section of wall to one side of a window. Plaster vomited from the wall, covering Ironman with white dust. Lyons held up three fingers, then did a quick countdown. Blancanales and Schwarz set up to answer the terrifying monstrosities outside.

When Lyons reached zero in his countdown, he didn't swing around to the open window, but simply pivoted and cut loose with his Beowulf on full-automatic. A volley of 350-grain, armor-piercing bullets sliced through the wall as if it were water and tore into the four armored killers in the street. Blancanales and Schwarz, having a better view of the street from their vantage points, held down their triggers, targeting an Iron Guardsman apiece. The tungsten-cored .50-caliber slugs punched through the wall and snapped into their targets.

The first of the Beowulf slugs only sparked on their armored targets, and Blancanales's heart dropped, realizing that they might not have the firepower to take down these steel-clad attackers. The Iron Guardsmen stood their ground and lowered their weapons when finally, unimpeded by the wall, one of Schwarz's bullets punched through the belly of his target. The armored gunman folded over, and distracted the other three. Even so, Lyons had to hit the deck as Fixx's warriors blew the wall he was hiding behind into a cloud of powder and smoke with their rifles.

"Carl! Get out of there!" Blancanales shouted as he remembered the high-explosive punch the murderous marauders packed. He and Schwarz ducked out of the room into a small kitchen.

Lyons, having no clear path to safety within the building, whirled and dived through the weakened wall just as a pair of grenades sailed into the room he'd just exited. Twin thunderclaps detonated at once, and the low remains of the wall sheltered the Able Team leader from the shock wave and shrapnel. Lyons wondered as to the fate of his partners even as he scrambled madly toward the cover of a parked Volkswagen. The steel-plated assassins tracked him, and their mighty rifles cut through the top half of the automobile. Only the chassis, seats and wheel wells had enough mass to slow their deadly weapons.

Lyons looked under the frame of the ravaged VW, and saw one of the armored killers dragging his wounded partner along. The two other indestructible invaders continued to pour streams of metal-chewing fire into the VW, keeping Lyons pinned.

"Shit," Lyons cursed as he pulled a grenade off his harness and yanked the pin. He launched it under the frame of the damaged automobile, then rolled over, tucking his chin to his chest. He hoped that his broad, armor-covered back would provide him protection from the shrapnel of his minibomb as it detonated. A piece nicked his scalp, and another dug into the back of one calf, but that was all the injury he suffered as more projectiles peppered his protected back, the trauma plates, polymer chain mail and Kevlar protecting him from serious injury.

From the wreckage of the safehouse, Blancanales and Schwarz opened fire on the stunned juggernauts. Lyons's grenade had staggered them, leaving them distracted. Even so, their body armor blunted and deflected most of their shots. Fortunately, it was only most of their shots.

One of the steel-clad killers dropped, his helmet punctured by a lucky shot, and the other assassin jerked as a heavy round struck him in the shoulder, a spray of blood spattering his gleaming chest.

The wounded marauder pivoted and pulled a pistol, firing wildly into the wrecked safehouse.

Schwarz grunted as a 6.5 mm round struck him in the chest, but his protective armor held against the armor-piercing round. Blancanales pushed the electronics genius to the floor before another bullet homed in on them and any unprotected limbs.

Lyons took the opportunity to pop up. Reloaded Beowulf in one fist and the GI-50 in the other, he opened fire with both guns blazing. A hail of half-inch bullets smashed into the injured gunman. The GI-50's rounds only sparked on the heavy, gleaming armor of the assassin, while some of the Beowulf bullets glanced off. Lyons let the pistol drop to the ground and gripped his carbine with both hands. The holographic sight atop the carbine centered on the assassin's head as he struggled, single-handedly, to reload his pistol.

Lyons pumped the four remaining rounds from his Beowulf into the juggernaut's head. The armored killer's head snapped back under the assault, and even though his helmet withstood the salvo, he toppled backward, neck twisted at an odd angle.

"Thou shalt have no iron men before me," Lyons growled as the killer dropped to the ground. A high-powered rifle round slammed into his upper chest and threw him to the ground. Lyons couldn't breathe for a moment, his lungs burned for oxygen and he felt his chest. No blood. He felt the nipple of the enemy bullet pressed against his armor.

A hollow thump resounded at the wrecked wall of the safehouse, Rosario Blancanales standing there with a smoking grenade launcher under his Beowulf. Struck dead-center with a 40 mm charge, the steel-clad hit man disappeared. In truth, the detonation rocketed the hardman through the door of the building he was standing in front of.

Schwarz limped to the damaged wall, pulled his GI-50 and emptied its magazine into the killer he'd gut shot. The injured assassin jerked violently under the hail of bullets, but he didn't get up.

Lyons finally caught his breath and tore open his armor. The delivery truck raced off down the street, but he was more concerned about the state of his chest. It didn't hurt to breathe, so no ribs had been broken, but he had a bruise the size of a pie plate across his deltoid.

"You okay, Carl?" Blancanales asked.

"I'm breathing, I see the sun and the enemy's not moving. I'm feeling fucking fantastic," Lyons answered. "Gadgets?"

"I hurt like hell," Schwarz replied. "But that's good. Dead men don't feel pain."

Lyons nodded, then touched the back of his head. His fingers came away from the wound, slicked with blood. "I took a hit in the leg, too."

"I'll check on it," Blancanales said.

"Go look after Jack first," Lyons replied. "I don't see him and he might be injured worse than we are."

"Don't you worry about little old me," Grimaldi interjected. He held bags of Able Team's gear in his hands, standing at the edge of the shattered floor. "Pol, catch this stuff. I don't want to mess it up."

"Just throw it down," Lyons said. "Then lower yourself carefully."

Schwarz looked at his own bruised chest, then shook his arm to test how well it moved. "Fixx and Skyline just escalated big-time."

"What next? A nuke?" Grimaldi asked, dropping to the floor.

"I wouldn't put it past her," Lyons replied.

Schwarz picked up one of their rifles. "I've seen it all, now."

"What is it?" Lyons asked.

The rifle appeared to be a slightly oversize M-16/M-203 with a twin-drum magazine. Schwarz ejected a shell from the breech and held it up. "Steel-tipped .300 Winchester Short Magnums. It makes a .30-06 look like a BB gun."

"That looks like a Beta-C drum, too," Lyons said as Blancanales ripped the Able Team leader's pant leg to get at the injury on his calf. "Those hold one hundred shots in 5.56 mm."

"Don't know how much they'd hold in .300 WSM, but something between fifty and seventy-five I'd guess," Schwarz replied. "Besides, they had grenade launchers."

"Yeah. I remember that. I was at ground zero, too, remember?" Lyons asked.

Blancanales held up a sliver of wire. "Your own shrapnel, Ironman. Trying to get a Purple Heart and run for President?"

Lyons flipped off Blancanales.

The Able Team medic chuckled. "All right, let's load up the van and get the hell out of here. I'll let you bandage that thing up in the car."

"Yeah. The Salvadoran cops are definitely going to wonder why World War III happened in this street," Lyons agreed.

Able Team and Grimaldi made themselves scarce.

Stony Man Farm, Virginia

"LATEST DEVELOPMENT from San Salvador," Akira Tokaido announced.

"Put the cam on the main monitor," Price ordered.

"They lost their cam and the laptop," Tokaido answered.

"Good grief," Price replied.

"Luckily, their satellite phone survived," Kurtzman interjected.

"Carl?" Price asked.

"Right here," Lyons answered. His voice filtered over the speakers into the computer center. "We just had a scrap with Fixx's hardforce."

"What happened?" Price asked.

"We won, but only barely," Lyons explained. "Fixx has even better armor available."

Price was incredulous. "You were attacked by tanks?"

"No. Men armed with some serious damn firepower and wearing stuff that looks like it came out of a comic book," Lyons replied. "Unless we hit them point-blank and straight-on with our Beowulfs, nothing could go through their armor."

"Unbelievable," Price said.

"How many of them were there?" Kurtzman asked.

"Four," Lyons answered. "And they had rifles that would make Cowboy drool with envy. AR-10s rechambered for .300 WSM, loaded up with AP and stuffed with high-capacity drums. Oh, and grenade launchers, too."

"The recoil on those things must be a nightmare," Kurtzman stated.

"We confiscated those monsters. Gadgets disassembled one and found inertial dampeners built in, and some pretty effective muzzle brakes."

"I'll let Phoenix know about this," Price said. "Get them on the line, Carmen."

"Working on it," Delahunt answered. "Got him."

"David?" Price asked.

"Yeah," McCarter replied.

"I'll let Carl explain the new development," Price offered.

Lyons went through a recap for the Phoenix Force commander.

"Bloody hell," McCarter said when the tale was over.

"You sound scared, David," Lyons retorted.

McCarter sighed. "You're assaulted by four men wearing enough weapons and armor to blow an entire building to rubble, you're wearing your Able Team special armor vests, and you still end up beaten, battered, bruised and knocked around, and you're wondering why I'm bloody concerned?"

"Well, when you put it that way," Lyons said.

"We are seriously outgunned. If Fixx and Skyline

have that kind of firepower to send after Able Team, that means that we'll be running smack into that shit when we hit her factory," McCarter explained. "Our P-90s can punch through a Kevlar helmet, but I don't know if it can handle the kind of armor those things have."

"I know 40 mm grenade launchers work," Lyons noted.

"We've got that, and Gary's McMillan rifle," McCarter said.

"Do you need more backup?" Price asked.

"Nothing would get here in time to make our deadline," McCarter returned. "I shouldn't have been so quick to let all of those Barretts sink to the bottom of the bay."

"We could try to get an air strike to help you out," Price offered.

"And risk a war between the U.S. and Mexico? Right. Like the Mexican president is going to believe ours when he explains that the reason why we blew up a refurbished automobile plant next to the largest city in the country was because it was cranking out remote-controlled robot killing machines and was protected by nearly invulnerable commandos," McCarter grumbled. "The whole world's going to look at America like it's lost what's left of its bloomin' mind."

"So you'll handle it?" Price asked.

"I'm making plans as we speak," McCarter stated. "It's not going to be easy, but we don't get called into action because the problem is a piece of cake."

"Good luck, David," Lyons offered.

"Thanks, Carl. I appreciate the info," McCarter replied.

"Do you think you can handle things on your end?" Price asked.

"We'll do our best," Lyons stated. "And if we don't…you are sending an aircraft carrier group this way, right?"

"Yeah, but Aaron predicts fifty percent losses to the fleet if we can't take out Fixx's automated defenses," Price responded. "And that's a conservative estimate."

"And a good time was had by all," Lyons returned. "All right, Barb. We'll take care of this mess."

"Sorry, Carl," Price apologized. "I hate dropping everything on your shoulders."

"Better ours than anyone else's," Lyons said. "Like the man says, 'those're the breaks.'"

"Just come back home," Price admonished, but the Able Team leader had already hung up.

Silence reigned in the Stony Man command center. There were eighteen hours left in their presidential deadline, and Price wondered if their teams would survive to even be called to the Middle East.

CHAPTER SEVENTEEN

The outskirts of Mexico City

Gary Manning tested his grasp of the bolt-action McMillan, working the handle and dry-firing the rifle. There was the possibility that he would have to use the big rifle in an antipersonnel mode after the report that Able Team gave. The sun hung in the sky, its blazing heat pouring down over the Canadian, and his hair was matted to his scalp with sweat.

"Your wrist okay, Gary?" Calvin James asked.

"Yeah," Manning answered. "I can handle the rifle all right."

"And your back?"

"You don't have to mother me, Cal."

James shook his head. "Sure, you rested, but not enough to put you back at peak condition."

"You heard what David said," Manning answered. "We might be going up against guards who are even better armored than the one's we've already fought. We're going to need the whole team in on this."

James nodded and checked the grenade launcher attached underneath his M-16. "Bad news all around. I just wish we had a little more time. Hitting them at the height of the day…"

"We don't have that time," Manning responded.

"He's right, Cal," McCarter interjected. He was testing out the balance on Manning's DSA-58 rifle. The Briton had doubted the power of even an M-16 to handle the heavily armored killers that Lyons had described, and wasn't heartened even by the power of the classic FN-FAL rifle, even with it's full-powered 7.62 mm NATO payload. He had replaced the forward furniture with a housing designed to mount a spare M-203 grenade launcher on the weapon, just to make certain he had enough punch.

Encizo and Hawkins had upgraded their M-16s to mount grenade launchers on the rifles, as well. Normally, only Calvin James took to the field as Phoenix Force's grenadier, but the assault on the factory promised not only human juggernauts, but the possibility of the Ankylosaurs pressed into security duty. The hurricane fence around the factory made it difficult to survey the grounds of the facility, and while Charlie Mott offered to give them a reconnaissance by helicopter, the memory of the mobile missile launcher that nearly killed Able Team in Arizona hung heavily in McCarter's mind.

"You're going to have to fly nap of the earth until we get to the fence," McCarter said. "Otherwise, they'll see us coming and shoot us out of the sky."

"All right," Mott answered.

"Once you drop us off, you get the hell out," McCarter said. "If Fixx was able to have one of those antiaircraft launchers in Arizona, she's definitely going to have more of those things here at her manufacturing headquarters. Barb offered us a naval air strike, but I'm pretty sure that Fixx has thought about that possibility, too."

"We're on our own," Mott mused. "And the helicopter we have isn't even armed or armored."

"You're going to have to be really good," McCarter told him.

"I'm not Jack," Mott admitted, "but I know my way around a joystick."

McCarter grinned. "All right."

The Briton double-checked the load in James's rifle.

The current U.S. Army issue 69-grain penetrators issued in the Middle East had proven insufficient against both human targets and enemy vehicles in countless firefights. Afghan and Iraqi opponents without body armor required five or more hits to kill with the rifle. Instead, Phoenix Force, anticipating trouble, had gone with 72-grain boattailed spitzer rounds. John Kissinger, Stony Man's armorer, had tested M-16s loaded with such bullets against not only automobiles, but against Able Team's heavy body armor. It would take a full magazine to damage the heavy vests enough to penetrate, which was a testament to the combined strength of Kevlar, polymer chain mail and ceramic trauma plates.

Would it be enough to knock down one of those steel-clad juggernauts that Able Team encountered in San Salvador?

It would have to do, McCarter decided. There was no

time to head home to pick up even bigger guns. His own DSA-58 was loaded with 168-grain, 7.62 mm ball, a legendary fight stopper and considered one of the heaviest battlefield cartridges since World War II. He'd seen M-60s loaded with such ammo blast jeeps and transport trucks into useless lumps of metal, but that was out of the three-foot-long barrel of the light machine gun. The DSA-58 had a stubby 14-inch barrel, designed for close quarters fighting.

"Death is just nature's way of saying you failed selection," he mused out loud, repeating the oft-quoted SAS saying.

"Why not just recite the 'Charge of the Light Brigade,' boss?" Hawkins asked.

"Just put on your armor, kid," McCarter said. "We're not dead yet."

"That's more like it," Hawkins quipped. "Just wanted to see if you still had that Cockney bad boy in you."

"He'll bite your ear off if you poke him any more, lad," McCarter warned. "I'd rather save him for Fixx and Skyline's men."

Hawkins grinned. "Point taken."

McCarter looked at the helicopter. It was a Hughes 500D, similar to the one that had been converted into a gunship for Fixx's assault on CIA headquarters.

The more he thought of it, it was probably Skyline who'd set up the attack on America's largest intelligence agency in an effort to knock out any foresight into preventing the El Salvadoran coup. Fixx would have been more interested in the Yuma proving grounds, taking out potential remote-controlled combat vehicles before they could be turned against her own automated battle machines. It would have been to the U.S.'s advantage to have unmanned combat drones take the fight to such mechanized defenses, putting Fixx back on the defensive. Certainly, Predator UAVs with their Maverick antitank missiles would be an equalizer in such a conflict. McCarter and Phoenix Force had been on the receiving end of such a remote-controlled attack before, when someone hijacked the controls of a Predator and turned its lethal firepower against the grounded team. Only luck and Gary Manning's expert marksmanship had kept the missile from killing half of the team.

He regarded Manning, who took the bandage off his wrist and fastened a shooting glove around his left hand. The Canadian flexed his fingers, making a fist several times.

"All set, old friend?" McCarter asked.

"I was born ready," Manning replied.

"Knowing you, that's not an idle boast," McCarter returned with a wink. "All right, gang. Mount up and let's get things ready for action."

San Salvador, El Salvador

"HOW'RE WE ON AMMO?" Lyons asked as Grimaldi drove Able Team toward Brujo's home.

"Standard .50 HP, we're well covered. I've only got three magazines of AP left over," Schwarz said. "That fight with the juggernauts was too much."

"How about the rifles we confiscated?" Blancanales inquired.

"About 150 rounds remaining," Schwarz explained. "Not much."

"It might just be enough," Lyons said. "Also, they've got grenade launchers, and they take Pol's 40 mm, which we have plenty of ammo for."

"Trouble is, I reloaded the ammo into two separate magazines," Schwarz replied.

"Less to carry. Who wants the Beowulf with three mags of AP?" Lyons asked.

"You can have it," Blancanales said. "Take mine with the grenade launcher."

"And we've got the standard HP-loaded Beowulfs loaded for anyone else," Schwarz added. "Besides, we'll take the .300s in case we run into any armor-plated opponents."

"If we do, then we can take their weapons and ammo, too," Lyons suggested. "So make it count."

"We'll try," Blancanales replied.

Lyons frowned as he inserted a ceramic trauma plate over the spot where he'd been hit with one of those steel-tipped .300 WSM rounds. He wanted to make certain that the armor of his vest wasn't compromised.

"You going to be okay on that leg?" Blancanales asked. "It's the same one where you dislocated your toe."

"I'll make it," Lyons told him.

The satellite phone warbled.

"Go, Barb," Lyons answered.

"Things just hit the big time," Price said on the other end. "The NRO gave us pics of the Salvadoran border. Honduras and Guatemala have been closed down. There are tanks already on the move across the major roads."

"Any hostile actions?" Lyons inquired.

"Nothing yet, but the carrier group hasn't reached the Salvadoran coast."

"Got a timetable?"

Price paused to double check. "Call it sixteen hours at full steam. They'll be sending planes in ten."

"The way that Fixx hit us with those super-soldiers, she's not being rushed to action by us," Lyons stated.

"You sure?" Price asked.

"Check the latest deployments to the Middle East," Lyons suggested.

"Right again, Carl," Price admitted. "Transport flights are dedicated toward resupply and delivery of support troops, and they just left en masse this morning."

"With that much matériel and personnel sent overseas, we won't have much left over to drop on El Salvador," Lyons explained. "Her timetable is still on schedule. We haven't affected a thing."

"Not exactly, Ironman," Kurtzman interjected. "The Honduran border is only at eighty percent effectiveness. Phoenix Force's hit on Puerto Peñasco interrupted a last-minute delivery of Ankylosaurs."

Lyons grinned. "Way to go, David."

"It'll still be a meat grinder for any conventional forces inserted by land, and the coast," Kurtzman began. "We can't tell. Those mobile units are too small and concealable."

"They weren't much taller than a man, and maybe twice as wide. You could hide four in a copse of trees easily," Lyons recounted.

"So you'll still have to get those destruct codes ready," Kurtzman admonished.

"Yeah," Lyons replied. "Unless…"

"Of course!" Schwarz snapped. "I took one out without a preprogramed code! Granted, it was against one that had been packed with C-4, but it might not have been packets attached to the unit that detonated."

"And we didn't include that information in our report to Rogers," Lyons stated. "And unless they have a tap on our communications with the Farm…"

"Give me Gadgets," Kurtzman requested.

"Able might not have to hit Brujo," Price stated.

"No, we still have to take him down," Schwarz answered. "He's the one directing the Salvadoran coup forces. He has to go down, and he has to go down in a way that's big, ugly and flashy. And we're not certain this would work against the Ankylosaurs, either."

"We'll try it anyway," Price announced. "You just be careful, okay?"

"Careful gets you killed, Barb," Schwarz replied. "What we will do is open a can of ass, open another can of whoop, stir thoroughly and throw Ironman in the mix. Anything that can swallow the cocktail is welcome to control Central America."

Lyons heard Schwarz bray with laughter. "What did she say, Gadgets?"

"Fuckin' A," Schwarz returned with a grin. "Welcome to Planet Ironman. I'm your guide, Mr. Wizard."

"Yeah, well tell the kids at home how to detonate those missile launchers, Mr. Wizard. Chances are, the Ankylosaurs will be garrisoned around them, and even if the initial detonation doesn't take them out, the radio pulse will drive their sensors wild enough to force them to attack the artillery units," Lyons suggested.

"Working on it," Schwarz replied.

VINCENZO BRUJO'S EYES opened, the lids rubbing across them like twin swatches of sandpaper. His head pounded, and he realized that he was suffering the aftereffects of his alcoholic binge. He cursed silently. It was all Eosin's fault. She'd drawn him into this maddening scheme. Now, a team of professional assassins who had gutted the infrastructure of ORDEN and the ESA were hot on his trail, and they weren't going to stop until his head was on a pike.

He sat up slowly, head throbbing angrily, punishing him for his excess. He wanted to tell it to shut up, but he knew he deserved it.

Brujo's greed had led him down the slippery slope he was on. And it was no longer just slippery. He was caught up in an avalanche of international mayhem that would end with him dead, either at the hands of the Cowboy Jihad, or when Eosin decided she was through with the drunken, ineffectual bastard she played like a mandolin.

"You stupid bastard," he cursed himself. "A pretty ass, a promise of power and everything you've spent years rebuilding is now at stake."

Brujo looked over to the nightstand and opened the top drawer. Within was a bottle of tequila, the same foul concoction that was responsible for his splitting hangover. Its sloshing contents called to him, reminding him that the hair of the dog was the perfect cure for his pain.

Instead, his gaze fell upon the wooden slabs sand-wiching chromed steel. He reached down and pulled out his .38 Super and racked the slide. A fresh round snapped into the barrel, and he flicked on the safety.

The hair of the dog that bit you was good for the ails of a hangover, but a high-powered bullet had proved a far more lasting solution. It had removed headaches in the form of crusading priests, nosy reporters and other forms of dissidents well enough for the past three decades. And he remembered Eosin's admonishment about the vulnerability of her head. She may have worn bullet-resistant polymers across her chest, but her skull was vulnerable.

One bullet, between the eyes, and Brujo would regain control of his hectic life.

He stuffed the locked and cocked .38 Super into his waistband, ran his fingers through the tangle of hair that stuck out at all angles, then left his bedroom. Two of his bodyguards looked at him, confusion coloring their faces.

"Who is the master of this household?" he asked them.

"You are," one of them said. "Why do you ask?"

"I am the master of this household. Good. And who told you to put me to bed like a child?"

"It was Miss Eosin," the other answered.

"And you follow her orders?" Brujo prodded him.

The bodyguard looked to his friend, who stepped back.

"It was in your best interest," the poor bastard answered.

Brujo lunged forward, wrapping his massive hands around the guard's throat. Twisting with all of his might, the Salvadoran supremacist wrenched the bodyguard's head around almost 180 degrees. Vertebrae snapped and cracked, and the man jerked spasmodically. Brujo let go and the corpse flopped to the floor, on his back and facedown, thanks to Brujo's strength.

"I decide my own best interests from now on," Brujo announced loudly.

"Is that so, Vincenzo?" Eosin's voice asked from down the hall.

Brujo whirled and brought up his gleaming, nickel-plated pistol. He fired two shots at head level before he could take in the sight that met him. Sparks exploded off of Fixx's helmet.

Eosin wasn't wearing the midnight-black, skintight uniform she had supplied for Brujo's reborn death squads. Instead, she was wrapped in gleaming chrome plates connected by dull, light gray polymer. Even though she had to have been behind enough armor plating to stop a cannon, the armor conformed to her every curve, compliementing her full, sensuous figure. She moved smoothly and freely, unhindered thanks to the polymer joints. She was flanked by two more men in masculine versions of those gleaming war suits, each carrying impressive-looking rifles. In Eosin's hand was a machine pistol, but it was casually pointed at the floor.

"What…" Brujo began.

The woman sighed. Her face was hidden by a mirror-polished faceplate, and a little red light suddenly cut in, poking out of her wrist. "I was originally going to use this to protect myself from the team when they attacked your home. Fortunately, I put it on in time for your little tantrum, Vincenzo."

"They will not follow you," Brujo challenged. "You cannot kill me!"

One of the men to the woman's right flipped up his helmet. Even framed by the open faceplate, the armored thug could have passed for Brujo's twin brother.

"Julio?" Eosin asked.

"They will not follow you," Julio mocked, matching Brujo inflection for inflection. "You cannot kill me."

The look-alike closed his visor just in time to deflect an angry bullet Brujo fired at him. Julio raised an armored middle finger in defiance.

"Plastic surgery, Vincenzo. I knew you were coming unhinged, and El Salvador is just too valuable to my project," Eosin explained. The red light on the back of her wrist was connected to a dot on Brujo's chest. The woman had a laser targeting scope built into her forearm armor.

Brujo stepped back as Julio and his faceless partner opened fire with their rifles. Brujo's "loyal" bodyguard exploded as .300 WSM rounds tore through his chest. The corpse slammed into the wall and left a sticky, bloody trail behind as he collapsed to the ground. Brujo's throat tightened and he raised his pistol against her.

"You've stolen my dignity, bitch." Brujo spit. "But I will die like a man!"

He fired at Eosin again, emptying the pistol. Bullets sparked on her metal-protected breasts and helmet-guarded face. The .38 Super locked open empty, and Brujo threw his pistol at the invulnerable witch who had destroyed his life. The gun bounced off her armor and he charged at her.

Eosin shook her head slowly, sadly, and Brujo felt his guts suddenly boil to life as if molten lava had been poured down his throat. He looked down and saw a line of holes across his white shirt, tiny little punctures from the 6.5 mm Bofors machine pistol in her hand. Brujo tried to take another step, but his legs wouldn't obey him. Something flashed from the end of Eosin's arm, and she slashed her arm across his midsection. The burning in his gut suddenly stopped after a final surge of pain.

He stumbled, crashing hard to his knees, but he didn't feel any pain from the impact. His intestines flooded forth through his wounded abdomen, and Fixx retracted a bloody blade into her armor's forearm housing.

Brujo howled in rage, incoherent. His brain had stopped working, only the desire to kill this chrome-plated temptress keeping his heart beating.

Eosin raised the Bofors and worked the trigger again.

Brujo's skull exploded and his decapitated corpse splashed forward in a pool of gore.

"You could have been big, Vincenzo," Eosin said with a sigh.

"Leave this pile of shit here. We've got visitors coming."

Julio and his partner nodded and went to their stations.

Washington, D.C.

THE WHITE HOUSE MEETING table was abuzz as Hal Brognola took the report from Stony Man Farm over his cell phone. The President glanced at Brognola, and frowned as he saw the reaction on the head Fed's face to the call.

The President walked over to Brognola in the corner as the Joint Chiefs and cabinet secretaries discussed the latest intel from Central America.

"What's the deal, Hal?" the Man asked him.

"Able and Phoenix are just about to make their last moves," Brognola explained. "If they can't do the job, El Salvador is going to be a hard nut to crack."

"Yeah," the chief executive admitted. "The NRO has been trying to determine how the coast looks, but going by what your people said confronted them in Arizona, I'm not too confident on any naval approaches."

"By the time we get a coalition in place, the enemy will have been firmly entrenched," Brognola added. "With coastal missile defenses like what we've projected, any embargo we put up is going to be tough to enforce. They can target our ships, yet let through entire fleets of freighters to resupply them."

"If it's any consolation, I don't think the Farm's teams are going to be needed in the Middle East," the President offered with a weak smile. "Our own armored divisions have proven capable of handling the Ankylosaur threat with minimal losses."

"Still too damned many," Brognola growled.

"I agree, Hal," the President responded. "The reinforcements and resupply are going to make things easier for our boys, but that's not going to help in the long run if we have to split our focus to cover the El Salvadoran crisis as well."

"It was a sucker play, and it suckered us good," Brognola told him. "Only the fact that we were tipped off, entirely by accident, had us looking in the right place at the right time."

"The CIA chief is busy trying to collate all of the Company's non-Langley computer records and resources to give us a better understanding of what we might be up against," the chief executive replied. "But take a look at him."

"He hasn't slept since Langley was hit," Brognola stated. "I've been there too many times myself."

"The Farm has suffered its share of attacks," the President mused. "After the shooting incident at the gate back in the nineties, they thought that they were fairly well off."

"Nobody expected gunships and platoons of bulletproof assassins to strike in the middle of Virginia," Brognola told him. "We were just lucky that we had someone there when someone hit that blind side."

"The enemy only has to get lucky once, Hal," the President admonished. "We have to be ready for anything."

"We are. Between Mexico City and El Salvador, my people will do everything they can to get us out of this mess."

The President looked at the map on the wall. "Right in our own backyard."

"That's why we're here, sir," Brognola told him. "To watch for the threats nobody else is looking out for."

"Thanks, Hal," the chief executive stated. He went back to his chair and called the meeting to order.

Brognola closed his eyes and took a deep breath. The deadline had been lifted on Able and Phoenix. The President had given them their full head, but it wouldn't matter. Right now, both teams were up against the wall facing off with a conspiracy that was only a step away from sealing the fate of Central America. If they failed, it would be a nightmare that would shake this hemisphere for years.

"Godspeed, boys," Brognola whispered. "Godspeed."

Mexico City

OTOMO GOLGO SKYLINE, checked on his men at the last minute. While Eosin had a small army of security guards hired for the factory, they weren't of the same caliber as his personal guard. The ninja master double-checked his own body armor. Unlike Fixx, who wanted to show off her technological power by parading around in a gleaming, chrome-accented suit of armor, Skyline preferred that the impact plates on his outfit-to-be decorated with mottled, dull-gloss shades of black and gray. He preferred stealth, and the low-profile uniform that Eosin had provided for him and his ninjas fit that bill perfectly.

Golgo also appreciated that these uniforms resembled the armor she'd provided to Brujo's men. These suits would need a heavy-caliber rifle to punch through, not the relatively lighter PDW rounds like those from a Bofors or an FN.

Unless their mysterious enemies were prepared to take on nothing short of a squadron of Ankylosaur tanks, there was no way they had the firepower to take down Golgo, his personal commander Tetsugomo, or the ten ninjas positioned around the factory.

Golgo smiled. The ninjas were armed with the machine pistols, insufficient to punch through their armor, but enough to slice through anyone else's gear. Unlike the failed assault on Langley, where he'd lost some of his best men, the enemy commandos wouldn't be able to turn their own weapons against them.

"Sir! A helicopter just came over the fence!" one of Eosin's security guards alerted him.

Golgo looked at the camera. "What about the launchers?"

"No good. They're too low to the ground," the guard stated. "If the thing rode any lower, it would need wheels."

"Damn," Golgo cursed. He activated his helmet communicator. "They're coming. Get ready. They surpassed our air defense."

He nodded as the helicopter drew closer. He preferred it this way. The commandos were going to see just how hard of a wall they were going to bounce off.

CHAPTER EIGHTEEN

Charlie Mott couldn't have kept the Hughes 500D lower to the ground if he'd gotten out and dragged it on a rope, and David McCarter blessed the hotshot ex-DEA pilot for it. He clutched the DSA-58 rifle tightly when he saw objects racing along the horizon. There were five of them, like black, puck-shaped scorpions, but moving so fast that they kicked up choking clouds of dust and sand in their wake.

"Ankylosaurs!" McCarter shouted out.

"Bail here! I'll take care of them!" Mott answered. "Gary, I need you to take out the last one."

"Sounds like one of your plans," Manning said as he elbowed McCarter in the ribs.

Phoenix Force dropped out the doors and hit the ground running. Mott flipped the Hughes up and swung it over toward the charging remote tanks as streams of autofire filled the air. McCarter could hear the man whistling Wagner as he dived at them.

"His radio's on," McCarter hissed.

The Ankylosaurs reacted instantly to the approaching aircraft, homing in on his transmissions. Mott jinked left, then right, swerving the nimble Hughes through blistering waves of high-powered weaponry. Mott's plan became evident when he dipped and threaded the needle between two of the combat drones. Head guns and tail cannons erupted, the robots trying to keep up with him. The miniature tanks swept each other with armor-piercing bullets and explosive shells. Their domed frames collapsed under the devastating assaults. One of them had its tail ripped from its back, while the other belched flame from a massive crater in its front end.

One of the Ankylosaurs jerked, coming under remote control and it swiveled toward Phoenix Force.

Manning hit the ground, braced the .50-caliber McMillan and stroked the trigger. A 750-grain slug punched through the tail boom, smashing the grenade launcher into useless scrap. Several 40 mm shells cycled toward the muzzle, striking the deformed tube and jamming it. Manning threw the bolt again and fired a bit lower as streams of autofire chewed the ground in front of him. Manning's second slug struck home on the tail boom, punching through a jammed shell in the launcher. The heavy bullet detonated the grenade, shock waves rippling through the tail boom and blowing off the back end of the Ankylosaur.

The streams of fire from the head guns swung off course, plowing into empty sand while Encizo and Hawkins charged forward. They got within 250 yards of the damaged combat drone and fired their own M-203s simultaneously. The twin high-explosive grenades im-

pacted with the staggered remains of the deadly machine
and flipped it onto its back like a gigantic turtle. The
head tore free as twisted head gun barrels blocked the
thunderous parade of heavy-caliber machinegun fire.

Three down, McCarter counted as he and James
swung their attention toward the remaining pair of Ankylosaurs. The joystick control of the command staff
lacked the automatic reflexes of the robots' central pro-
cessors. One of the machines far behind on the learning curve winged its partner with a salvo of
rocket-propelled grenades, but the explosive shells
glanced off the curved frame of the other drone. The
human pilot didn't return fire. It knew the difference between friendly fire and a blatant attack, unlike the automatic pilot of the machines.

So much for a free lunch, McCarter mused as he leveled his grenade launcher at the base of the one that accidentally hammered its compatriot. McCarter's
grenade struck underneath the bulk of the war machine
and detonated against one of its axles. Six-ounces of
high explosive tore the support strut off the undercar-
riage and shredded the wheels on a second axle. The machine tipped, and its discus shape dug into the sand.
Before the Briton could celebrate, the robot's two remaining sets of wheels powered it around, tail boom and
head guns swiveling to target him. James fired his shell,
striking the Ankylosaur between the dual horns of its
head guns, the minibomb caving in the robot's skull and
splaying its barrels wide on impact. Rocket-propelled
shells from the monstrosity's tail whipped out wildly,
chewing up the landscape. Hawkins and Encizo ran

away from the line of fire as the combat drone cut loose blindly.

The undamaged machine hit its engines and ignored the unarmed helicopter. The five humans on foot had proved to be a far more dangerous threat, and its operator directed it toward them.

Mott saw this and brought the Hughes down hard on top of the Ankylosaur. The landing skids bent double, and the tail rotor slammed hard into the grenade-launching boom on the back of the battle robot. The head of the Ankylosaur dug into the ground, its twin spearlike head gun barrels catching in the sand. Wheels powering forward, the machine snapped off its own head unit and tossed Mott and the helicopter off its back.

The Stony Man pilot struggled with his machine, but luckily the Hughes was so low to the ground that when it nosed in, rotors snapping against the earth, Mott was unharmed by the impact. The headless Ankylosaur plowed on, as if to grind Phoenix Force beneath its massive weight.

"Gary!" McCarter called. "Stop it!"

"Right," Manning answered. He swung his rifle away from the approaching combat drone and fired a single shot. Suddenly the remote-controlled drone swerved, as if it had lost all sight of its enemies. Stripped of weaponry by Mott's collision, as well as its cameras, all it had left were engines and wheels. It zoomed past McCarter, close enough for the Briton to see that a damaged camera dangled from the remnants of the minitank's tail.

"What did you do?" McCarter asked.

"Took out the security camera," Manning answered.

The crippled machine's grenade launcher locked empty, and it spun in frustration.

"Redundant cameras. Charlie accidentally took both sets out when he took out its weapons," James commented.

"Go check on him," McCarter ordered. "Gary…"

"I spot six guards at the corner of the main building," the Canadian answered. "They've got rifles."

McCarter nodded and dropped prone beside his friend. "Let me take them. Save that fifty for when we need it."

"Go right ahead, boss," Manning replied. He swept the factory compound as McCarter targeted the distant gunmen.

Even with a short barrel, the chopped FN FAL had far more reach than the security force's M-16s. It was akin to shooting ducks in a barrel, but McCarter didn't doubt that the gunmen he cut down with a half dozen shots would have had any compunctions. After all, they'd taken to the field in the aftermath of a swarm of tanks. McCarter finished with the gunmen and got to his feet.

"Good shooting," Manning complimented him.

"I'm not completely useless with a rifle—" McCarter returned.

"Missile," Manning suddenly cut him off.

"Artillery!" McCarter bellowed, and he looked to see the arcing trails of rockets pierce the sky. He turned and saw James pulling the stunned Mott out of his pilot's seat, then broke into a full run toward the two men. He reached them just as the first warhead speared into the ground with an earthshaking detonation. Mc-

Carter grabbed a fistful of Mott's flight suit and James had his Jet Aer dagger out, slashing at his safety harness. The whole process felt like it took a year, but a second later, all three Stony Man operatives hurled themselves from the wreckage of the helicopter. Its bulk shuddered as another explosive rocket slammed into it, the mass of the crippled machine shielding the fragile men in its shadow.

"Gary…" David gritted.

Manning swept the rooftop of the factory and found that each of the four parapets along the side of the building facing them had fallen away, revealing squat launchers as tall as a man. Two-man crews worked feverishly to feed fresh shells into the artillery pieces, and Manning pulled the trigger on his McMillan. The 750-grain .50-caliber slug smashed one warhead in the hands of a loader and detonated it. The resultant blast destroyed the launcher and hurled the operating crew off the rooftop like rag dolls.

The remaining three pivoted as if they were one unit and homed in on Manning.

"Christ," Manning cursed as he ran for the shelter of a destroyed Ankylosaur. Missiles dropped from the sky, and the shock wave pushed him along against the wrecked shell of the combat drone. His back was killing him, and in taking cover, he slammed his left hand against the broken hull of the minitank. Pain flared in his arm, jolting all the way up to his shoulder and his McMillan spilled into the dirt.

McCarter and James cut loose at the rooftop artillery crews, but their rifles didn't have the reach of Manning's big Fifty. All they did was pepper the wall of the building with slugs that lost their battle with gravity.

"Too far," McCarter growled. He spotted a lone shape race toward Manning. Rockets slammed into the landscape, hurling clouds of dirt into the air, obscuring the battlefield.

The Briton cursed, when he heard Hawkins's drawl cut over the radio. "Hey, Gary. Sorry I'm too late to pop an Ankylosaur, but you did promise to let me play with your McMillan."

"Go right ahead, T.J.," Manning offered.

The Southerner picked the fallen rifle off the ground and pressed the fiberglass stock against his shoulder. "Which setting on the scope is mine?"

"Dial it to four," Manning instructed, and Hawkins did so. The crosshairs in the heavy Bushnell moved lower and to the right, suiting the ex-Ranger's shooting style. Locked on, Hawkins adjusted for wind and bullet drop, then let fly with a shot at the rooftop.

One of the artillery launchers exploded in sparks as he struck it in its control panel's guts. The deadly payload on board was unharmed, and the two crewmen took cover behind the machinery.

"Move!" Manning bellowed, but Hawkins grabbed the Canadian by the shoulder and held him down.

"Wait…" Hawkins replied.

The line of artillery shells fell haphazardly around them.

"Of course. They're painting us with a laser," Manning stated. "And they kicked up too much smoke to aim accurately."

"As if the launchers were aiming themselves," Hawkins replied. "Those guys are just feeding them rockets."

"Can you see the laser unit?" Manning asked. He flexed his hand and fist, twisting it in a circle to get it back in working order.

"I'm looking for it," Hawkins replied, searching through the Bushnell scope.

"Found it," Encizo called.

Manning smiled, glad that the other members of Phoenix Force had put Aimpoint scopes on their M-16s. Though the rifles only had minimal magnification, it was still enough to allow them a good view of distant targets, like snipers or enemy soldiers with laser target indicators.

"Third window from side two," Encizo pointed out. "Level five."

Hawkins adjusted his aim on the building and spotted a man with a large projector in his hand through a half-open window. He pulled the trigger on the McMillan and when he rode out the recoil of the massive bolt-action, he saw that the window was empty.

"Did I get him?" Hawkins asked.

"Yeah," James said. "That Fifty is some scary shit."

Hawkins grinned. "I might buy one for myself."

"With what paycheck?" Manning asked.

"I could buy it used from you," Hawkins returned. "You're rich."

Manning picked up Hawkins's scoped M-16/M-203. "Tell you what. I'll trade you."

"Sweet deal," Hawkins answered.

"All right, let's move in!" McCarter called. "Before they get someone else on the laser designator."

SKYLINE WATCHED in disbelief as the members of Phoenix Force and their pilot rushed toward the factory. They had cut through his force of Ankylosaurs and crippled their artillery rockets. He could have shifted the command modules for the launchers on the other parapets, it would only take a minute, but he'd lost one of his men with the laser designator, and it would take precious time for him to get operable artillery modules up to the roof.

"Invaders approaching on foot!" Skyline warned. He picked up a matched pair of Bofors machine pistols and made sure they were loaded. Spare magazines hung in belts on his hips, and the little hammer-shaped guns were looped over his shoulders on slings.

He lowered his faceplate and took to the stairs, pausing as he ran across a couple of his nonarmored staff. They were Fist of God mercenaries who had accompanied him from Panama to bolster the security force of Fixx's manufacturing plant.

"Guard the remote-control center," Skyline ordered. "If the enemy gets in there, destroy everything that you can."

"What about the invaders?" the two Christian Identity goons asked.

"We'll handle them. But if they get that control room, it's all over," Skyline warned. "Defend it."

The militiamen rushed past him to the control room. He hoped that they would be able to hold the line against the invaders.

Skyline pushed the thought from his mind. They would have to split up to get past him, and even if they did, he had his eight best men in armor that could defeat all but the most powerful of rifles. The American commandos were doomed the minute they stepped inside.

He disappeared down the stairwell, ready to make them bleed.

CALVIN JAMES ACCOMPANIED Gary Manning as the pair rushed into the main production center. Lines of Ankylosaur shells sat on conveyor belts, assembly robots hanging or poking up from the floor, the armlike structures silent.

"Shit," James hissed. "It looks like there must be fifty of these things."

"This is just the chassis assembly area," Manning said. "The whole production line shows—down."

James ducked behind a six-foot-tall robot as autofire lanced at him. Bullets sparked on the yellow frame of the assembly armature and hydraulic fluid burst out like green blood. Manning cut loose with his M-16, ripping apart the hidden shooter. Another gunman perched behind a mostly completed robot fired over the top of the curved dome, forcing the big Canadian behind cover.

James leveled his rifle and spotted the rifleman's feet underneath the frame of the Ankylosaur and triggered his weapon. Shinbones and calf muscles exploded under the ex-SEAL's assault and the would-be killer toppled to the concrete floor, wailing in agony. James triggered his weapon again and the burst shattered his skull.

"Gary?" James asked.

"I'm fine," Manning responded. "These guys aren't even wearing the second-stringer armor."

"Yeah. Light resistance so far," James mused. "I don't know…"

Suddenly the tall black man whirled as he spotted movement out of the corner of his eye. "Gary!"

Before he could bring his rifle to bear, the scrape of a boot on the crosswalk above him gave James all the warning he needed to roll under the conveyor belt. Automatic fire chopped through the air and splashed against the belt and its rollers. Armor-piercing ammo punched through heavy rubber and tore pockmarks in the concrete. James rolled out from behind the cover of the supports for the rollers, heavy girdered steel, and triggered his M-16 to fire back through the belt, then squirmed back to cover. Heavy feet crashed into the belt over his head, and the Phoenix Force medic rolled to the other side of the production line as more automatic fire chased him.

Reaching the cover of a manufacturing armature, James shielded himself from a follow-up burst and rapidly reloaded his rifle. The wraith in black somersaulted across the top of the conveyor belt before James could charge the breech of his rifle, and the Phoenix Force medic reversed his weapon. Instead of the standard fiberglass stock, his rifle, as were the others on his team, had been replaced with a tubular steel collapsing stock. It made the long-barreled weapon easier to store and handier to maneuver. The steel stock also had the added bonus of having enough strength to shatter glass or to break a neck with a hard strike. James crashed the tubestock of his rifle across the attacker's neck and hurled the marauder to the floor.

The gunman struggled to recover his weapon, attached to his armor by its sling, but James pressed his attack. The steel stock rebounded off the armored assassin's helmet, but the curved shape of the headgear deflected most of the blow. The killer let the machine pistol hang on its sling and stabbed outward with a hard punch that caught James in the stomach. Fortunately, the ammunition pouches on James's vest also absorbed most of the blow, but the Phoenix Force commando wouldn't get a second lucky chance. A triangular blade snicked out of the back of a forearm housing, like a built-in sword, and the razor-sharp tip ripped across James's chest.

James ducked most of the slash, but the slice parted several layers of his armor. He kicked hard, striking the man in the knee, but only succeeded in knocking the armored swordsman off balance. The ex-SEAL swung his M-16 around and loaded the chamber. The juggernaut lunged forward, wading through a stream of rifle fire that glanced off the curved and angled surfaces of his protective uniform. James blocked the triangular blade with the frame of his rifle and kicked the bullet-proof ninja in the stomach. That was enough to knock the wind out of him for a second, and James drew his Jet Aer dagger in one smooth movement.

This was his last option, and the Phoenix Force knife fighter threw all his weight against his blade-packing adversary. The point of the fine dagger struck the armored killer between his shoulder and neck, piercing through the high-tensile polymer fibers just under his helmet and collar. Five inches of steel sank into the assassin's neck, and the killer jerked violently. His departing spasm opened up James's right biceps as the forearm sword connected. James let go of his dagger as the weight and leverage of the corpse ripped it away from him.

Bleeding and winded, James hastily reloaded his M-16 when he looked over to see Manning's battle with his own opponent.

The armored ninja dropped on Gary Manning's back like a ton of bricks, and the impact jarred his sore and battered muscles. The brawny Canadian dropped to the concrete, but caught himself with his right forearm, sparing aggravating his sprained left wrist any further. Manning jerked his left elbow into the killer's side with enough force to throw the man onto the production line.

The juggernaut scooped up his machine pistol and opened fire, point-blank, and Manning barely hit the floor behind a tool cabinet. A stream of 6.5 mm holes perforated through the cabinet's sheet-metal wall, showing the Canadian that his protection was flimsy. Manning let out a grunt, then threw his shoulder against the rolling tool chest. It was five feet tall, and weighed at least one hundred pounds, and with Manning's bulk and strength behind it, it shot forward like a missile and hyperextended the ninja's gun arm, snapping the elbow joint. Manning staggered backward, his chest a mass of bruises under his body armor. The Bofors PDW ammo had been stopped by the combined resistance of the tool chest and his Kevlar, but Manning still hurt.

The Canadian threw the tool cabinet aside, grabbed the ninja's wounded arm and twisted with all of his might. Even battered, bruised and worn down by days of pain and exertion, he was still able to make the armored assassin howl for mercy as Manning folded his arm like a chicken wing. The killer kicked and struggled, trying to reach his holstered pistol with his off hand, but Manning wrapped one burly arm around the helmet.

"You know what I like about you armored creeps?" Manning growled. "The easy twist-off tops."

The assassin kicked and struggled, trying to escape, and the Canadian wrenched on the helmet violently. Vertebrae exploded with the sound of shattering bottles.

Manning slumped against the conveyor belt, breathing hard. A wave of nausea swept through him and he exploded on the floor, bile erupting from his lips and nostrils.

"Gary?" James asked.

Manning stood, wiping his mouth and chin on his sleeve. "You look like hell, Cal. Let me get that arm for you."

James looked at his bleeding arm. His whole sleeve was soaked through, and it was numb. "I was just going to ask if you were all right."

Manning looked back at the broken marauder. "All things considered, I feel fabulous."

James leaned back and let Manning bandage him up.

"WE'VE GOT an update," Hawkins announced. "These suckers have sword blades built into their forearm housings. Also, they're black, like the other armor, and don't seem to hinder their…"

Encizo normally would have allowed the youngest Phoenix Force member to finish passing on the intel, but the Cuban reacted with blinding swiftness, hauling him out of the way of a figure in the shadows. The glint of light along the forearm blade had given the assassin away, and Encizo caught it before Hawkins was skewered. With a powerful kick, Encizo smashed the wrist of the assassin, pinning the killer against the shelving unit.

Out of the shadows of several other aisles in the warehouse, two more black-clad killers stepped into the open, machine pistols spitting fire. Encizo grunted as a 6.5 mm round struck him in the shoulder blade, stopped by the combination of protective heavy body armor and his own powerful muscles and the heavy bone of the scapula. The impact stunned the stocky Phoenix Force warrior, however, and the pinned ninja was freed.

Hawkins, flat on his butt, swung the McMillan rifle around and fired from the hip. The massive rifle kicked like a shotgun, but its muzzle brake and excellent design of the fiberglass stock kept the recoil from hurting him. Instead, the juggernaut who had been Hawkins's target was bodily lifted off his feet and hurled through several boxes of parts.

The marauders stopped and looked at their comrade, who lay still, sprawled with his limbs twisted to unnatural angles. The Southerner rapidly worked the bolt on his McMillan Fifty and triggered it again, but the two assassins ducked out of sight. Encizo lurched to his feet, left arm numbed by the armor-piercing bullet. He was certain that his shoulder blade had been broken, but

Hawkins had bought them some time. He also had proved that the juggernauts were vulnerable. Blood poured from the ninja's shattered chest plate, and tangled arms and legs only twitched as a dying nervous system misfired.

"I've got you covered, Rafe," Hawkins said, back on his feet. He loaded another big M-2 round into the breech and scanned the darkness.

One shelf shifted and the Phoenix Force warriors lurched out of the way. Above them, the shadow of a ninja leaped from one unit to another. Encizo, having battled ninjas on more occasions than he cared to remember, spun to face the second surviving killer as he used his partner's distracting misdirection.

"Surprise," Encizo snarled and he held down the trigger on his M-16. The barrel was only inches from the assassin's belly, and when the 72-grain hunting rounds struck the high-tensile polyfibers, they held, for a moment. However, against a full 30-round magazine, unloaded at point-blank range, even Fixx's best work was insufficient. Had Encizo aimed higher, at the chrome-and-ceramic reinforced chest plates, or to the left or the right only a little bit, the stream of ultrasonic bullets, striking at a full 3200 feet per second, would have glanced off molded polycarbonate. Instead, Encizo had gone for the seam, an impossible shot at anything longer than an arm's length.

The ninja's head shook wildly as his guts were blown to shreds. Hawkins spun in reaction to the newcomer, but it was unnecessary. The marauder was dead on his feet. Encizo kicked the corpse to the ground and hauled

Hawkins back to cover. One shelving unit shook violently, and Hawkins threw his weight against it when Encizo tripped. Hawkins struggled against the heavy weight, possessing neither the massive musculature of Gary Manning, nor the broad, powerful arms and shoulders of his Cuban friend. Boxes tumbled off the framework, one bouncing off his back, and Hawkins stumbled.

The last ninja clambered to the floor with spiderlike ease and leveled his weapon at the stunned Southerner. "Surprise this, you fools."

Hawkins looked up, breathing hard. "Wait!"

"For what?" the marauder asked.

A thunderbolt exploded from between Hawkins's legs, and the steel-clad killer jerked violently, his leg torn off at the hip. The murderer's head bounced off the concrete.

"For my partner to take advantage of my own distraction," Hawkins said.

"We'll have you smoking ninjas on a daily basis at this rate, T.J.," Encizo quipped, letting the McMillan drop to the floor. "Man that thing kicks!"

"You'll be okay?" Hawkins asked.

"Yeah, the feeling's coming back to my hand," Encizo replied. "Load my M-16 and we'll continue the hunt for these bastards."

Hawkins nodded and helped his wounded partner.

CHARLIE MOTT WAS on David McCarter's heels, armed with a borrowed Phoenix Force P-90 machine pistol. "Built-in swords, night-vision optics in the helmets, radios…"

"Quiet, Charlie," McCarter admonished. He checked the load in his FN FAL, the compact .30-caliber rifle having proved invaluable in killing two of the armor-encased assassins when Mott's P-90 proved ineffective. After this, he had three more magazines of twenty shots apiece. It had taken an entire magazine to kill two of the armor-clad killers, and he'd burned up more going against "normal" security forces. "Seven big guns down. Lord knows how many to go."

It was a long, slow walk up the stairwell. McCarter would have taken the steps four at a time in his usual, headstrong fashion, had it not been for the fact that he was hauling a rookie along with him. According to Hawkins's report, he and Encizo had run into lighter resistance after taking care of their trio of ninja opponents. And from their tactics of stealth and misdirection, there was no doubt that these men were ninjas.

McCarter sighed. "Bloody ninjas."

"It beats the rise of the machines outside," Mott quipped.

McCarter glared at the pilot, shutting him up. Mott cinched his old, battered, yellow baseball cap down tighter, its bill poked backward to allow himself the most peripheral vision up, down and to the sides as possible. "There's a radio tower atop this building, so there's a good chance that the remote-control command center is stationed on the top floor."

"And if it isn't?" Mott asked.

"The others are searching other sections of the factory. Still, Manning scoped out the building and he saw a bundle of cables go over the side of the roof and into a top-floor window," McCarter stated. "Chances are that we'll get lucky."

"If we were lucky, we wouldn't be stuck in the middle of Terminator vs. Predator," Mott muttered.

McCarter managed a smirk and reached the top landing, FN FAL leading the way. He reached for the door handle, then jerked back, throwing Mott aside. The metal door shook as armor-piercing rounds punched through it. McCarter cut loose with a double tap, spiking two high-powered rifle rounds back through the door. Mott took cover behind the stony protection of a flight of stairs and ripped off a long burst with his P-90. McCarter motioned for him to hold his fire.

"Don't waste ammo," McCarter told him.

Mott grimaced. "I think I twisted something diving for cover."

McCarter sighed. "Hold the fort, then."

"Screw that," Mott snapped. He hobbled to his feet. "I've seen too many of these movies. It's the dumb shit who lags behind that gets eviscerated when the hero tells him 'stay here and out of the way.'"

McCarter nodded. "If I have to move, I'm leaving you behind."

"I'll keep up," Mott replied.

McCarter cracked the door open, the pilot pressed against the wall to his side. No gunfire ripped through the opening, but the Briton reached back and snatched off Mott's baseball cap.

"Hey," Mott complained softly. McCarter stabbed the bill with his pocketknife, then poked the combination around the corner. An explosion of gunfire shredded the battered old headgear.

The Phoenix Force leader snapped his Browning from its holster and dived through the doorway at knee height. As he sailed above the floor, he spotted the two gunmen responsible for rendering Mott sans chapeau, two Americans with machine pistols, perched in the doorway of a room full of electronics. McCarter popped off a single 9 mm round into the face of the left-hand guard, brains sneezing out of his skull riding 124-grains of copper-jacketed lead. McCarter hit the floor and rolled, zipping a 115-grain full metal jacket bullet into the groin of the right-hand sentry. The guy folded over in agony.

Mott swung around the corner, P-90 tracking, but only saw the wounded gunman. He held his fire.

"Guard him," McCarter growled.

"What?" Mott asked.

McCarter glared, and the pilot did as the Briton ordered.

Mott stood next to the gagging guard, keeping his muzzle pointed at the wounded man.

McCarter had a feeling. He wasn't a man who believed in premonitions, but he'd been in combat enough, received enough calls from his gut instincts that he couldn't discount the theory of his body reacting to threats that his conscious mind wasn't aware of. Perhaps it was a shape in his peripheral vision, or the scrape of a boot, but whatever it was, the British lion was on edge and he returned to the stairwell.

He leaned over the railing, then jerked out of the way as a black shape blurred from underneath the landing. Automatic fire lanced into the ceiling, barely missing McCarter's head, and he fired four quick shots into the concrete at his feet. The .308 rifle bullets punched through the stone and elicited a grunt. McCarter wasn't buying it and he threw the rifle down on its sling. With a lurch, he vaulted over the rail and swung under the landing in an explosive burst of speed. The black-clad figure on the level below had only just begun to creep up the steps to catch the Briton off guard when McCarter slammed into him, feet first. Their bodies crashed against the wall and bounced off. McCarter landed on an upward slope of stairs, while the hardman tumbled back against a downward rail.

Skyline's machine pistols had been knocked from his grasp by the brutality of McCarter's impact, and his first reaction was to extend not one, but two forearm sheathed swords. McCarter scrambled to swing his rifle around, then threw the frame of the weapon up to block one slashing ribbon of deadly steel. The Phoenix Force leader barely danced out of the path of Skyline's second blade. McCarter twisted his rifle and hammered the folding steel stock against his adversary's faceplate with all of his might.

Rattled, the ninja master stumbled, but not before his blade nicked McCarter's forearm. Wincing, the Phoenix Force commander drew back, swung his muzzle down and pulled the trigger. A solitary 7.62 mm NATO round struck Skyline in the upper chest, and bounced off, embedding in the concrete wall of the stairwell.

Skyline lunged forward, the point of his forearm dagger slicing McCarter's shoulder as he swerved out of the path of the strike. The Briton pulled the trigger again, and this time the bullet glanced off the curved slope of Golgo's helmet.

The point-blank rifle shot staggered the armored assassin, and McCarter chopped the stock of his rifle into the ninja master's stomach, driving him back farther. Skyline swung again, the edge only knocking the knit wool cap off of McCarter's head. The Briton lowered his head and slammed his shoulder against his opponent's chest, and immediately regretted it. The cut on the limb split farther, sending a jolt of pain down his back, and it felt as though he'd struck a brick wall. Still, Skyline toppled backward toward the railing.

A forearm blade flashed up, and McCarter stopped it, catching Skyline at the elbow. The armored marauder tried to bring his other blade around, but the Phoenix Force commander wrapped his other hand around his adversary's wrist.

"Stalemate," Skyline taunted. "But you've been through hell. I'm fresh. I'm wrapped in invulnerable armor. And I've been waiting for you."

"Show me what you've got, Skyline," McCarter hissed.

"You recognize me?"

"You talk too big to be a peon," McCarter grunted, straining against Skyline's strength. The ninja master was right. McCarter had been battling across several days against dozens of enemies. Even now, the armored killer was gaining even more leverage.

Suddenly, Skyline's armored faceplate hammered against McCarter's forehead. Jolted, the Phoenix Force commander staggered back, stars flashing in his eyes.

"Congratulations," Skyline taunted. "Not many people know just who sent them to hell when I do the job." He wrapped his hand around one of his bouncing machine pistols. "Bullets or blades?"

McCarter kept silent, blood pouring from a cut on his forehead.

"Hey! Shithead!" Charlie Mott bellowed. Skyline whipped around and flinched as a wave of P-90 machine pistol fire slammed into him. Skyline lowered his arms as he realized that the tiny subgun didn't have the power to affect him in his armor.

"Maybe I'll kill your cavalry first, you Cockney bastard," Skyline said with a laugh.

"Maybe you'll learn to fly on the way down," McCarter snapped. He hurled himself into the armored assassin and carried him over the railing.

The two bodies sailed through space, and it took all of McCarter's speed and agility to hook a handrail on the way down. Gravity wanted to tear the Briton in two, but he hung on with every ounce of strength he had left. Meanwhile, Skyline bounced from railing to railing like an armored table tennis ball until he struck the floor with a sickening crunch.

"Holy-moly!" Mott exclaimed.

McCarter looked down and saw Skyline attempting to rise. One gauntleted hand struggled to wrap around the stock of his machine pistol. The Phoenix Force leader shook his head and with his free hand, tore a grenade off his harness. He bit out the pin, feeling his tooth crunch on the metal, then let the minibomb drop. He spit the cotter pin down for good measure.

Skyline, a.k.a. Otomo Golgo, watched as the little round ball flared as hot as the sun in his visor, instants before the shock wave smashed in his faceplate.

McCarter wrapped his arms around the railing and looked up. "What the bloody hell was that?"

"Giving you a breather to carry out your cunning plan?" Mott asked.

McCarter rolled his eyes. "Dropping my own bloody arse down a stairwell is a cunning plan. Get down here and help me up!"

Mott raced down the steps to the Briton's aid. Mc-Carter smiled inwardly. No, it wasn't the most cunning of plans. But then…it worked.

David McCarter sighed and held on as he waited for Mott to help him back onto the stairs.

CHAPTER NINETEEN

El Salvador

Euclide Potts, the commander of Fixx's Iron Guard, stepped onto the porch overlooking the driveway. Encased in impregnable armor, he felt like a god. And the FX-300 assault rifle in his hand was a thunderbolt worthy of Zeus himself. Granted, it was Angela Eosin herself who was the true goddess, possessed not only of the brilliance to fabricate such awesome weaponry, but of heavenly beauty and the power to twist armies and nations around her slender fingers.

But those who serve the gods also sit at the Pantheon's table. Sure, he'd risked his life for the woman who sought to change the face of the Earth. But the rewards were astronomical. He owned houses around the world, drove the fastest cars, and when he wasn't attending to his mistress' needs, he savored the flesh of some of the most sensual women on the planet.

Potts smirked under his armored faceplate. Yes, it

was good to be a goddess's right-hand man. Whatever he desired, he sampled. And when he was finished with it, he could cast it aside without a second thought, dropping it in the refuse bin of broken dreams and shattered hearts. It didn't matter to the lead Iron Guardsman. He'd done enough bleeding for generals who said he was forbidden to sleep with whomever he wanted to sleep with, to fight for causes that were simply ploys to make some rich oil barons wealthier.

Fixx wasn't full of that bullshit. She wanted to make the world a better place—for her. If someone got in the way, it was Potts's job to take them out. Just like these assholes who called themselves the Cowboy Jihad.

Potts frowned. He remembered when he was in military intelligence. The Cowboy Jihad was the name of a mysterious group claiming credit for the destruction of the Syrian embassy in Lebanon. Artillery rockets loaded with poisonous gas, produced by the Syrians themselves, had been intercepted in Lebanon, en route to destroy much of the Israeli border, guaranteeing the beginning of a near apocalyptic conflagration. Imagine the surprise of the masterminds, waiting at the Syrian embassy, when their own rain of doom came crashing back down on their heads, obliterating them.

Syria made lots of noises, but since an aberrant terrorist group had claimed responsibility, claiming that the Middle East had best beware, a true international incident had been defused. Things had been tense, and the world breathed easier when relations in the region returned to their normal state of cold peace. Angry glares were still exchanged across the borders in that region, and if Fixx had her way, both sides would be allowed to destroy each other in balls of nuclear flame.

Fixx had arranged for another couple of situations recently, attempting to hurl the region into chaos. Potts hadn't been involved, but both had failed due to dogged outside interference. He wondered, absently, what would have happened if he had applied his considerable skills to those missions.

He would never know. Potts lived in the present, and he fought to concentrate on the here and now. The wall of the estate was thick and high, preventing the possibility of breaching at any point other than the main gate. The top edges of the walls were covered with broken glass and ringed with concertina wire, promising to snag and slow down anyone foolish enough to climb over. Any helicopters coming over would be met by Eosin's modular missile launcher, configured for antiaircraft combat.

That just left the gate, and any truck that made it through the wrought-iron bars would run right into a cordon of Ankylosaur combat drones, under the command of a trained team of Fixx's operators. Unless these cowboys possessed a tank, there was no way in hell that they would survive a gauntlet of 40 mm grenade launchers, 25 mm cannon and .50-caliber machine guns.

And if that happened, Potts had also deployed thirty of Brujo's bodyguards, Colonel Logan's Fist of God militiamen, and finally, Potts and three members of the Iron Guard.

It was a ring of steel and fire that no man would dare brave.

Logan walked up, wiping the sweat off his forehead. "Don't you get hot in that thing?"

"It's the latest in environmental design. I've got a cooling unit on my back that chills water and pumps it through capillaries in the armor," Potts replied.

"I could use one of those," Logan admitted.

"Stick around, Colonel. Who knows, you might just make an excellent Iron Guardsman," Potts offered. "I lost four of my men today."

"Yeah. I heard," Logan answered. "I think an operation similar to this one took apart what was left of my California contingent awhile back."

"That's why you're so eager to ride Fixx's coattails in Central America," Potts stated.

"Yeah. I want to be able to see my enemy coming," Logan snarled. "That way I'm ready to give them a fight. I'll go into heaven a warrior, standing tall, no matter what."

Potts nodded. He forgot how goofy these Christian Identity bastards were. While Potts had been a churchgoer himself, his priests were more interested in tolerance and moderation, not like Logan's white supremacist freaks who saw the Zionist Occupation Government around every shadow. Potts wondered if he should have offered Logan a spot on the Iron Guard, considering how these militia maggots considered people of alternative lifestyles let alone skin color. He doubted Logan's sincerity toward Eosin, obviously a Hispanic woman of dark, rich skin and deep, sultry eyes.

Then again, Logan seemed to be practical. He kept his beliefs in his pocket when it came to the people who gave him guns and money.

Potts just doubted how long that would last.

Gunfire crackled at the gate, and Potts imagined that maybe this Cowboy Jihad would give him just enough cover to arrange for Logan's liquidation.

That's when the two-and-a-half-ton truck slammed through the gate like a meteor. It burst down the road at blinding speed. The Ankylosaurs whirled into action immediately, their weapons spitting out spears of flaming death at the big steel truck. Smoke erupted from the engine, though, and the vehicle continued its headlong charge toward the main house. Potts couldn't see anyone inside the cab, and he couldn't make out what was in the truck bed. He took a tentative step forward.

As soon as the truck was in the center of the cordon of Ankylosaurs, the vehicle disappeared with a blinding flash of light. The world collapsed into silence for a long, dreadful moment. Potts braced himself, hoping that his helmet's audio filters would protect him from the deafening shock wave that he knew would come instants later.

Suddenly, the Iron Guardsman was lifted off the ground and hurled back into the doors of the estate's manor, heavy oaken doors shattering to splinters as his armored form smashed through them.

CARL LYONS HATED having to resort to terrorist tactics, but sometimes, when you're up against the wall, you just had to fall back and pull whatever you had out of your ass. Able Team had raided a fertilizer supply store, stealing a heavy cargo truck and tons of fertilizer. It wasn't the first time they'd turned thousands of bags of nitrogen into a heavy-duty bomb. This time, however, the truck bomb had a little more punch, thanks to a dozen kilograms of C-4 high explosives and several radio detonators. A 2x4 and a piece of rope to hold the steering wheel and accelerator in place, and their guided missile was set.

Schwarz hit the detonator as soon as the truck was in the middle of the formation of Ankylosaur combat tanks. They might have been immune to small-arms fire, and anything short of a dead-center hit from an anti-tank rocket, but against Hermann Schwarz's improvised bomb-building capabilities, there was no contest. Even as far back as the plantation wall, the detonation nearly shook Lyons from his feet.

Grimaldi drove past with the side door of the van open, and Lyons jumped into the rear to join Blancanales and Schwarz.

"Showtime," Lyons growled.

"I don't know," Schwarz mused. "I still think we should have used plutonium. Go nuclear before she could, and all that."

"And miss the fun?" Lyons asked.

"Besides, we forgot our lead underwear back at the Farm," Blancanales said. "And you know Ironman wants a confirmed kill."

"Shit, he can go wander around in high radiation," Schwarz complained. "He already is a father. What about the next generation of geniuses waiting in my loins?"

"Nut up and do it, Gadgets," Lyons snapped.

Schwarz nodded as Grimaldi drove through the shattered gate. The wrought-iron doors had been no match for seven tons of metal and fertilizer blasting along at 70 mph. But as soon as they got into the gate, Grimaldi had to swerve off the main road, grinding the tires into soft grass and churned sod. A crater, two feet deep and a football field in diameter, made up most of the front lawn of the estate.

"That was fertilizer?" Grimaldi asked, unwilling to drive into the crater.

"Floor it and cut across the bowl," Lyons ordered.

"My own special recipe. I added gasoline and plastic bags to the mix," Schwarz explained. "An improvised fuel-air explosive."

Blancanales whistled as he saw one of Fixx's minitanks embedded in the top of a wall, ten feet up. "Have I ever mentioned just how glad I am that you're not a postal worker?"

"Innumerable times," Schwarz said with a grin. "But I never get tired of it."

Grimaldi drove over the lip of the crater, and Lyons held on for the drop to the bottom. As soon as the tires hit the compressed dirt, the pilot floored it and the van shot across the center of the bowl, a smooth-blasted hole of destruction that was a free path to the manor. "Good God."

Lyons kept his eyes peeled. The Iron Guardsmen had proved tough nuts to crack, and while they might not have been immune to the power of Schwarz's bomb, they could have been far enough away to have survived. The front of the manor house was partially collapsed.

Grimaldi reached the far edge of the crater and hit the brakes. "We're not getting up over that without help."

"Leave the van," Lyons ordered as he leaped out. A bloodied defender—Lyons couldn't make out his nationality through caked gore covering his face—rose and fired a shot that struck the Able Team leader in his body armor. Lyons pulled his GI-50 and punched a half-inch hole through the gunman's face, shattering his skull with the massive handgun.

"See, if you'd used plutonium, we'd miss all this fun," Blancanales chided.

"It's the little things in life," Schwarz quipped.

"Split up," Lyons ordered. "If there are any survivors, smoke 'em if they want to fight."

"Or if they're Fixx or Brujo," Blancanales added.

"That, too," Lyons stated. "Keep in radio contact."

A lone Ankylosaur rolled out into the open, flopping lazily over clumps of sod in its path. The three Stony Man commandos froze for a moment, when their communicators crackled to life.

"Let me see if I have the hang of this, guys," Akira Tokaido mused out loud.

The remote-control combat drone pivoted, then charged toward the manor house, guns blazing. Whatever was left of the front doors and the walls around them were blown to rubble by explosive shells and heavyweight slugs.

"Yeah, you got it, Akira," Schwarz said into his ear mike. "Glad David got back to you with the control frequencies."

"Not only for those, but for the automated missile launchers, as well," Tokaido answered. "Right now,

Hunt, Carmen and Aaron are weeding out the Salvadorans' new armored divisions. Check this out."

The missile launchers on the roof of the mansion erupted, columns of smoke spiraling upward.

"You might want to stand back," Tokaido warned.

"Damn kid," Lyons grumbled as Blancanales and Schwarz crouched against the falling antiaircraft missiles. Warheads detonated on landing, chewing massive chunks out of the roof.

"Okay," Tokaido said. "Now the Navy can pick you boys up by helicopter."

"You could have just shut them down," Lyons pointed out.

"This is more fun," Akira admitted.

Lyons looked at the flaming roof, huge holes blasted in it, then shrugged. "I keep forgetting, you're just as crazy as we are."

"You honor me, man of Iron," Akira said flamboyantly.

"I come to bury Fixx, not to honor you," Lyons explained, and he raced into the building.

HERMANN SCHWARZ GAVE the armored figure on the ground a gentle kick. Its helmet, and its head, rolled free from the shoulders, and he could see that the square of metal wasn't the Iron Guardsman's collar, but a piece of his truck, effectively forming a guillotine blade. Schwarz shuddered and tightened his grip on the FX-300 rifle.

"Heads off to you," Schwarz said with a nervous chuckle. The remains of gunmen assembled outside the main house were strewed, sometimes left whole and untouched, seemingly, others blasted to pieces.

He walked up to an eyeball that sat on the grass, glistening. Schwarz knelt and looked at his reflection in it, fascinated by it. It was a blue eye, so it must have been one of the Fist of God militiamen, although it also could have been a pure Spaniard who had inherited it from his European ancestors. Schwarz shrugged. No matter.

In the reflection of the eyeball, he saw a fast-running shape. It was the only warning he had, but Schwarz whirled to meet his attacker. Covered in his own blood and crazed with rage, Colonel Matthias Logan tackled Schwarz before he could trigger his rifle, and the two men wrestled for the weapon. Schwarz saw that strips of Logan's face were missing, teeth visible through the hole that used to be the supremacist's face.

"Burn in hell, you bastard!" Logan bellowed.

Schwarz twisted to free his rifle, but the colonel had the strength of a fanatic, madness and shock combining to push his muscles past their old pain-induced limits. He kicked Logan in the groin, but it was like lighting a match next to a bonfire. Insane and stripped of half of his face, Logan didn't notice as his testicles were crushed by Schwarz's knee kick.

Instead, the Able Team commando fell back, pivoted and let go of the confiscated rifle. Logan went flying from the surprise maneuver. With animalistic ferocity, Logan spun and leaped at Schwarz, fingers curled like claws. The electronics genius ducked and slipped under Logan's lunge. He hammered the madman under his solar plexus. Air exploded from the colonel's lungs, along with a spray of blood from the ruined stringy flesh of his face. Schwarz reached down and grabbed Logan's belt buckle and lifted the Fist of God leader, flipping him over his back.

Schwarz leaped down onto Logan's chest, driving his boot heels into the man's rib cage. Bones snapped like twigs under the force of the impact, and the colonel vomited more blood, croaking weakly in agony.

Schwarz drew his GI-50 and delivered a mercy round.

"I guess Carl can close your file now," Schwarz said as he continued to make certain that the Salvadorans and the Fist of God militiamen were all dead.

ROSARIO BLANCANALES cut back to the entrance of the manor and stepped over the shattered doors. He'd looked for other entrances, but they were either locked, or he had to close them down because frantic defenders opened up. Blancanales wasn't taking any chances, and he fired a grenade into those windows, collapsing sections of wall into clumps of rubble, unpassable. He was tempted to just step back and blast a new door, but he wasn't certain how many of the Iron Guardsmen were alive, and the one thing he knew worked with decisive force was a 40 mm grenade.

He wasn't even sure if the steel-tipped .300 WSM rounds would do the job.

Instead, Blancanales stalked back to the main entrance that Lyons had rushed through. He looked up in time to see Schwarz put a bullet through the head of a body. He wondered who the target was, but had more important things to do. He stepped over a pile of debris at the door, then felt something clamp around his ankle with a grip of steel. Blancanales tried to twist free, but instead, he was hurled off balance. The eldest Able Team member crashed to the floor, then struggled to get back to his feet.

He turned to see a man—Potts—rise from the rubble, wood crashing to the floor around him. Blancanales pulled the trigger on the FX-300 rifle, spraying the Iron Guardsman with a salvo of high-velocity slugs. The .300 WSM was designed originally as a hunting round for large game, but the U.S. Military chambered select long-distance sniper rifles for the cartridge. Steel-tipped slugs were selected because they could cut through all but the heaviest protective vests worn by paranoid enemy commanders, or shoot through an armored limousine.

Instead the FX-300 burst raised only sparks on Potts's armor, simply dusting off his gleaming chrome under multiple impacts.

"Did you make that bomb?" Potts growled.

"No, my partner did," Blancanales admitted. "But if you want a piece of him, you're going to have to get past me."

Potts shrugged, then snapped out the blades on his forearm shields. Mirror-polished swords glimmered in the half light of the blasted lobby. "Your funeral, old man."

Blancanales was tempted to drop his trigger finger to the 40 mm grenade launcher, but Potts was too close. The blast would crush Blancanales as easily as it would his adversary. Instead, the Able Team warrior dashed toward the stairs. Potts took off after him, and nearly sliced off Blancanales's leg with a vicious swing. As it was, fresh blood poured down the back of the Able

Team veteran's leg, a small scratch that didn't reach an artery, but was still a reminder that Blancanales was working on borrowed time.

He swung around and hammered the buttstock of the captured rifle into Potts's faceplate. The metal helmet bounced back, and Potts staggered backward off the bottom step. Even if his mobility was unhindered, being smashed in the head with a rifle butt was still going to hurt. Blancanales reversed the rifle again and opened fire.

Potts squirmed out of the way, the marble floor tiles exploding into clouds of dust from the onslaught of the heavy slugs. With a wild leap, Potts grabbed the rifle barrel and wrenched hard.

Blancanales let go, rather than get caught up in a wrestling match over the weapon. He reached back and swung the Beowulf off its sling and cut loose with a point-blank burst of 300-grain hollowpoint rounds. Potts jerked backward with a jolt under the firestorm, skidding across the floor. Blancanales continued up the stairs at a full run, then dove for cover. Decorative marble columns that supported the main staircase's handrail detonated as Potts tore into them. The thickness of the stone protected the Able Team veteran, but one rifle bullet clipped him just above the elbow, and another cut a furrow in his thigh. Blancanales continued to crawl up the stairs, getting distance between himself and the armored maniac down below.

"Stand still and fight, you coward!" Potts bellowed.

Blancanales looked at the distance between them, then sneered. "All right. You want me to fight?"

Potts laughed as Blancanales poked the barrel of his

Beowulf between two columns. The Iron Guard commander spread his arms, as if to welcome the ineffectual bullets against his armored chest. "Go ahead! You hit me with that at point-blank, and I withstood it. Give it to me!"

Blancanales nudged the barrel farther forward, and Potts froze, his laughter dying away as he looked down the 40 mm muzzle of the grenade launcher strapped underneath the Beowulf. "It's yours. Take a bite."

This time, when the shock wave threw Potts through the mansion doorway, it carried him in pieces.

CARL LYONS heard the detonation of the grenade and looked back over his shoulder as he stepped through the hallway on the second floor. He keyed his communicator, but received no answer. Chances were, in all the excitement, his partners had lost their earplugs. In violent-enough action, it was easy to lose the communicator earpieces. He was tempted to go back to check on his teammates, but he realized that he had a job to finish up here.

He turned back and negotiated his way around a toppled tree in a clay pot. As he stepped over, he caught a flash of movement ahead of him and tensed. A rifle slug slammed into his chest and bowled him onto his rear, his lower back striking the trunk of the tree. He managed to hold on to the Beowulf rifle, though, as he looked at the amazing sight of a silver goddess stepping down the hall, an eye of red fire burning at him.

"So, Cowboy, is this the Jihad?" Fixx asked.

Lyons fought to suck down air, when Fixx's weapon

spoke again. A powerful force tore the rifle from his hands and slammed it into his gut. He folded over and Fixx stepped up to him, kneeling so that they were face-to-face. She plucked the rifle out of his lap and tossed it over her shoulder.

"Don't you know it's polite to answer a lady when she asks a question?" Fixx asked, brushing the steel tips of her gauntleted fingers across his craggy cheek.

"I'll answer them when I hear a lady ask them," Lyons growled defiantly.

Fixx giggled like a schoolgirl at the response. "You are just so cute."

Lyons tensed for the slap he knew was coming, and wasn't disappointed. Fixx was strong, and with the added steel wrapping her fist, the blow felt like a jack-hammer against his jaw. Fresh, molten fire poured from the tip of his chin down his throat and seized up his chest. Lyons's eyes crossed in pain, and when he reflexively clenched his teeth, the agony tripled.

"Aw, poor baby," Fixx whimpered. "That jaw looked a little red. Did somebody break it?"

Lyons breathed deeply, spittle flying from his lips. His brawny fists clenched in rage, and he was unable to speak.

"I guess I might have done that. Sometimes I forget that I'm wearing steel knuckles," Fixx explained. She grabbed a clump of his blond hair, cocked her fist and punched him in the forehead. Lightning flashed in Lyons's brain, and when his eyes focused again, the outside world registering on his agonized senses, he found himself on his feet.

Fixx held him up by his vest, and her visor had been pulled back to reveal her dark, beautiful, Latin features.

Lyons tasted bile on his tongue, and tried to focus on the acidic taste, or on the pounding agony jolting through his jaw. He needed anger and strength.

"You're actually quite good-looking," Fixx explained. "Granted, I beat the hell out of you, but I'd bet you'd clean up nicely."

Lyons exploded into action, pummeling her stomach with three quick punches. The Able Team leader staggered and tripped over the fallen tree, his knuckles aching where he'd punched her unyielding armor. Fixx looked at him in astonishment.

"You're a fighter, too," Fixx admitted. "I have to admire that, even though you're way outclassed. Wait… you're the guy who went toe-to-toe with our boy at Dulles, aren't you?"

"Yeah," Lyons grumbled. It hurt like hell to talk, but the pain cleansed his mind, gave him a focus. He felt the berserker railing against the chains of control in his mind.

"So, what, you're going to make a habit of getting your ass kicked by us?" Fixx asked. "Although, getting stomped twice in your lifetime really couldn't be considered a habit."

Lyons knelt on all fours, straddling the tree, his mind racing to push the sight below him through all levels of his consciousness before is rage took over. "Come a little closer, witch, and we'll see just what an ass kicking really feels like."

Fixx laughed and snicked out her forearm blade. "Go ahead and get your knife, or your gun, big man. I'll give you a fighting chance, and I'll leave my face unprotected."

Lyons took a deep breath. This time he was sure that

the rifle round had broken a rib. The pain and breathlessness were all too familiar. The berserker, though, didn't give a damn. "Going to be a shame to ruin that face."

Fixx blew him a kiss. "Turn me on, dead man."

"Just wanna ask, where's Brujo?"

Fixx stepped aside, and Lyons saw a bloody puddle in the hall. "I gave him his severance pay."

Lyons grinned. "Good. You get to have it all."

"All of what? You talk…"

Carl Lyons exploded into action. He gripped the sapling and swung it around like the hammer of Thor. The trunk smashed against Fixx's helmet and snapped her head around. The "silver goddess" pirouetted and slashed with her sword, catching the tree trunk on Lyons's backstroke. The blade bit through the wood and imbedded halfway in.

The woman's cheek bled freely where a branch had slashed her dark skin. "Be a good soldier and die!"

Lyons twisted the tree trunk and pulled Fixx off balance. Using the tree as leverage, he tore the blade out of its forearm housing, but the woman recovered and snapped her other blade free. The point thrust forward and tore into Lyons's belt. It jammed in him, and when Fixx pulled free, she had a Beowulf magazine speared on her arm sword.

"Not a soldier," the Able Team leader snarled, blue eyes wild with hatred.

Lyons stabbed the tree forward, its broken pot slamming into Fixx's chest and driving her back into the wall. Her free hand scrambled for the machine pistol hanging from its sling, but Lyons stomped on her wrist.

The bones held, protected by their barding, but it kept Fixx from unleashing a point-blank burst that would tear out Lyons's guts.

Instead, Fixx kicked him in the ankle he used for support, and Lyons crashed to the ground. She pulled the trigger, but the Able Team leader rolled out of the way and drew his GI-50 in one movement. Instinct made him fire for her center mass, and Fixx jerked violently as half-inch bullets crashed into her chest plate. Lyons was about to follow up with a head shot when the woman kicked the gun off target. A .50-caliber hole appeared in the wall, and she stiff-armed her machine pistol to Lyons's face. He lunged forward and caught the armored weapons designer at the knees.

The two bodies tumbled down the hall as a stream of 6.5 mm armor-piercing slugs ripped plaster from the ceiling. Fixx snapped her head forward and broke Lyons's nose with the impact, but the berserker was well past feeling new pain. Instead, he wanted to share all his rage and hatred with her. He grabbed her wrists and pulled backward, flipping her onto the stairs.

In the foyer, Blancanales and Schwarz looked up to see Fixx tumble into view, and they cut loose with their rifles. The woman covered herself as the bullets sparked off her gleaming chrome. She swung the machine pistol around again, and the two Able Team partners dived for cover. The floor took another pounding of assault-weapon fire, and Schwarz prepared to launch a grenade when Lyons pounced on the armored woman.

The electronics genius held his fire, not wanting to blow up his friend, and together, Lyons and Fixx tumbled down the steps. The Able Team leader hammered her with his fists, ignoring the crackling pain with each impact. Fixx pounded against his shoulders and head, but even her steel-clad fists didn't cut through the red haze of bloodlust that had taken over Lyons.

All he could think of were the soldiers slaughtered under Rogers's command, murdered because they were just part of a distraction. Dead men who were doing their duty for America, who would never go home to their families. He thought about the rampage the Hand of God unleashed in the Middle East among other American servicemen. It was fuel for the fire, and his fists landed with more and more force.

When they reached the bottom of the landing, Lyons was spent, and Fixx was coughing up blood. Her steel-clad knuckles had split his skin in a dozen places, and one eye had swollen shut, and when he pulled back off of her, he could barely stand. Schwarz and Blancanales rushed to his side to hold him up as he stood over Fixx.

"You cowboys win," Fixx whispered. "But there's more out there."

Lyons reached clumsily into Blancanales's holster and drew his partner's GI-50. "Don't worry. I'll make sure you have a reunion in hell."

Fixx snorted, blood trickling from her nose. "I'll see you there, freak." As she lurched up toward Lyons, he pulled the trigger on the GI-50. Fixx dropped to the stairs.

"Save me a lap dance," Lyons snarled.

Schwarz and Blancanales supported their teammate

as they walked him outside where Jack Grimaldi had flagged down a Navy helicopter with a smoke grenade.

"Our ride's here," Schwarz told him.

"Great. I can't wait to get to Iraq," Lyons said.

"Carl, you look like shit," Schwarz argued.

Lyons looked at Fixx's corpse on the stairs. "But I feel great!"

EPILOGUE

Able Team and Phoenix Force didn't have to go to Iraq, and after the war they waged against Fixx and Skyline's conspiracy, Brognola was able to request that the President grant them a month to relax and recover from myriad injuries. It was just as well. As soon as the Stony Man cyberteam got the command codes for the Ankylosaurs, they took command of the surviving minitanks in the arsenal of the Hand of God operatives in Iraq.

The Hand of God and their allies among the insurgents were faced with a bad case of killer karma as the remote-control combat drones cut loose in orgies of destruction. Those who escaped the out-of-control robots were flushed into the waiting rifles of U.S. servicemen, directed to the weapons stashes by Kurtzman's triangulation of the stored hell weapons. Even those wearing the black body armor that Fixx designed had their tickets punched by Marine snipers armed with heavy-caliber rifles.

All told, 250 of the conspirators behind the diversionary attacks were slaughtered by the vengeful might of the American armed forces, along with a little nudge from the electronic intelligence command center at Stony Man Farm.

El Salvador was a different mess. When the Ankylosaurs turned on their handlers, the former ORDEN and ESA thugs broke and ran in terror. They had been told that they were going to be invulnerable warriors, sweeping their nation into a new era of racial purity. When they were attacked by their own machines of terror, their so-called invulnerable armor suddenly too weak to deal with the awesome firepower of the combat robots, they fled. Military units that had experienced mass defections had most of their men return, and the commanders, many of whom were in on the attempted coup, quickly swept all charges under the carpet. A storm was coming, and the old guard did their best to cover their tracks.

Those who died in service of the coup were promptly bulldozed into mass graves, if there was anything left of their corpses, the plots plowed over, and their names promptly forgotten.

The poison of corruption still rotted in El Salvador, but like every time that Able Team had paid a visit to that troubled nation, it had been cleaned up a little bit. There were fewer thugs to do the bidding of the bosses, and Joaquin Malina showed up at INTERPOL headquarters, naming names and begging for protection.

The struggle for justice in Central America continued. Battered and bruised, the warriors of Stony Man

Farm were bandaged and stitched back together, told to rest and relax, and they disappeared to the four corners of the world to unwind as only they could. Until the next call to arms.

TAKE 'EM FREE

2 action-packed novels plus a mystery bonus

NO RISK
NO OBLIGATION TO BUY